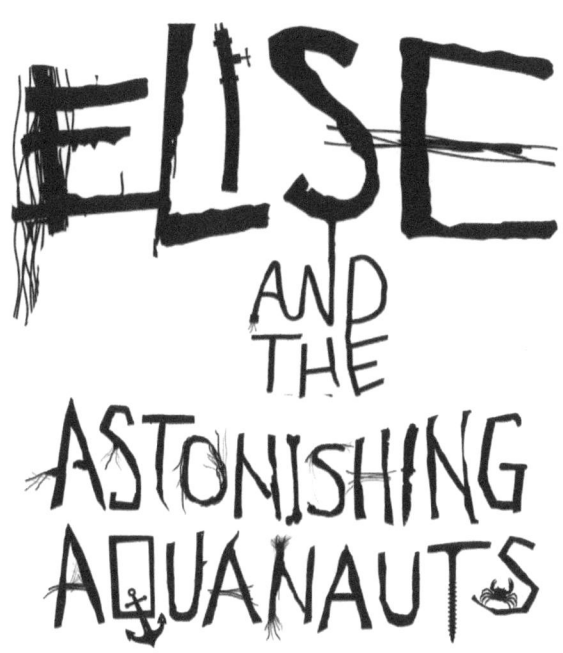

ELISE
AND THE
ASTONISHING AQUANAUTS

STEVEN WELCH

This book is a work of fiction. Names, characters, places, and incidents are products of the author's imagination or are used fictitiously. Any resemblance to actual events, locales, or persons, living or dead, is entirely coincidental.

Cover art and interior formatting by Damonza

Published by Cave Branch Press

Also by Steven Welch
Elise and the Butcher of Dreams

About the Author

Steven Welch grew up in Daytona Beach, Florida. He was raised on comic books and pulp paperbacks, sitting on his Mom's lap as she read aloud stories of the weird and impossible.

He's been a theme park creative director, radio morning show host, actor, convenience store clerk on the midnight shift, improv comedian, and line cook.

Welch has had the good fortune to travel from Ecuador to India announcing water-ski shows with a roving band of water-ski warriors, mystical drinking shamans, and renegade cultural emissaries known as The Stars of Florida.

His family is his light.

For Sammi

Special thanks to Jules Verne, Lester Dent, Stan Lee, Jack Kirby, Jacques Cousteau, Don Buffa, Bill Whalen, Cindy Welch, and Ruth Cobb for the inspiration.

CHAPTER ONE

Dad

'And the cathedral was not only company for him, it was the universe; nay, more, it was Nature itself. He never dreamed that there were other hedgerows than the stained-glass windows in perpetual bloom; other shade than that of the stone foliage always budding, loaded with birds in the thickets of Saxon capitals; other mountains than the colossal towers of the church; or other oceans than Paris roaring at their feet.'

—Victor Hugo, Notre Dame de Paris, 1831

THIS IS THE story of a young girl who risked everything to bring back the ocean.

Did she succeed?

Well, as her friend Jules once said, "There are no perfect endings, but there can be good ones."

*

He chased her through the surf, and they laughed as they ran and played on the last day of her Dad's life.

The sky was as blue as the sea. There were flashes of white from seagulls and gold from the sun.

Warm water splashed around their ankles.

He was carrying more weight than when he was young; there was gray in the unruly hair, but his eyes twinkled, and he was still a boy in a man's body.

He was her Dad.

She was Elise St. Jacques, eleven years old and blond as the bubbles in Dad's cheap beer.

The beach stretched on for miles of white sand and palm trees.

Her Dad barked and growled as he chased her through the surf. "Mad dog! Mad dog!"

Elise laughed so hard that her belly hurt. Dad was closing in, and she knew there would be a fierce tickling or perhaps even a bionic airplane spin if she didn't get away.

He was on her, and Elise was lifted into the air.

Yep. Bionic airplane spin. The blood rushed to her head, and the beach became a blur, images repeating and repeating as her Dad spun tight circles with her in his arms.

They both fell into the surf, disoriented and slightly nauseous.

The water was warm and little minnows nibbled at their toes.

Soft curling waves broke near them every few moments. Elise could feel the crunch of periwinkle shells under her hands. She sifted through the sand and watched as the little shells popped up then burrowed back into the mud.

Where did they go? How deep was their little world? What was it like there, in a place of shiny crushed shells, of flowing water, of darkness and sudden light?

"Hey, Goofus. What are you thinking about?" His voice was deep and rich. He could magically create all kinds of funny voices, weird characters, and funny dialects. She didn't understand exactly what her Dad did for a living, but she knew that he used his voice for commercials and shows. Nothing big, nothing famous, but that's what he did. It was kind of cool and made for spectacular bedtime stories.

Elise smiled at her Dad. Goofus. That might annoy her when she got older, but now it made her laugh.

"I want to be a periwinkle," she said.

"Ok. You're a periwinkle."

With that, Elise dove face-first into the watery sand, digging as if she was a pony-tailed mollusk. She came up, cheeks covered in mud.

"Changed my mind. There might be monsters under there."

Dad stared at her for a moment.

"You never know, I suppose."

Elise's eyes grew wide.

"You mean there might be monsters under there?"

There was a silent heartbeat, then her Dad laughed.

"Nothing that Les Scaphandriers couldn't handle, right?"

"Right."

"So you're afraid of monsters? I thought I taught you better," her Dad said. He splashed her with water.

"I'm not afraid." She splashed him back.

"Well, it's ok to be afraid as long as you can control the fear and make it dance. Right?"

"Just like Jules Valiance."

"Exactly. They say he once played tag with giant electric crabs just to know what it felt like to get the shock pinch."

"Awesome. Tell me."

And so, her Dad spent a few minutes telling Elise the thrilling and unlikely tale of Jules Valiance and the dreaded electric crabs, of the mad chase among the sunken sky taxis, of the flirty little mermaid who teased Jules as he swam, and of the last-second rescue at the hands of the rest of Les Scaphandriers, the League of Astonishing Aquanauts, the greatest secret of the sea.

France had led the way in oceanic research, and Elise's Dad was a geek for that sort of thing. The brave souls who dared the depths wearing copper helmets and breathing air from hoses were known as Les Scaphandriers, and her Dad had been obsessed with them. His den at home was adorned with sepia-tone photographs of bold expeditions, of strange sea creatures, and of submersibles welded from iron and steel.

It wasn't much of a leap for her Dad to spin bedtime stories for little Elise that transformed these vintage marine explorers into something fantastic and larger than life.

By the soft amber light of her night-light, Dad had told Elise hundreds of tales of The World's Below and Between, of its heroes and villains, of its strange creatures, of the legendary Scaphandriers and their amazing champion, Jules Valiance.

*

Who is Jules Valiance?

To the world at large, Jules Valiance is a man of supreme intelligence and absurd courage, the leader of those Astonishing Aquanauts, Les Scaphandriers.

He is strong and lean, his hair a mass of blonde dreadlocks, his green eyes sparkle like gems in a weathered face forged in copper by countless tropical suns.

Legend and birth records show that he was raised in Antibes and honed his aquatic skills at the hands of oceanic masters, both infamous and obscure.

Blessed with a remarkable singing voice, he can shatter garden gnomes with his pitch and, given time, transform sugar into taffy.

The martial arts skills of Jules Valiance are a unique style of savate infused with gleanings from Elvis. This makes him one of the most dangerous and unpredictable men alive. Strangely, his first and third toes are deadly weapons.

He is one of the few men in the world who can speak the

language of the dolphin, specifically Atlantic Bottlenose, thanks to relentless practice and the peculiar deviation in his septum.

Jules dated Madonna, just for a day, and created "break dancing" during an unfortunate incident with an amorous sea wasp.

His bouillabaisse is legendary but can only be eaten once. No one knows why.

Jules Valiance has no use for mimes or chicken nuggets.

*

Jules Valiance was epic.

"Time enough for stories later, Goofus. Let's grab breakfast."

The warm air felt good on their skin as they stood and made their way back to their beach towels.

Elise loved the weekends. No school, just going to the beach with Dad. She had never known her Mother. It was just the two of them in the world, and that's all she knew, and that was fine. These were the best days, endless in the moment and then as quick as a hummingbird wing.

These were the days she dreamt of as she slept. These were the times that kept her warm, like the sun on a beach afternoon, that drifted in and out of her thoughts, haze on a hot summer road far in the distance, always there and always out of reach.

These were the days she missed, the days with her Dad, but he died on that day at the beach.

His heart gave out in the surf as he swam.

Elise was playing in the waves, and she turned to see him floating face down in the water.

At first, she thought it was a game, but it wasn't.

This wasn't a game at all.

Dad didn't move. He didn't breathe.

We take life for granted, as a given, as a constant, but it isn't, not at all.

Bad things can happen fast.

She screamed, and strangers came to help, but Dad was dead, and there was no saving him.

Elise went into shock, and the people had to pull her away from her Dad's body. The rest of the time was a blur of faces and flashing red lights and horror and things she didn't understand.

He was gone, and he never came back.

It can happen quickly, as you know, that fade from light to dark.

She had no Mom that she knew. No other family. Now she had no Dad.

She was alone, but her Dad had created a will, and it sent Elise to Paris, a place she had never been, a language she didn't speak, a country she understood only in bits and pieces from his stories.

He always told her he would live in Paris when she left him for college. He told her it was the best place in the world.

A city of light, Dad had called it.

Now there was just darkness. Airports. Strangers.

Trains. Cold rooms. Miami.

New York. London. Days blended into the night and then again into morning.

Then, Paris.

And that's how Elise St. Jacques ended up at Le Jardin de la Jeune Fille.

The Girl's Garden.

*

CHAPTER TWO

Le Jardin de la Jeune Fille

THE GIRL'S GARDEN was a hidden building on a cobblestone side street deep in the Isle de la Cite, and it had been there for over 150 years.

Elise had been there exactly 346 days, but she felt as if she had been there since the beginning.

The brick was faded white and gray with dark wood along windows and doors hand-carved by craftsmen long since dead. It looked out over the tiny café where Elise could watch old men sip drinks and argue with each other over newspapers. From her window, she could see the bookstore full of mystery, the boulangerie Le Bat, the office, the produce displayed like tropical flowers outside of the corner shop.

Our Lady of Paris, the Cathedral of Notre Dame, was a stone's throw away, and her bells rang to welcome every new day without fail.

Elise learned that in France, the first floor of a building was what Americans called the second floor. Why there was such a difference, she didn't know, nor did she care. It mattered, though, that the window of Elise's room on the third floor could open just a crack and would invite the wonderful smell of Monsieur Belfre's baked bread to drift in on the rise of the sun.

It would have been nice if Elise could eat Le Bat's bread rather than the stale stuff served with each meal in the clattering cafeteria.

She rolled to her side and considered her room. It was big enough for one, but there were four girls to a room at The Girl's Garden. Elise was given the bed by the window, not out of kindness, but because it was the loudest and draftiest. The street sounds of cars and delivery trucks would begin at sunrise every morning except Sunday, and on Sundays, the girls would all go to Notre Dame for prayers.

The other three girls were sleeping.

They were awful.

Juliette snored and was prone to talking in her sleep. Her words, half muttered, were difficult to understand. Now and then, though, it was clear she was having a conversation about dental floss. On awakening, she never remembered dreaming about dental floss.

Juliette was the nicest of the three, less prone to cruelty towards Elise but not a friend. The nicest thing about her was she tended to ignore Elise.

Agnes, on the other hand, was unpleasant, heavy and dull in a sinister way. She wore atrocious, pink-rimmed glasses and had enormous teeth that seemed to take up most of her face. Biot did her bidding and would just as soon insult Elise as look at her. The insults were always in French, and as Elise had grown better at understanding the language, the two had made their comments more cruel.

Their words, spat out over meals, in class, or at the play yard, cut like broken glass.

"The idiot American can't do anything properly. Her father killed himself of shame at having such an ugly and stupid daughter. Better if she had died with him. Better for the whole world."

In the dim light, Elise could make out the dark wood of the armoire, the sheen from the posters that decorated the walls, and the skeletal coat rack.

Somewhere outside her window, a car horn made a brief noise. There was a tick tick tick of a clock, the beating of her heart, the soft whisper of her breath.

Elise was wrapped in the blanket her Dad gave her when she was small. This was one of the few things from the old days she still possessed. The blanket was special, not just because of memory, but because of its soft fabrics patch-worked together into unusual patterns, its mosaic of embroidery that seemed to be stitched of gold, and its toughness.

The blanket had not a single blemish or torn thread, despite everything it had been through. Dad made her promise she would always sleep with it to keep away the monsters.

When Elise had arrived at The Girl's Garden, the Sisters had taken away all of her things.

The Sisters ran the Garden with ruthless and cold efficiency. That first day, Elise had been terrified, confused, and without hope. The Sisters had done little to make her at home.

They snatched away her belongings and rifled them for contraband. They berated her for mistakes beyond measure. One of them had grabbed the blanket. Elise wouldn't let go, and she kicked and screamed with all of her strength.

A towering woman that Elise came to know as Sister Viverette saw the uproar. There had been a heated discussion, and then they had made the one exception. Sister Viverette returned the blanket to Elise and promised that there would be no more trouble.

They had taken all of her things, but not her blanket.

As the days went by, Sister Viverette made a point of checking in on Elise when darkness came and the girls were settling in for bed. While she smiled little and often seemed unsteady because of too much wine, Sister Viverette was the one person at The Girl's Garden who showed Elise any kindness at all. In fact, it became routine for the Sister to tuck Elise in and make sure that her special blanket was wrapped tightly for the night.

There was little comfort at this new home, and Sister Viverette was stern, but those moments of kindness before sleep meant a great deal to Elise.

*

The alarm clock rang before the sun came through the window. It was a noisy old thing, an antique round creature of glass and brass they would need to wind before going to bed each night. The sound was a tray of silverware rolling down a cliff.

Elise eased out of bed, holding her blanket around her. The others were moving as well. Biot was quick to be first, always skittering like a spider. Slow Agnes sat on the edge of her bed and stared dully at the wall. She looked like a pig that'd been struck between the eyes by a bowling pin. Juliette staggered to the armoire to retrieve her uniform.

Morning rituals at The Girl's Garden, as mechanical as the alarm clock and nearly as thrilling. Elise winced as her feet hit the cold stone floor. There was a Turkish area rug, but it didn't extend to her bed.

Dressed. Teeth brushed. Hair combed. Face washed. Blanket tucked away. Books gathered and placed in a bag that dropped over her shoulder. Ten minutes, no more.

Elise walked down the narrow old wooden stairs to the second level, then to the floor.

The room opened into the foyer of The Girl's Garden.

Sister Viverette stood at her station like a vulture standing guard over the corpse of a dead hog. She was thin and tall, with skin the color of piano keys and just as cold. Her black dress covered her neck to toes except for those skeletal hands and that pinched face. A thin chain held a golden cross and a small medallion around her neck.

Elise could catch a glimpse of the little medallion when being tucked in at night. It was an old-fashioned diving helmet of tarnished brass, no bigger than a fingernail. Strange thing for a Sister, Elise thought.

"Bonjour, Elise St. Jacques," said Sister Viverette, "your tripe and chutney is getting cold. Depeche toi."

"Jen ne comprends pas?"

"Hurry, please."

Elise dashed past her and moved toward the cafeteria. Her French was getting better, but she was still far from fluent.

Elise sat with the other girls, a hundred or so, at the long dining tables of The Cafeteria. The room was quiet for such a crowd and activity. A bit of light poured down from the glass-domed arcade-style ceiling of the room. The air smelled of cumin and starched clothes.

And yes, the tripe and chutney were cold.

The chutney sat on her plate like a spatter of jellied insects next to a little puddle of pig innards that Sister Viverette called tripe. Elise hated tripe and chutney day. Who eats pig guts and chutney for breakfast? Honestly, until coming to this atrocious place, Elise had never even heard the word "chutney" before. Now, every Tuesday morning, she began her day with a not-so-steaming pile of spiced whatnots and a chunk of stale bread.

Dad had been a great cook, or at least Elise thought so. He would make wonderful meals for the two of them, sizzling plates of bacon and eggs, biscuits and sausage gravy, homemade pizzas hot out of the oven with cheese caramelized and crunchy.

Now, tripe and chutney.

Yay.

*

A day at The Girl's Garden was supposed to be a voyage of discovery into the world of impending womanhood. Here, so Elise was told, pathetic orphan girls would journey step by step along a path of intellectual and cultural enlightenment that would take them from hopeless poverty into the posh hallways of power and privilege. Learn to speak other languages, master the art of cleaning floors, develop your dishwashing techniques, and navigate a hundred different variations of bullying that ranged from the innocuous comment to the flat-out backyard beating. What great fun!

Nights were hers, though. Once done with the day's labors, Elise could settle into her room, into her bed, and she could try to remember who her Dad had taught her to be. More than anything, though, lying in bed at night, she could see the thing that gave her the most comfort in her world.

In her mind, she could visit Jules Valiance in The Worlds Below and Between.

Her Dad's tales had captivated Elise for as long as she could remember. At night, tucking her in, he would weave another yarn of the heroes and monsters of this strange world. When she was old enough, they had begun a project together. Using sticks and twine and found objects, they created a tiny little world, a place of wonder and imagination.

To the outside eye, it might seem meaningless chaos. To Elise, using her imagination to paint the picture, it was the endless, marvelous, mysterious world of her father's stories.

Cat's eye marbles became the legendary singing spheres of the frozen sea. Twine was the carnivorous Sargasso weed that devoured sea gerbil huts. Cotton, stretched and pulled, were the dome clouds of the Prawn God's Kingdom. Broken watches, an egg carton, and some duck feathers were transformed into the magnificent and absurd steam spewing Abyssal Wagon. It was in this that Jules and his team would have their wildest adventures, sailing and soaring and diving through the Seven Seas, dodging ravenous Volcanic Mega-Squids, exploring the Slug Pits of Sumatra, wooing mermaids, and doing those things that could only be done in the Worlds Below and Between.

What had happened to their wonderful, ridiculous project? Thrown away, probably, with everything else.

"Aller au lit, Elise."

It was the voice of Sister Viverette. Time for sleep. She was a tall thin shadow, and she weaved to the bed on unsteady legs. Elise could smell the wine on her breath and heard the woman's old knees creak as she bent down to straighten the bedsheets.

"Oui, Sister."

Cold fingers tightened the blanket around Elise and brushed the hair back from her face.

"Pleasant dreams."

"Thank you, Sister."

The woman closed the door as she left, and the room became dark.

Elise returned in her mind to those fantastic stories and dreams.

Voyaging in her imagination to these worlds, Elise could feel her father, hear his voice, see his face. For a moment, she felt warm. Then, in the still darkness of that cold room, in a foreign place of strangers and indifference, the awful memories of that day on the shore came back as they always did.

The rushing tide, the screams. He was there, and then he was gone. Sometimes she hated him for going away. She hated him for filling her head with fantasies and lies, then leaving her alone.

But this night, Elise didn't think of those things. She didn't think about the cruel girls, the strange foreign city, the cold room, lost dreams, or the day Dad died.

Elise St. Jacques lay in the gloom and thought of The Worlds Below and Between, diving into its mysteries, swimming through its complexities, soaking in those old stories of Les Scaphandriers.

So, she allowed herself for just that night to think about the good days.

After a time, though, it became harder to drift through those fantasies. An hour passed, then two. The magical worlds faded away.

The room grew cold. Elise felt numb. She wrapped her blanket tight around until she was a mummy swaddled in its soft, beautiful fabric.

"I'll do this now, but not tomorrow, or ever again. I swear it."

And for the first time in a long time, Elise St. Jacques cried. Then she fell asleep, and her blanket's beautiful embroidery began to glow.

*

CHAPTER THREE

Ten Years Gone

WHO WAS THROWING sand against the window?

Elise had been having the most unusual dream. There had been darkness and bears riding scooters and something with skeleton fingers tugging at her skirt. She hated skirts.

It was cold. She curled up tight against the chill. Her arms and legs moved slowly, despite her best efforts, as if they weren't interested in listening to her.

She tried to open her eyes and found it to be a struggle.

Stop throwing sand. She wanted to go back to her dream and make it better, maybe push the bear off of the scooter.

All right, it's too cold.

Elise pulled at her blanket, and it came apart in her hand.

She raised up, eyes wide. What had they done to her blanket?

The room was dim. The sound of sand continued to slam against her old windows. Elise tried to gather her blanket and saw it was falling apart, like cotton candy or spider webs in the wind.

Her heart felt like it was being knifed. They had destroyed her blanket. How did they do this awful thing? She sobbed and took a deep breath.

She coughed. There was dust in the air.

Now awake, she heard outside the roar of high winds. A storm?

She peered out of the window next to her bed, dizzy, almost toppling back to her pillow, but couldn't see much.

There was a dim red haze, and the window was caked in dirt.

The wind was blasting sand against it like a horrible snow. Her heart was pounding, eyes and throat itching because of dust, shrouded in the remains of her blanket.

"Wake up." She told herself it was a dream gone bad, and she needed to wake up or be suffocated.

Something smelled disgusting. Rotten. Elise was scared.

"I need to wake up. Wake up now. Wake up.

Wake up."

What was happening?

She reached for her light on the nightstand next to her bed and pulled the string.

Nothing.

The power must be out, she thought.

So hard to see in the room. So dark.

She pushed away the remnants of her blanket and scrambled out of bed, feeling her way. The other beds were empty, and the room a shamble of dust and cobwebs. The rotten smell was getting stronger as she moved about, disturbing the still air in the room.

Where are they? Where is everybody?

Fine, I will not wander around a nightmare in my pajamas, she thought, fear becoming anger.

She looked at the remains of her blanket for a long moment. It was a dusty gray shroud, thin as hair, the vibrant embroidery just a memory. What had they done? Her teeth bit into her lip in anger and sadness.

"I'll make them pay for this."

My beautiful blanket. Dad's blanket.

She pulled on jeans, boots, and a sweater.

Elise ran out of her room into a tornado of dust and nearly plummeted out of her hallway into the street three floors below.

The wood at her feet was rotten and gave way under her boots.

She backpedaled, sending chunks of the floor flying, grabbing the door jamb for support.

The rest of the building was gone.

Her doorway opened out onto a pit where the Girl's Garden had once towered. The air was red chaos with wind blowing sand sideways. She struggled to see through the storm.

Elise teetered on the edge of her door jamb, fifteen meters above the street, her room and the floors beneath just a tall, jagged column of wood and stone.

Freezing wind slapped her face, and something more, the sand, as if thrown by a giant.

It hurt.

Why am I dreaming this?

She became tangled in rusted support metal beneath the rotten wooden floor and fell backward into her room. A splinter of wood sliced her hand, but the pain was nothing.

What Elise was seeing overwhelmed everything else.

Paris was engulfed in a storm of wind and sand.

And something more. Fireflies? No.

Sparks of light filled the air, shutting on and off. Sparks.

Electricity. The air, the sky, was charged with lightning.

The old building across the street from where The Girl's Garden had stood was burned out and skeletal, what she could see of it through the red fog of the sandstorm. Dunes of sand were piled high, like crimson snow. The blood-red haze made it impossible to see beyond, but huge flashes of light, like the heat lightning she remembered from her time in Florida, erupted in the distance.

Thunder, sharp and brittle, barked and shook her to the core.

She felt the rumble in her heart.

Elise held her bleeding hand up to her face. It hurt.

"Oh, crap."

She scrambled back into the darkness of her room, dizzy from fear and confusion. Wait.

Dizzy, yes, because the floor felt like it moved. Impossible. Floors don't move.

First, I need to wrap up this cut.

She opened the chest in the corner of the room and pulled out a black scarf. There was a thick layer of dust everywhere, and it made breathing difficult. Elise ripped the scarf in half, wrapped a piece around her lower face as a bandana so she could breathe without sucking in the dust.

The other half became a tight bandage for her wound. The cut wasn't too bad, but she didn't want it to get full of that awful dust.

She looked around, taking stock of her surroundings.

Dust. Lots of it.

Wait. The candles. She searched her bedside table for matches and found a box. A strike, and a lit candle revealed more in the gloom.

There was something big and moldy on one of the other beds. Agnes's bed.

She walked closer, inspecting it.

Elise weaved again, like Sister Viverette after too much wine. Why am I so dizzy, she thought.

The mold was the size of a person and spread out like spilled old molasses, dripping down the sides of the quilt. It smelled horrible. Tiny white mushrooms were growing here and there. Elise looked closely, and her stomach lurched.

At the top of the bed, stuck in this puddle of mold, there was a pair of pink-rimmed glasses. And buck teeth.

Elise wanted to scream but couldn't find her breath.

This was Agnes.

Ok. Screaming and acting the fool wasn't an option.

This nightmare was different, true, but if she was to be an active participant in her own nightmare, she was going to take charge.

Lucid dreaming, that's what they called it, right?

Elise ran back to her bed and grabbed her backpack. It was a tough old thing, dusty but still intact.

Inside of it was a couple of her books, a water bottle green with mold, her flashlight, some odds and ends.

Oh. Snack bars.

Sweet. Guess it was true; junk food could survive the apocalypse, at least in dreams.

Elise jammed socks and underwear into the bag, along with a shirt and jeans. Oh, and her toothbrush. Dad had always badgered her about brushing her teeth.

She forced herself not to look back at the bed, where the body lay molding.

But what if it was moving?

What if Agnes was up and about, reaching out with drippy, gross fingers of mold and mushroom?

"What if I stop freaking myself out? How about that?"

Her backpack was heavy but not impossible.

Time to get out of here. Anywhere but here.

"Let's see the rest of my nightmare."

And that's when something wet and heavy moved in the darkness of the corner of her room.

The feeling you should look over your shoulder, that something awful was behind you?

Elise had that feeling. Her heart raced. She forced herself to look back into the darkness.

The stinky lump of Agnes still moldered on the bed, but there was a shadow behind it. A tall, thin shadow.

"Hello?"

Nothing.

She couldn't breathe, and her skin was alive with fear.

"Hello?"

The thin shadow moved, and when it did, there was something unnatural in the movement.

Terrified, Elise scrambled to the door that opened out into the storm. She looked down beneath the crumbling, rotten door jamb, and the whole world felt once more like it was spinning.

The street so far below was draped in sand and spark.

The roar of the wind was strong, and she couldn't hear if the shadow was moving. That made it worse because it could be on her before she knew it.

Time to move.

She strapped her backpack tight and dropped to her knees, looking down into the room below. Dark, but maybe safer than this.

Elise looked back. The shadow was no longer dark against the far wall. It was low and slow, moving along the floor. Toward her.

Her fingers gripped the metal bars that had supported the stone of her floor. The cut on her hand stung. She slung her left leg down into space, holding tight. Then the other leg and she was hanging by ten fingers out over the pit below.

Now what?

If she dropped straight, she might make the floor below.

Or she might miss by an inch and plummet.

Elise saw a beam of wood close to her left hanging from the debris of her floor. She held herself now with her right hand and reach out with her left, clutching a deep gouge in the wood.

Deep breath.

Like a monkey, she released her right and swung to the beam.

Not bad.

Then the beam shifted under her weight and dropped a few inches.

Bad.

If the beam fell out of the stone building, she would die.

The floor wasn't directly below her.

It was a foot to her right. She would need to swing over and drop and hope nothing gave way.

A warm, disgusting breath tickled her neck through the cold of the storm's air. She glanced back into the face of the shadow, and in the blackness of that face, there were teeth like knitting needles and dozens of tiny red eyes.

Elise didn't hesitate. She pushed off against the wooden beam and dropped as far to the right as she could, landing with a hard bounce against the floor below.

Run.

Elise moved to survey the room. It was a shamble of dust, just like hers had been. No corpses, no weird walking shadows.

And a hole in the back wall.

She ran to the hole. It was big enough to fit a skinny girl with a fat backpack, and there was a streetlamp just beyond, within reach.

"I can climb out onto the lamp post and make it to the street. No problem.

But then what?"

A thump. Elise turned to the sound.

The shadow man had dropped into the room and stood smiling a horrible hungry smile, a thin silhouette against the storm.

It slinked towards her.

Elise was through the hole in the wall and out onto the light post before she had time to blink.

She slid down the pole like she'd seen firefighters do in old movies and landed in the street, ankle-deep in soft sand.

She raised her middle finger up to the teetering tower of rubble that was all that remained of the Girl's Garden, turned, and ran as fast as she could into the dark, storm-swept streets of her Paris nightmare.

The last gossamer shreds of her blanket drifted away behind her.

The shadow watched her go, and its many eyes did not blink.

*

CHAPTER FOUR

The City of Light

WHERE WAS EVERYONE?

Her instinct was to call for help. It's what you do when you're a kid, and you're lost or scared.

You call for help, but it was so loud on the street she didn't imagine it was possible for her voice to be heard.

She tried anyway. Her call came out like a mouse fart.

This felt like one of those nightmares where you try to scream but can't find your voice. It was hard to take a deep breath for fear of sucking in sand, even through her makeshift bandana. There was no way her voice could carry over the roar of the wind.

The sand was getting in her eyes and hurting her face where it struck. She struggled to see. The air was thick with the sandstorm, and she didn't know if it was day or night.

Strange and horrible bolts of lightning struck and danced and crept like white fingers across the horizon. There was a deep red glow above that might have been the sun or might have been a full moon.

Tiny sparks erupted all around her, like fireflies.

She tried to touch one and got a painful shock, like when you are walking on carpet on a cold day and touch a friend on the shoulder.

Shielding her eyes, she looked back at the Girl's Garden.

It was a skinny tower of rooms with the sides of the building shaved away, as the last piece of a big three-layer cake, teetering, looking like it might fall at any moment.

And then it did.

The last of the Girl's Garden came apart into a million pieces as it fell towards the street below, imploding then exploding in clouds of debris.

Was that a scream?

The roar of the old building's death overwhelmed all for the briefest of moments, then became a tumble of noise echoing across the island.

Elise dashed away as the billowing waves of dust rolled over everything, whipping to and fro in the ferocious wind.

The old buildings continued to her left, just down the Rue Chanoinesse, past the smoking rubble where the school had once stood.

She ran and ducked into the first alley to get out of the storm.

The passage was dark but peaceful. She continued through past rusted garbage bins and piles of debris covered in sand.

"Notre Dame is this way. Towards the Seine. There must be people there."

The relative calm of the alley allowed her to gather her thoughts as she walked.

"So, I went to sleep. Middle of the night, big sandstorm hits, which is weird because wouldn't the weatherman predict something like that? Guess they really don't know what they're talking about.

Maybe a nuclear bomb went off, and everyone is hiding to stay safe. The wind causes our old building to collapse. Good riddance."

Faded posters lined the old walls, hard to see in the gloom.

The air was still.

Reddish light at the end of the alley hinted at the street beyond and the Place du Parvis, the square at the mouth of the cathedral.

This was Ground Zero for the city of Paris.

"Doesn't explain the shadow that chased me. Or the blob of poo that looked like it might have once been Agnes. Doesn't explain it at all."

She pinched herself so hard she thought she might pee a bit.

I'm wide awake.

She picked up the pace and popped out of the alley into the fury of the sandstorm.

There she was. Our Lady of Paris. The cathedral of Notre Dame towered above the Place du Parvis, and beyond her would be the great river Seine, the life of Paris, the flowing, wonderful, ageless river that brought the glory of a thousand years from the sea to France.

Elise loved the cathedral. Those great bells, Marie, Emmanuel, and the rest, that rang out each morning like angel calls. Her towering gothic walls of countless sculptures telling stories of love, faith, sacrifice, and compassion. Her guardians, those great gargoyles with views unmatched of the city of light, those stone eyes forever open, always on watch against the end of days. The only place more magical than at the cathedral's feet was in her, in the golden vast vaulted chamber of worship and hope where humanity's genius for building things became one with our thirst for beauty and boundless imagination.

When the Allies and the resistance came to Isle de la Cite in 1944 to liberate her from the Nazis, it was the sound of Emmanuel that heralded liberty to all of Paris.

Elise had learned of this in her studies, and what a glorious sound Emmanuel must have been.

She was a wonder, and Elise was not surprised to see Notre Dame still stood.

She will always stand, she thought as she ran from the alley, through the sandstorm, across the empty square, and up the steps to the cathedral of Notre Dame where the promise of shelter and sanctuary was sure to never be broken.

Here, in the heart of Paris, in the essence of hope and faith, there would be help.

*

CHAPTER FIVE

The Marionette Man

ELISE STOOD ON tired legs at the entrance to the cathedral, The Portal of Last Judgement.

The freezing sandstorm howled at her back.

The portal was a wonder of carved wood and metal, and Elise had entered the cathedral through that door many times since she came to The Girl's Garden. Sunday mornings, of course, when the girls attended service, but also in those quick moments when she could sneak away and explore the neighborhood, if only for an hour or so.

Elise hesitated because the nave beyond the Portal of Last Judgement was dark. It felt unnatural. The cathedral had always called to her, and she had come to know her way around the vast gothic interior. There was always light, whether it was the sun coming through the rose windows or the hundreds of candles that brought a warm glow to the night, a necklace of stars tended to by the Priests and the faithful.

She mumbled a curse, felt guilty for blasphemy in a church, then moved into the gloom.

There must be someone in here.

It was so quiet. Our Lady of Paris kept the scream of the

sandstorm at bay, as if telling it to "shut up, this is a place of holy purpose, and we don't need your noise here."

Her eyes adjusted as she stood still just inside the cathedral.

There was a dim light, after all, a crimson wash that played in from the stained-glass windows high above and along the cloisters, and even from the great south rose window. Shafts of soft light revealed the rows of benches before the choir.

Behind her were the mountainous organ and towering pipes. Even the sanctuary in the far distance was revealed in the bloody light. The buttresses high above her head remained in black, though, and the darkness was unnerving.

Anything could be lurking up there.

The sand had invaded even here, in Notre Dame. There was dust at her feet and sand the color of parchment was everywhere, sometimes in little dunes as high as her ankles.

She walked forward and deeper into the cathedral.

Now that her ears were adjusted, she could hear the wind, the ticking of sand against the windows, and soft creaks and groans from the lady herself.

There was no movement.

Elise had half expected and half hoped there would be a congregation inside, huddled in the safety of the great church, sharing food and water and stories of survival. If there was a place in all of Paris where people could be safe, this was it.

"Where are you? Is anybody here?"

Speaking above a whisper in the cathedral was rude, so her voice was timid and low.

Yes, but circumstances were weird. What if there's something bad in here? If I call out like an idiot, maybe there's a friend, and maybe there's something else. Maybe me calling out is like ringing the dinner bell at The Girl's Garden, and all of these skeleton corpse zombie shadows will rise from the pews and come after me with a thousand eyes and teeth like knitting needles.

And maybe I should stop freaking myself out, she thought.

"Hello? Is anyone here?"

Louder.

"Is anyone here?"

Louder still and this time with tears as the fear and the confusion overwhelmed her.

The sound of her trembling voice echoed in the cavernous place, bouncing from wall to wall and beyond, then disappearing into the silence.

What if I'm alone?

There she was, Elise St. Jacques, a terrified speck in jeans and a sweatshirt standing alone in the cavernous heart of the cathedral of Notre Dame, washing in ribbons of bloody light and dancing motes of dust, a single frail child in an eternal space.

"I'm just a kid!"

She felt silly and stupid.

Who cares if I'm a kid?

Who cares?

Something moved above her in the blackness, and it made a sound like bones grinding against rock.

Elise looked up.

He came down from the ceiling on strings like a spider down a web.

Elise didn't even have time to jump back. There was a giggle, a dirty smiling face an inch from her nose, breath like one of those awful sausages the ladies served on Thursdays, the kind made of innards stewed in the juices of a cow's stomach.

Then, just as quickly, the man ascended back into the darkness.

Well, that just happened, thought Elise.

Another giggle from the darkness above. An odd springy sound. Then, a shrill voice.

"Once more into the breach."

He descended with a mad and ferocious howl. Elise stood her

ground, and he was there again, a dirty old man's face with gums where teeth had once lived, smiling at her madly, white spittle flying from his thin lips.

"Bonjour, ma fille," the old man said, and then he was yanked back to the ceiling.

"I'm not French," Elise shouted as he went.

There was a moment of silence.

"Neither am I."

He descended slowly this time, tugging on a series of ropes at his waist that allowed him to control his speed. It made a creaking sound as he went. Elise studied him, afraid but too curious to run.

The man was dressed in a ragged and filthy blue suit.

He wore a necktie. His hair was gone, and his bald head was dark with soot.

He was harnessed into a complex system of ropes. Wait, not ropes, really. They were ropes fashioned out of scraps of clothing, fabrics, even in some places plastic bags. These strings were attached to something hidden at the ceiling, and he was attached to them like a marionette.

He was a marionette man, and he dangled a few feet above Elise, just out of reach.

"The guidebook said this would be a two-hour walking tour," the man said in a thick Liverpool accent, "English speaking guide, comfortable pace, ice-cream licking, and historical anecdotes delivered in a breezy and whimsical manner."

The man scrunched up his face.

"Bollocks."

"Who are you?" asked Elise.

"Clean as salt, fresh clothes, your own teeth, not scarred up with suction marks, the better question my dear is, who are you?"

"Elise St. Jacques."

"You're making it up."

"Am not."

"Are too."

"Stop it."

"You're not real," the man said, "don't think I know? Think I just tumbled out of the old turnip truck, eh? Just another spiteful little spirit, just another bit of undigested rat, there's more gravy than grave to you, child."

"That's Charles Dickens."

"No, it isn't."

"Yes, it is."

"Oh, no, it isn't."

With that, the marionette man ascended and let out a rude fart as he went.

"Now you're just being gross," Elise shouted into the darkness.

"You want a gruyere with that chardonnay?"

"What?"

"You want cheese with that wine?"

The strange marionette man opened his arms wide as he descended and addressed the cathedral.

"Savior, why do you send me an idiot ghost when I've been so good at cleaning your house? Why do you vex me so, oh great and holy ghost in the sky what has done us a real trick?"

Once more, he dangled inches from her face.

He tooted again.

Elise had been scared. Now, she was annoyed.

Besides, she thought, this old freak was so wrapped up in his own twine there was no way he could catch her before she got away.

"My name is Elise St. Jacques. I was trapped in the stupid girl's school down the street, and now I'm no better off than I was before. I'm twelve years old, and I'm not scared of you."

"Well, good. No reason to be scared of me."

"Well, good. Now, why are you dangling from the ceiling?"

"Where else should I dangle? Safe as houses in here, and not a speck of wind or spark of lightning."

"Where is everyone?"

The marionette man was startled by the question.

"What?"

"The people. What happened to the people? Where is everybody?"

"Not following you, kid. You mean, the people people?"

Elise was so frustrated that she could scream.

"What happened to Paris?"

"Oh. Where have you been, little one?"

The marionette man descended. There was concern in his eyes, but more than that, there was wonder and fear.

Elise stepped back. The man didn't unharness from his strange contraption, but he was practically standing on the floor of the cathedral.

"Where did you come from, girl?"

Elise was silent.

"You don't know where the people are? You don't know what happened in The Great Turn?

There are at least three thousand three hundred and thirty-three odd and horrible things that have happened since my holiday went daft, and that's just me. Multiply the odd and horrible by the twelve million people who lived in the city and by the seven billion people who lived in the world with their flat screens and Big Macs and iMacs and terrorism and refrigerators and video nasties and polar bears and Googles and hypermarkets. Odd and horrible to the infinite, that's what this is. They say the ocean just got sucked away like water down the bathtub drain. How can that happen? Where are the bloody people, you ask? Good bloody question, I say. What happened to bloody Paris? What happened to me? What happened to my Cecile? What happened to my family? What happened to YOU?"

His shout rang out like a gunshot through the cathedral halls.

Elise waited for the echo to recede before speaking.

"I don't know. I woke up. That's all.

I went to sleep, and I woke up, and everything was changed. Is this a dream?"

The marionette man chewed on this for a bit, then he began to reel himself back up and away from Elise.

"Maybe it's you. It's been ten years gone, child. If what you say is God's truth to my ear, if you went to sleep and woke up to this mess, you haven't aged a day in all that bloody time. You're a devil, and God help us, maybe it's you what done this to the world."

Fear swept over his face as he lifted away. Elise had seen fear like that before, in her mirror after her Dad died.

"You go away from here, girl. You go away from here and leave me alone."

Like a spider scurrying back into its web, the marionette man disappeared into the gloom above, the only sound the creaking of the pull that kept him aloft.

The red shafts of light from outside Notre Dame became brighter. Elise had no idea what time it was, but it looked as if the sun might be on the rise.

She needed a better look at the city, and she knew just where to go.

*

CHAPTER SIX

The Crab and Le Bat

HER LEGS WERE numb from the climb.

To the left of the front facade of the cathedral was a corkscrew stairway that had led Elise three hundred and eighty-seven stone steps up past the giant bell and on to the top of Notre Dame's South Tower.

Elise had been there many times, and she knew this was one of the best views of Paris, one of the best views of anything in the whole wide world.

The foul dust hadn't drifted into the stairwell passage.

Inside, it was clean and quiet, and she felt somehow safe. The glow of the rising sun led her upwards.

Elise stepped out into the cold and onto the platform at the top of the cathedral of Notre Dame. The wind was dying down, and the dust wasn't so bad. The lightning was gone. The sun was rising, huge and red, off to the horizon, and its light made the city the color of a fresh rug burn.

Oh, but she could see. She could see for miles. The sandstorm was just a whisper, and she pulled away the torn cloth that covered her mouth so that she could breathe freely.

Off to the north was Montmartre, to the south the towers of St.-Sulpice. Beyond was the Eiffel Tower, that iron and steel dagger aimed at the heavens. Elise walked along the rooftop observation area.

The safety cabling that had been in place to keep you from falling was battered and bent and even torn away in some places.

The gargoyles and chimeras still kept watch over the city, but their skins had been scoured and pockmarked by the sandstorms. This made her sad. She wondered for a moment if she could gather blankets, climb out, and cover them up to protect the gargoyles from the storm.

Probably a bad idea.

Elise had named them on her many trips to the top of the cathedral. There was Edgar and Ian, and over there was the chimera she called Ruth. Ruth the Truth, because in Elise's imagination, Ruth was the chimera who held all the centuries-old secrets of the Isle de la Cite, of Paris herself.

Wait, that one's new.

There was a sand-covered something off to her left, far along the edge of the cathedral. It was stone still as any of the other gargoyles, but she recalled nothing ever being in that spot.

Sand drizzled from it as if it had moved. Elise froze. It shifted slightly.

Oh, it had definitely moved. This wasn't a gargoyle at all. A bird? A bird covered in sand from the storm? No, not a bird. It was as big as Elise.

The thing shook like a dog shedding water after a bath, and sand flew everywhere.

Elise ducked behind the wall of the roof, and her heart felt as if it was going to jump out of her chest and run away.

She heard a clacking sound, like crab claws, and that was enough. Elise scrambled backward and dove for the stairwell.

Before she ducked back down the steps, she dared a quick look at what was perched on the edge of the cathedral.

It was a plump, red crab the size of a big dog, and it had eyes on stalks that were looking right at her.

Elise ran out of Notre Dame at a sprint and into the street.

She dashed past a bent and battered streetlight and around a corner. She ran hard, not looking at anything but what was ahead of her.

Heart pounding, throat dry from thirst and dust, she burst through the open door of the neighborhood boulangerie, Le Bat.

Light from the rising sun spilled into the old bakery, captured by the dancing motes of dust thick in the air. Elise tried to catch her breath, then wrapped the torn cloth back around her mouth to block out the dust.

The old bakery had been a wonderful, warm, funny place.

When the girls were allowed to visit Le Bat, which wasn't often, fat Monsieur Belfre had always greeted them with laughter, hugs, and sweet snacks. Elise remembered little of her time in America, but she knew the bread there wasn't anywhere near as good as what she had fresh from the oven of Monsieur Belfry.

The smell was still there, faint, a yeasty ghost that tickled her nose and belly.

Elise took a moment to take a bite from one of the snack bars that had been buried in her backpack. Once this was gone, there was no telling where she might get food. She was thirsty too and finding water might be an even bigger problem.

The glass case that had held countless baked delights was broken and empty. Chairs were overturned. The old cash register was gone, as was the little television that had sat on a shelf in the corner.

Elise walked through the gloom, looking for anything that might be of help. Behind the bakery counter was sand piled an inch high, little dunes of it led to the back, and Elise cautiously moved toward the darkness.

"Oh."

Stop and think, why don't you?

Elise slipped her backpack off and dug into a side pocket.

Her flashlight. It was a twisted light. You spin the back, and it powered the little light bulb for a few minutes, no batteries needed. Dad had given it to her.

She gave it a series of twists.

The beam of the flashlight pierced the darkness.

Elise moved on, picking her way past cardboard boxes brittle from the arid air. The light revealed trash, old newspapers, bags of flour that had been ripped open and emptied.

Newspapers? Elise grabbed at a paper partially buried in the sand. She pulled it up and played light over its yellowed surface.

The newspaper was Le Monde. Elise knew that those words meant "the world." In letters the size of her hand, the front page screamed "La Fin." The end.

There was a single photograph, poorly focused and at an odd angle, as it had obviously been taken in a dire situation. A mother and her baby huddled behind soldiers who were aiming their weapons at the sky while people ran around them in panic.

What was in the sky? What were they firing at? You don't shoot at an asteroid or a sandstorm or even a bomb from the sky. You only shoot at something alive, right? Something you could kill with a bullet.

All right, the sun was up, and it was time to find help and to figure things out.

Elise stepped back into the street. She stayed close to the old buildings as she made her way toward the Seine.

*

CHAPTER SEVEN

The Graveyard of Boats

PARIS HAD BEEN a city of life, light, and music.

Now, there was nothing except the shuffle of sand and a light whisper of wind. There weren't even birds. Elise had always delighted in the pigeons that swarmed the area around Notre Dame, dive-bombing tourists and eating out of your hand as if posing for photos.

These were all gone, or eaten, or hiding, or grown the size of elephants because of radiation or whatever.

The river Seine was close behind the cathedral. Elise ran across the street, heading straight for the water. If nothing else, she could boil water from the river so that it might be safe to drink.

But there was no water.

The Seine, the mighty river and lifeblood of France, was a dry and barren bed of sand. Elise sat on the edge of the Quay and stared down at the dunes stretched as far as her eyes could see in either direction.

Here and there were lumps in the sand, and out of those lumps peeked torn sails, masts, decks. The boats of the Seine were buried here, from the tiny little skiffs to the mightiest of the cruisers, buried in a nautical graveyard.

Curious, Elise clambered down the steps, down to the Seine.

The sand was soft but not too bad.

She walked out onto what had once been a river. Her boots sank an inch or two, and she was careful to step slowly. No need to drop into some kind of quicksand.

A riverboat rested on its side under dunes of dust.

She approached it cautiously, looking for any sign of movement. Nothing moved except the shifting sand.

Elise stood looking up into the side of the ship, the broken glass of a long porthole just overhead.

A skull stared back down at her.

She felt cold, colder even than the chilly air around her.

Eye holes, black and empty, staring down, judging, asking, condemning.

A single gold tooth gleamed from the back of the paperwhite jawbone.

It couldn't hurt her, and she knew that, but the hair on the back of her neck stood up anyway.

Someone had been riding in the boat, enjoying a cruise or doing some work, or trying to get away down the river. Now they were dead.

But, this person had been in the boat, on the water, right? How did they die? She was puzzled.

There was a hole in the side of the boat a few yards to her right. She shuffled over and took a look inside.

Just metal and wood and fiberglass or whatever it was boats were made of, all jumbled up and broken. Not rusted, though. Scoured by the sand until the metal was shiny and the wood was smooth.

More bones were scattered about the cabin, just beyond her reach. And something else. A snack machine? Yes, a vending machine.

So, how brave are you, Goofus?

Elise ducked low and moved into the ship. Her backpack snagged on something above her, and her heart froze for a beat.

She yanked it free and pulled it down from her back, carried it low along the sand.

It was dark in the corners, but soft red sunlight spilled through holes here and there, lighting more of the path toward the vending machine.

The machine lay on its side, the back facing her. The dead were off to her left, strapped into benches. Skeletal corpses, still dressed in tattered clothing, still draped with day packs and earphones. A few weathered guidebooks were scattered about in the dust.

So, this had been one of the tourist boats.

These people had been on a tour of the Seine when something awful happened, and it happened so quickly they didn't even take out their earbuds to stop listening to the English or German or Spanish translations.

The world had ended in a flash.

Elise moved around the fallen vending machine and tripped, falling face-first into the sand, into something hard and pointy.

Ribs. She had fallen into someone's ribs.

Elise was brave and old for her years, and her courage came from anger, a strong and deep place.

But she was still only twelve years old.

She screamed, and once she started screaming, she couldn't stop. Screaming, scrambling away from the bones, she cried so hard she thought her cheeks would break. She knew her screams would attract something terrifying, she knew it, but she couldn't stop.

She couldn't stop looking around, frantic now, at the bones jutting out from the sand all around her, the skulls, the fingers, the leg bone she had tripped over; it was all too much, too horrible.

Elise curled her knees to her chest and buried her face in her hands to try to stop the screaming, her sobs convulsing, the tears dropping into the sand, probably the only water the river had known in years, her tears, the river Seine.

She looked down at the tiny rivulet of tear water she had made.

The Seine, now just the tears of a little girl. This struck her as funny, and her screams stopped. Crying still, she began to laugh.

How about a boat for my tears so I could sail away from this place, she thought.

Elise took a few minutes to compose herself. Her fall had kicked up dust from the sand, and she waited for it to settle a bit before moving around. When the motes had gone back to rest, she stood and shook away the sand and the fear.

The glass door on the front of the vending machine was cracked, half-buried in a little dune. But inside, oh inside, the treasure!

Bottles of water. Chips. Candy bars.

Chewing gum.

Elise picked up the leg bone that had tripped her and swung it like a cricket bat. The glass cracked more but held. She swung again, and then again. On the tenth swing, her arms and shoulders aching, the slice on her hand stinging, sweat burning her eyes despite the cold, the glass shattered.

Let's find out how much my backpack will hold.

*

CHAPTER EIGHT

Watching The Girl

THE NOISE. SUCH shrill noise.

It had no sense of smell but could see a bit, and most of all, it could feel.

Tendrils, whiskers, antennae, reaching, sensing, discovering, following the tracks in the sand, following the tracks in the sand until the noise began, the high and awful sound.

The child thing was making the noise.

Was it wounded? We must see.

It sounded as if it were horribly wounded, as if a limb had been removed or it had been stepped on but not killed, just left to suffer.

"Oh, and my eyes are on stalks so I can see around corners."

The human child thing is making the wounded sound and sitting in the thing of wood and metal and bone.

It is not injured. Why does it make the wounded sound?

"Oh. I smell water. I smell saltwater."

The thing is leaking saltwater from its little eyes, and oh, the saltwater smells lovely.

I must tell Ozwold. He will be back soon from his strange scampering, and I will tell Ozwold, and we will go to the girl to find out if she knows where to find more of that lovely saltwater.

*

CHAPTER NINE

Candy Store

A BUS WOULD have been nice.

Or the metro. Of course, people who could help her would have been nice, too. Or just people. Rude people, bored people, annoying people. Any kind of people would have been wonderful.

The backpack was so full and heavy with her scavenged goods that her backed ached. Elise walked to the west along the Left Bank, having crossed the bridge that led to Shakespeare & Company, the old bookstore. This was not the original location, but it was still a wonderful place full of books of all kinds. A charming fountain stood in front of the store, but now it was dry and overflowing with sand.

Elise peeked into the broken windows and saw a scatter of paper in the darkness. This made her sad once again, and then she became angry at her sadness and punched herself in the thigh.

She stepped away from the store and walked back to the road along the Quay.

Now the sun was high and bright, an orange ball ringed by halos of red. The wind was gone, and the city was quiet. She could see well now, the dust no longer clouding the sky.

Overturned cars littered the road, some almost completely

buried in drifts of sand. There was one of the red tourist buses, still standing where it had stopped as it had collided with a tree.

Elise slipped off her backpack and clambered up to the second level of the double-decker. She ran to the front for a better view of the city and what lay ahead down the street.

Devastation as far as the eye could see. Tangled cars, buildings scarred black with fire damage, trees broken by wind or something else. No life, no movement anywhere.

Paris was dead as those skeletons in the ship.

Well, I'm not going to end up like that.

*

What would you do if you were the last person on earth?

Elise had sometimes considered what it would be like after a zombie apocalypse or a meteor strike or just some weird dimensional shift that wiped the slate clean and left the worldwide open for her.

Eating candy would be good. Unlimited candy, if you could find it. Maybe there would be electricity and you could watch every movie ever made. You could read every book, listen to every song, play with every toy as long as it wasn't something built for two. You could stay out until all hours, and nobody would be there to tell you to clean up, study, go to sleep, brush your teeth, you could poop where you please, you could throw rocks through windowpanes and joy ride in fast cars with the wind blowing in your hair, so free.

Of course, the reality of it was a bit more of a kick in the knees.

No electricity, not much candy, sand and dust wherever you looked, and you weren't alone, not really. There were scary things and a man who dangled from the ceiling of Notre Dame like a farting puppet.

So, Elise entered what had once been a tiny candy shop on the Left Bank and shut the door tight behind her.

This would do for tonight.

The lock was good, the windows small and unbroken, half-covered in dust. Light could get in, but not by much. The store was small and uncluttered, with a wooden bar that ran the length of the place.

Even the glass here was unbroken.

There was no candy in the case. Not a problem. She had snacks galore for now. What she needed was a safe place to hide, and this would work.

A twist of her flashlight, and she moved up the small steps to the first floor. Not too dusty, not too scary. There was an apartment with a single bed, simple furniture, and a bathroom. This had been someone's home. Probably the candy maker. Elise thought it must have been a woman, an older woman because the decorations in the room were colorful and frilly and of another time. She had never known a grandmother, but this is what she imagined a grandmother's apartment would look like.

There was a framed picture by the side of the bed. A child's school photograph, a boy Elise's age, maybe younger, smiling, dressed in a PSG jersey.

I wonder where he is? I wonder where they all are?

Elise dropped her backpack to the floor.

She heard the voice of her Dad, that rich, deep voice.

She couldn't hear what he was saying, but it warmed her. It gave her courage and hope.

The adrenalin she had spent, the horror, the fear, the chaos she had felt, the confusion and wonder, all of these things pulled away at the courage and endurance inside of her like strings pulling the marionette man back to the top of the cathedral.

Elise pulled blankets around herself and tucked away behind the bed.

Hidden, she fell sound asleep for the first time in the new world.

*

CHAPTER TEN

The Man of Many Eyes

THE WINDS CAME at night.

That's how it worked now.

Sleep was fitful in the candy store. It's hard to rest easy, no matter how tired you are, when you're afraid of the world around you, so Elise was half-awake when, after sundown, the sandstorm came back.

There was no slow build, no warning. The still of the evening was blasted with a roar of hard wind as if a giant had flipped a switch, and Elise jumped up to the window.

Visibility dropped to nothing, only the tiny sparks in the air, Hell's fireflies. Then, that roaring, crashing lightning filled the sky.

Dust devils formed along the street below and whipped along like violent ghosts. The shock flies seemed to fly into the dust devils, and Elise watched, fascinated, as they became little tornadoes of electricity. They were beautiful, but she thought it might be smart never to get too close to one if the opportunity presented itself. Such was static electricity in a sandstorm at the end of the world.

Something else moved in the gloom and frenzy. Elise shrunk down so that only her eyes peeked over the windowsill. There was a massive creature lurching and shambling down the street, as big as an elephant, with tentacles that reached out and probed as if seeking food.

Elise moved quietly as she could away from the window.

She covered herself back up in the blankets and old clothes, concealed and safe as could be, and tried to go back to sleep.

*

Morning light drifted in through the window, and Elise woke up. She heard no sound, no howling wind. Just like that, the sandstorm had died.

She stretched and went to the window.

The last time she had gone to sleep, it hadn't worked out.

Perhaps this night's sleep would wipe away this new, horrible, unkind world.

Outside the window, the sand outside was still, a red snowstorm covered Paris.

Oh well. At least there was no sign of the giant creature she had seen the night before.

The street was perfectly calm.

She made a breakfast of a blueberry health bar and a can of soda she had pulled from the machine.

"Brush your teeth," she said to herself after, "We're not animals here."

A twist of the water faucet in the tiny kitchen produced a rattle of pipes and a belch of dust and nothing more. She brushed and rinsed with the rest of her soda.

There was water in the toilet, and she relieved herself with a proper flush.

"Oh. Shouldn't have done that." She suspected water would be precious, and there went most of it from the water bin at the back of the toilet.

Elise stared out the window at the landscape below.

She felt safe in the candy store, but she knew she needed to find help. If the weird guy in Notre Dame was still alive, there must be others, less weird, somewhere.

"I can't stay here."

*

She was careful to walk close to the buildings along the Left Bank, along the Quai d'Orsay, as she made her way west. She didn't want to leave footprints out in the open.

Also, she could scavenge as she went, popping into promising shops. She had more than she could carry now, having found bottles of water and plenty of snacks.

Elise had used some of the water to clean the cut on her hand. It helped, and once clean, the cut wasn't as bad as all that.

There had been skeletons, of course. Bodies dried by the wind and sand. Some of the cars held them, and she came across a dead man dressed in rags hanging by a rope from a sand stripped tree. The leathery skin was like jerky, and the rope made a little creaking noise as it swung in the soft breeze.

The sky was strange, with no clouds, just the red haze of the sun. The dust in the air obscured visibility.

But just after noon, there it was.

The Eiffel Tower.

She had been afraid it was destroyed, that whatever had come to destroy the city had toppled her, but the tower was still in one piece, still proudly pointing to the heavens, still there.

The Girl's Garden had never taken the girls to the tower.

That would have been too much like fun, she supposed. On the weekends, though, when they were taken to the museums or other sights, she had seen the tower. So amazing, so tall, a perfect place from which to see the entire city.

That was her plan. Get to the top of the tower. From there, she would see forever; she would find help.

Elise stood for a moment in the shadow of an old market building, resting her legs. Walking in the sand was difficult, and her thighs burned.

Something near made a sound like the hiss of a bicycle tire being emptied.

Then it moved, just behind her, in the shadows.

Elise turned and saw a shadow, a shadow that moved, a shadow with many eyes and sharp teeth as long as your fingers.

"Run! For God's sake, girl, run!"

An old woman dressed in a heavy brown coat was standing back down the avenue, screaming at Elise.

Elise was too scared to move.

"Run!"

The shadow slithered out of the darkness and scrabbled on all fours into the street, toward the screaming old woman. The sound attracted it, the call to run.

Elise watched in horror as the thing dashed to the woman like a spider on four legs chasing down a tasty bug. It happened so quickly. The woman tried to run, but the shadow thing was on her before she could turn.

Elise ran. She didn't stop to watch what happened, she didn't look behind, she ran as fast as she could and tried to block the horrible sounds out of her ears, the sound of the old woman being killed.

Run. Run.

Run. She knew she was leaving tracks, and she was slow in the thick sand and weak from fear. This was that nightmare where something is chasing you, and your feet are stuck in mud, and you can't move.

Into the alley, down the side street, less sand there, easier to run.

She dashed down a street to her left, then cut through an alley to the west, ducking and dodging and finding places where the sand was thin on the pavement.

There was a clattering sound above her. She looked up, and

there was a big shadow pacing her along the rooftop, along the gutters.

Elise ducked into another side street. This part of the Left Bank was older and rife with little paths, thank goodness. She looked up.

Still there. Whatever it was, it was following her, keeping pace, hunting her, making weird noises like spikes on steel and...a chirping sound?

She looked behind, and there it was. The Shadow Man.

It had found her.

It was red with sand. No, not sand. It was red, but that wasn't sand. That was the old woman, or what was left of her, dripping from the Shadow Man.

Elise screamed and cursed and ran as hard as she could, but now her legs failed. Fear seeped into the muscles and paralyzed her.

She tripped and tumbled, got up and ran again, looked back.

The Shadow Man was meters away.

This was it, oh crap, this was it.

"Daddy, Daddy, Daddy!"

Even in the moment, it felt silly, like a baby, calling for Daddy, but so scared, so scared, so stupid.

She fell, not feeling the pain as she hit the street.

She rolled onto her back, ready to kick as hard as she could, ready to fight.

The Shadow Man stood over her and smiled, dripping with the old woman's fresh blood.

Elise could see now that it wasn't really a shadow. It was slimy and black like a snake or an eel, smooth and terribly thin.

The skinny hand reached out for her, for her face.

Elise kicked it, and it moved back, startled but still reaching for her.

And then there came the strangest noise, the sound of an angry monkey.

The Shadow Man heard it too. It looked up just as the giant

crab and the angry monkey dived from above and landed between it and Elise.

The monkey had fins and was covered with scales, and it was riding the colossal red crab like a cowboy rides a horse.

*

CHAPTER ELEVEN

Not Today

THE CRAB RAISED pincers the size of coconuts and serrated with edges like a knife as if daring the Shadow Man to approach.

The monkey, if that's what it was, pointed at the Shadow Man and howled.

They stood their ground between the Shadow Man, dripping with blood, and Elise lying helpless in the alley.

The dark figure moved to the right, trying to get around them, to get to Elise.

The monkey and the crab blocked it.

The crab was deep, dark red with undertones of blue, the fat shell covered in spikes and bumps, feelers waving above what must have been its face, eyes on stalks.

The ape, almost as tall as Elise, seemed more a creature of the sea than of the jungle. A light belly gave way to a dark brown back, all covered in wide scales, with fins like a fish that ran the length of its spine. When it roared, which it did constantly, a tall row of spines stood up from the scaly scalp.

The Shadow Man hissed and slapped the howling sea monkey with the back of a bloody hand. The blow sent the ape flying across the alley and hard into a wall.

It bounced and didn't move.

The crab raised up on thick legs and attacked, sweeping claws back and forth, trying to strike.

The Shadow Man was too quick, and it reached for the crab with those thin fingers.

Snap.

The crab was quicker than Elise thought possible, and with the sound of carrots being chopped, it brought up a huge claw and neatly lopped off several of the Shadow Man's fingers.

A hiss turned into a thin, wet scream.

Something heavy jumped over Elise as she rolled away from the fight. The monkey.

It was awake, alive, and now it was shrieking and climbing onto the Shadow Man's back, biting and striking with its fists.

The crab moved again between Elise and the Shadow Man.

It was protecting her?

The monkey and the black creature rolled and scraped in the dust of the alley, sending spatters of blood flying.

The Shadow Man got its hand around the monkey and lifted as the sea ape violently, madly, struck and tried to bite. The monkey was slammed against the wall.

An accordion sound, then a loud crack, and the sea ape went limp, its neck broken.

Elise couldn't see the crab's eyes or its face if there was one she could understand, and the thing didn't make a sound or even change colors, but she knew it was furious and hurt.

The crab was on the Shadow Man before Elise could take a breath.

Claws like twin scythes went to work, slicing and hacking.

The Shadow Man screamed again, but the scream stopped, and then there was just the wet sound of the crab dismembering the thin, ebony demon that had killed its monkey friend.

Dark blood spray as if from a garden sprinkler, and Elise felt it hit her face.

She stood, backing away, then running to the far end of the alley, trying to get as far away as possible.

She stopped to look back.

The crab was done with the Shadow Man.

It sidled to the dead sea monkey.

The long red feelers, like tentacles, reached out and seemed to sniff or touch or sense the sea monkey. This went on for a few moments as if the crab was trying to decide what might be wrong with its friend. Elise sensed an overwhelming sadness from the creature.

Then, those hideous pincers picked up the carcass of the dead ape with great care and draped it across the wide shell of a back.

"Thank you," said Elise.

The thing didn't look back at her. Elise couldn't tell if it had even heard her voice or that it would have understood.

The great crab moved away, leaving the dead Shadow Man lying still in the cool of the alley. Elise watched the crab leave, then turned and walked back into the street.

What a strange world this was turning out to be, she thought and wiped the blood from her face. There was a touch of warmth on her skin from the red glow of the sun.

She looked up into the sky.

Wait.

Is that a balloon?

*

The bag was bright blue and trimmed with gold that sparkled even from a distance. A basket big enough for perhaps two people dangled below the bag, although it was difficult to judge as the balloon was so high.

The glorious blue hot air balloon floated above her, gliding to the west. She could hear the "pssshhhh" of the flame keeping it aloft. She could pick out a single figure that seemed to ride in the basket.

Don't wave. Don't yell. You don't know who that is or what they might do to you.

Elise stepped back behind a sand dune and watched the balloon.

Ok. There were people here in this new Paris. There was the weird marionette man. There was the poor dead woman who had tried to warn her of the Shadow Man.

Now there was someone piloting a blue hot air balloon.

Elise had seen horror and felt helpless overwhelming fear on that cold morning, but now, the sight of this incredible surprise, this wildly strange thing, lit the tiniest spark of hope in her heart.

She had been rescued by a giant crab and by a howling sea monkey that had sacrificed its life in battle with a demon, and now she watched someone piloting a balloon a thousand feet above, someone that might help, that might tell her what had happened to the city.

Well, I'd better follow the balloon.

So, she took off walking fast.

Where was it going? What if it was going to just drift off and away?

She quickened her pace, finding strength and energy in hope, staying alert to her surroundings but glancing up to track the balloon.

Wait. No way.

It looked as if...

Maybe it was just a coincidence, but...

It sure looked as if the blue balloon was flying toward the Eiffel Tower.

*

CHAPTER TWELVE

Ozwold

THE CIRCUS WOULD miss Ozwold.

I would miss him, too, although he was loud and rude and pulled on my feelers as a joke.

Ozwold was brave and good.

He was a good soldier and even better on the trapeze.

That's how he will be remembered.

*

CHAPTER THIRTEEN

Renny and Robert

THERE WAS AN arcade.

Before the big indoor shopping malls or department stores, the people of Paris would shop along the arcades, covered passageways lined with shops of all kinds, vendors, merchants, cafes. You could buy your dinner ingredients, have a glass of wine, chat with your neighbors about whatever neighbors chatted about, you could even smoke a cigarette back in the old days when cigarettes were everywhere, and nobody knew how bad they were for you.

The wreck of a car had been moved to the mouth of the arcade, along with wire and boards and debris. A wall. Somebody had walled off the entrance to the arcade.

Elise ducked low and tried to see into the arcade passage, lit as it was by the red sunglow that spilled in through the long, broken glass arcade ceiling.

She had no intention of stopping. The balloon was her main concern. But she thought she had heard a noise down the arcade, and the wall of debris was mysterious enough to catch her attention. Somebody had deliberately created the wall, so perhaps somebody was still there, down the passage, in the arcade.

What if they weren't nice?

Crap. What to do?

She dashed back into the street and looked towards the tower.

The blue balloon was gliding to the second level of the tower, over a hundred meters above the Champs de Mar. She could no longer hear the muffled whoosh of the flame, and she couldn't see who or what was piloting the thing. Even the bright blue of the balloon, in that distance, became a dingy brown through the red haze of the sky.

But it was targeting the tower.

She heard the noise again from beyond the wreckage wall, and this time it sounded like a voice. Or voices.

Just a peek.

Elise crouched low and went back to the mouth of the arcade.

She found a hole, a space just big enough for her if she removed her backpack. She dropped her bag into a little huddle of debris, so it was concealed, then slipped through the hole in the debris wall and into the arcade.

Shafts of dim light and old shops to her left and right.

Voices in the distance, arguing.

There were people here.

Elise walked toward the voices, and as she approached, their words became clearer. They were speaking in French, which made it difficult for her but not impossible.

She was good at filling in the gaps of her understanding, and more often than not, she was right.

"Do you think the National Team is just around the corner, waiting for you to cheer like an idiot?"

"There must be a stadium, and if there's a stadium, there's a team. Wouldn't have a stadium without a team."

"You're out of your mind. Who's on the team? Dogs and old women?"

"Maybe. Maybe local boys, maybe a busload of Japanese tourists, maybe, yes, it's dogs and old women. I don't care. Do I look like I care who is on the team? I care that there is a team."

"Japanese tourists were the first to die. Too busy taking pictures."

"Bigot! Racist!"

Elise stood at the door of the little cafe. Tables were set outside, and these were clean of dust and decorated with plastic flowers. A golden glow came from candles inside of the cafe, and two old men were revealed in the amber light, sitting at a table with a bottle of wine between them, half-full glasses in front of them, cigarette smoke drifting up from a big black ashtray.

"Bonjour," she said.

The two men stopped arguing. The thin one with fat eyebrows looked like he was going to jump out of his skin. The other, small and heavy with thick glasses and thicker lips, made a little gasp and stood.

A machete appeared in his hand, pulled, Elise supposed, from under the table.

"Mon Dieu. Une fille."

Elise stepped back, ready to run.

"My name is Elise. Who are you? Parlez-Vouz Anglais?"

"Renny," said the thin one, "it's a little girl. What the Hell?"

The small one with the machete waved the blade in the air, trying to be menacing but failing in the attempt.

"Who are we? Who are you?"

"I said my name is..."

"Yes, yes, yes. You said your name is whatever. Little girls have all been eaten, so don't tell me you're a little girl. You're something awful in disguise, and I'll whack you."

"I haven't been eaten. Right?"

The thin one took a drag on his cigarette.

"She has a point. Maybe she's from the Orsay."

The one with the blade made a snorting noise.

"There are four people in the Orsay, and that was a year ago, so now it might only be mad Justin and his imaginary friend. I say she's one of those fiends pretending to be a little girl."

"Sit down and drink your wine, you old queen. If she's a murderous fiend, we're dead already, so we might as well have a smoke and a talk."

He pulled a chair over to the table and motioned for Elise to join them.

"I'd rather you put down the big knife. And I'm sorry, but can you speak English?"

"Put down the blade, you fool."

The small, heavy one grunted and sat down, slipping the machete back under the table. He picked up the bottle and poured wine into a dirty glass.

"Fine. So, this is death, come to meet us with weepy little eyes and blood on her face, making us speak English. A horror. Let's toast to our demise and find out what our assassin has to say before she turns all monstrous and eats our livers."

Elise watched them. She knew bullies and cruel people from her time at the Girl's Garden, from Agnes and the teachers and that awful man who trimmed the hedges and made rude comments. These two were old, hopeless, and a bit dim, but they were people, and they didn't seem to be cruel.

She sat down at the table and offered her hand.

"So, again, I'm Elise. Who are you, and what happened here?"

The old men looked at each other with a comical "seriously?" expression.

The thin one spoke first. In English.

"I'm Robert. My fat friend who likes to think there's a football tournament just around the corner is Renny."

Renny lit a cigarette.

"We blocked off the arcade. We hide up there, on the first floor above the cafe. Safe enough."

Renny blew smoke.

"Where have you been hiding, and why is there blood on your face?" he asked.

"I wasn't hiding. I was asleep. I woke up, and Paris was gone. Gone and different. Something tried to kill me just now, and this is its blood."

Four bushy eyebrows shot up at the same time.

"Impossible."

"To death and violent little girls." The two old men raised their glasses in a toast and drank their wine. Robert made a noise in the back of his throat and offered his glass to Elise. She shook her head no.

"Cigarette?" Robert held out a pack of smokes. Renny snorted.

"She's ten."

"What's it going to do, kill her?"

"Twelve," said Elise.

They both raised their hands in apology.

"You claim," began Renny, "you don't know what happened. That you woke up and Paris was gone."

"Yes."

"It's been ten years, girl."

"Elise. And that's impossible."

He pointed at the cafe wall to his right.

There were countless little scratches on the wood, single digits carved out in fours then crossed through with a heavy line.

It was a counting of the days, and it covered the wooden wall.

Robert ground his cigarette butt out in the ashtray.

"She's mad, Renny," he said in French.

Elise was silent because she could not argue the point.

"Yes," said Renny, "of course, she is. Aren't we all?"

Fat old Renny leaned over to Elise and spoke. His voice was low and measured, and his eyes did not blink.

"I woke up too, with a dog and a mother who cared for me, in my little apartment in the 18th. There was a terrible sound, and wind threatened to blow down our building.

The television was showing a movie about the end of the world, but it wasn't a movie, it was the news, and it was happening all over the world at once. It started with the ocean. The ocean disappeared, all of it, in a flash. Then, there was no reason, no warning, just things coming up from the ground and dropping from the sky and no bullets, no bombs, no warships in our mighty French army could stop them. By the time I had finished my coffee, I had watched America fall on my little flat screen, and by the time we had made lunch, there were screams outside of my apartment, and my dog was barking, and my mother was screaming. I looked outside of my window, I lived on the third floor, and I saw these things, these awful things, chasing my neighbors through the streets, tearing into them, killing them, going door to door. I saw the Seine drain away. I looked up, and I saw them in the sky."

He stopped and took a breath, then a sip of wine.

"By the time mother had prepared dinner, our city had fallen. Our world had fallen, for all I knew. The sky turned the color of mud, and the wind was a hurricane. And days became weeks, and we tried to find peace, but first, they killed and ate my dog, and then they killed and ate my mother, and then I found some people who could help, and the things got most of them too. And as time went by, there was just Robert and this little place that escapes their notice, and we sit in here and smoke and drink and pray we're not found so we might die a peaceful death in our sleep as drunken old men."

"So, girl," he said, "the marks on the wall over there represent the nine years, five months, and twelve days Robert and I have been in this place. But it has been ten years since that morning when I woke up to the end of the world, and I still do not know what happened or why. In the movies, you know, they show you the alien invasion, the zombie horde rising up, the meteor falling from the sky. And there's always a scientist or a hero who will tell you what is going on, what planet or what Hell the villains are from, and how they are to be stopped, and at what terrible cost. But this did not happen as it does in movies or in books, or in songs about the end of all things. This happened after breakfast and before lunch, and I have no idea why."

And with that, Renny stopped talking and sat back in his chair, staring at his hands.

There was a low whistle from the wind beyond the street and a light ticking from a clock sitting somewhere in the darkness. There was the smell of cigarettes and of old men who had not washed in a long time. Elise took a moment to consider what Renny had just said before she asked,

"And what about that balloon?"

*

CHAPTER FOURTEEN

Take the Blade

ELISE WOULD HAVE felt this was foolish if she were more self-aware.

She would have mentally kicked herself.

These two harmless old men had been leading a perfectly peaceful life, hidden away in their little cafe, and now she was escorting them outside to look at a big blue balloon that might have been a figment of her over-heated imagination.

But she was excited to have someone with her as they made their way outside, and self-awareness was sometimes a rare commodity for Elise.

She picked up her backpack from its hiding spot and strapped it to her back.

Renny and Robert followed her, crouched low, looking this way and that like squirrels crossing a street wary of the inevitable car to come and squash them.

The distance from the cafe, through the rough barricade, down the passage, and into the street was short, less than a hundred meters.

It felt like a journey of a thousand miles.

"There. It was flying there. Toward the tower."

Elise pointed up and to the west, into the blob of orange that might have been the sun.

"I've never seen or heard of a balloon. Are you sure it wasn't a jelly?"

"A what?"

Renny shrugged his shoulders.

"It's what we call them. They float; they have lots of arms, some as small as your hand and some as big as a house. Air jellies."

"Take you up screaming as soon as piss on you. Horrid things," Robert added.

Elise thought about what she had seen.

"No. It had no arms, and it was trimmed in gold. I saw the flame that kept it in the air."

"Well, be that as it may, we're not going up there. I'd rather sip my wine and die of lung cancer from my old cigarettes, thank you."

"You don't mean it."

"Maybe not, but still."

"Cancer is just another thing that eats you, you know. Just more slowly than a monster."

"You're clever, for a little girl."

"And you're annoying and need a bath," said Elise, "but are you coming with me?"

Robert seemed ready to continue, but Renny put his hand on his friend's shoulder.

"No."

Elise didn't understand.

"Someone flew a balloon to the top. We need to go see who it is."

Renny shook his head.

"We've seen enough."

"I haven't."

"Then you'll die, Elise."

Renny turned and began walking back to the cafe.

Robert hesitated, then smiled and dropped to a knee in front of Elise.

"Come with us. We'll keep you safe as best we can; there's food and wine enough. And Renny isn't as bad as he seems."

"Yes, I am, I'm awful, and I don't want a little girl living with us. Let her go, Robert."

"Shut up, you old pisser. Come on, girl. You're a fool, and you'll die a fool's death if you go much further by yourself."

A long moment passed.

Sometimes when you play solitaire, you can't help peeking at the next card. When you run, you want to take one more step. When you dream, you want one more moment in bed.

"I'm going to see what's at the top of the tower. From there, I will see for miles and miles, and maybe I can find even more people. So, thank you, but no, I'm going."

Robert shrugged.

"Fine. I don't like kids anyway."

"But one favor. I want you to take this."

And that's how Elise came to own a sharp knife.

*

CHAPTER FIFTEEN

Scynda

WHAT HAD HAPPENED here?

A battle, a birth, a murder?

Scynda moved down the side of the building, every bit of her skin the color of brick, the texture of mortar, so she blended with the city around her.

If you looked at the building, you would not see her unless she wanted to be seen, and if she wanted to be seen, you only had a gnat's breath to live.

She wasn't just invisible because that was a cheat and of no proper use.

She was unseen.

She became.

That was her gift as a special and blessed child of the First Sea.

There was no finer thing than to be there, in plain sight but unseen, stalking, smiling in anticipation of feasting, a part of all and yet a part of nothing.

When a world was turned and drained, Scynda arrived on The Shock Tide, along with her dark assassins and other, stranger things.

This world was rich, and the hunting had been wonderful.

So little resistance. Now though, there was this amusing puzzle of blood and tissue.

She slithered to where The Man of Many Eyes was lying in a wide splatter of its own...self. Her skin was brown, then gray, then she relaxed and became as silver as the belly of a dead fish. This was her natural color, and she knew it could be used because whatever had killed the lurker, The Man of Many Eyes, was long gone.

Her eyelashes wave to and fro because they were tentacles as long as a frog leg, and they helped her sense things.

Tiny hairs along her arms began to feel the air as well.

What was that? Something different.

The smell of blood, of course. And fear. Fear was a smell, and it was strong here. But something else?

Her skin opened and reached out too, each cell so hungry, so in control of its own ways and yet a slave to her will. A new smell? A quick ripple wave of blue passed along her surface. Yes, a new smell. Crab, yes, dead sea monkey, yes, but something else.

Human. Young and female. Harsh, clean smell, not like the rest, a fresh smell, the smell the human's had when the change had come. A fresh smell didn't belong in this world.

I must hunt and kill this clean new thing that doesn't belong here before it does any real harm.

She stood over the remains of the lurker.

She was Scynda the Mirror, the seeker, the arrow in the night, the leader of the Men of Many Eyes.

She became as black and red as the alley at her feet.

Others appeared, moving quietly, almost gently, but with awful purpose, dark, slender, sinister men with mouths full of knitting needles and so many, many eyes.

They were the Lurkers, The Shadow Men, The Men of Many Eyes, and they formed a circle of seven around Scynda.

She looked as human as human, as sleek and beautiful as a painting in one of their old museums, but as awful as horror on the face of a newborn. Scynda raised her arm, her cells sniffing the air for any sign.

And then she smiled and pointed to the west.
The Lurkers moved off, on the hunt.
Scynda became the color of the dust and followed.

*

CHAPTER SIXTEEN

My Field of Slugs

ELISE ONCE PLAYED a video game where you were a frog. It was an old game, something her Dad might once have played.

She moved towards the Eiffel Tower like the frog in that old game, dashing from side of the street to side of the street, from pile of rubble to wrecked car to overturned public toilet to sand dune. And all the time, she was hoping she didn't get squashed because she didn't think there was another round in this game.

The air was getting colder. The red fire of the sun was sinking lower and lower, and shadows were growing longer.

A rusted carousel made deep squeaking sounds as it moved in the breeze. There were sandblasted unicorns and mermaids; the color removed left the sad sculptures bare and gray ghosts.

The park was a desert, of course, and there were dunes piled high, with pointy tips, like sandcastles. Some were as high as her waist, while a couple of these stood a good ten meters from base to tip. They were weird, and she steered clear of them where she could.

She kept her head on a swivel, always looking for movement.

She had tied the long machete to a bit of rope and wrapped the rope around her waist. The blade was in a sheath of old leather. It didn't make her feel any safer. But it was there if things got bad, and she felt she could use it.

Elise loved animals but had no qualms about eating meat, so killing something wasn't a concern. At her age, the connection between the ham in your croque monsieur and the pig in the petting zoo was tenuous. She smiled and felt warm inside when she saw a puppy but had no problem at all dissecting a frog in science class or killing a spider on the wall.

Of course, the frog doesn't fight back, but still.

As you know, there's a surprising coldness that can manifest at the most unexpected times in the heart of a child, and perhaps the universe saw fit to put it there as protection against what might lay in wait.

There are moments when children need to be dangerous.

*

By the time she had dashed and ducked and hid and scrambled to the Champs de Mar, the wide park at the foot of the Eiffel Tower, the sun had disappeared behind the skyline of dead Paris, and Elise was exhausted.

Night was cold, and the winds came, sandblasting all in their path. Lightning came too, along with the shock flies and dust devils of electricity that danced and haunted the land.

Elise shivered and munched on a candy bar as she hid tucked away inside a twisted pile of burnt-out cars. Getting deep into the wreck without getting cut or stuck had been a trick, but now she was squirreled away in a little steel den where she felt as safe as could be, and to top it off, she had, through the maze of metal, a clear view of the tower.

Once, the Girls of the Garden were taken on a bus trip to the Museum of Science at night. On the way, Elise had marveled at the beauty of the Eiffel Tower as it sparkled, a million lights all twinkling in synchronization, illuminating the night, firing the imagination.

There were always so many tourists, thousands of them, always a crowd.

It was always a dream for Elise to be in the tower and go to the top, to see the city at her feet and all around her.

Now it was dead, a skeleton against the roar of the sand-storm night.

How can I get those lights back on, she thought.

She didn't once think of being back with Robert and Renny at the cafe.

But where was the balloon?

It wasn't tied to the top of the tower, nor was it sitting on the second deck, not that she could see.

Of course, seeing was a problem as the night wore on.

The sandstorm was so thick visibility was limited, and the air was alive with the sparks she had come to understand as static elec-tricity, the painful result of so much sand whipping against so much sand at such high speeds.

There would be no taking the tower tonight. Too dark, too dan-gerous, too much storm and sand.

She was twelve, she was brave, but she wasn't stupid.

Elise had taken a blanket from the old woman's candy store.

She wrapped it around her and curled into a ball, back against a cold wall made of someone's Peugeot, and fell fast asleep.

*

She had been buried alive.

What time is it?

It was pitch black inside of her hiding place, and her view of the tower was gone. She reached out and touched sand.

The sandstorm had buried her in the night.

Elise felt a moment of panic and pushed her hand out further. Her fingers went through the dune, and she felt the cold morning air. Light shot through the sand as it sifted away.

This was a good place to keep safe, and she would remember it.

She tidied up the candy wrappers by burying them and then took a sip from a water bottle.

Elise stepped out of the wreckage and looked about.

The morning was tranquil, with the wind just an echo.

The sandstorm had created new dunes here and there, and the white powder had accumulated over and around her hiding place and made it look as if the cars and debris were dusted with confectionary sugar.

She missed the morning sound of birds. The pigeons were such a part of Paris, such a part of the soundtrack. Their absence made her sad.

And then she heard someone singing.

It was far off, so distant, but it was a voice, singing, and it was singing "La Vie en Rose."

Her heart jack hammered. Where was it coming from?

Elise walked across the sand-covered expanse of the Champs de Mars toward the tower, trying to figure out where the song was coming from.

She was a tiny thing in the shadow of a giant, a speck on a vast ocean of sand, so small and dark and obvious.

She was walking backward, looking around, when her foot tripped over something, and she fell.

It didn't hurt. The sand was soft. For a moment, she considered making a sand angel. Then she looked to see what she had fallen over.

The lump, half-buried in sand, was brown and slimy, like a garden slug, but the size of her backpack. It roiled and quivered, sand sticking to its sticky skin.

Elise froze and watched the thing as it rolled over and presented hundreds of little pink tentacles, each boasting a fang like a cat's tooth. At the center of it was a hideous mouth.

She was running before she could think. She stumbled again and was up fast. Another of the things. Then she focused, looked around, not at the sky, not at the tower, but at the sandy desert all around her.

There were hundreds of these brown lumps, these sand slugs with claws. Thousands.

They were everywhere, some covered with sand and just bumps in the dust, others in the open, squirming and dirty like worms.

Stand still. Figure it out.

Okay. They didn't move quickly, at least not yet. Giant slugs, but she was quick, and if she was careful, they couldn't hurt her.

Watch your step, she told herself, as she made her way across the park's lawn. Just watch your step, and it will be fine.

The voice was still singing. Elise let the voice calm her, and she walked with care, avoiding the slugs, walking toward the tower.

The rising sun cast light from the east, and then she noticed that the things didn't like the light. As the sun touched them, they squirmed and wormed their way into the sand, hidden.

Just like earthworms. They come out at night then bury themselves in the day.

Well, that doesn't help, she said to herself, just as she stepped on something squishy.

The slug wrapped around her boot in an instant.

She felt sudden, heavy pressure as it squeezed her calf, and then dozens of pointy things tried to push through her thick boot.

Elise grabbed the machete.

She couldn't hear the singing through her own cries of horror.

She brought the blade down softly at first, afraid to cut herself, then harder, with desperate strength, when she felt one of the claws penetrate the boot and touch her skin.

The machete cut the slug open like a watermelon, and something that looked like white spaghetti noodles in broth spilled out all over the sand.

It released her and fell dead.

Elise ran, avoiding lumps in the sand, hoping for the best.

That was one of the most disgusting things ever, she thought.

Seriously. Who has guts that look like spaghetti noodles in broth?

One of the sand pyramids stood in her path, with slugs to either side. She dashed to the left of the hill, her shoulder slamming into it as she went, her feet dancing to avoid the slugs.

Sand poured down from where her shoulder had struck the mound.

And then, so did the ants.

She looked back in horror. Ants? Yes, like ants, but big, the size of her thumb, and blue as a robin's egg. They were swarming out of the sand pyramid in a frenzy.

It was an anthill. Those piles were anthills.

Elise ran faster, not looking back now, her breath like ragged sheets of fire.

And then she was standing on a concrete slab at the base of an iron leg the size of a city block, and then she was through an iron gate she slammed hard behind her. A faded sign said, "No Admittance Without Pass."

A year in Paris and I've never been in the Eiffel Tower.

Time to change that.

*

CHAPTER SEVENTEEN

The Grand Ball at the Top of The Tower

THERE ARE THREE levels to the great tower. The first is at nearly two hundred feet. The second is more than a hundred feet above that. The third, the observation platform at the top, was nearly a thousand feet high.

The Tour Eiffel was built for the World Expo in 1889 out of 10,000 tons of iron. A man named Gustave Eiffel designed her, and she went up in an astonishingly short time, only two years.

This beacon, this impossibility, was viewed by a few Parisians of the time as a grotesque effrontery to the beauty of the City of Light.

Author Guy de Maupassant famously ate lunch from the tower's restaurant as, in his words, it was the one place in Paris where he could not see this "tall, skinny, pyramid of iron ladders, this giant and disgraceful skeleton."

She was a radio tower, a landmark, and a marvel. A man named Franz Reichelt died in 1912 when he attempted to fly from her first level wearing his scientifically designed spring-loaded flight wings. He left an impression in the ground six inches deep. He also left quite an impression with the crowd of thousands who watched him plummet. The tower is painted anew every so often, she grows six inches in the heat of a summer day, movies and television and song have practically made her a cliche, and Hitler had been eager to survey Paris from her summit, but The Resistance cut the elevator cables, and Der Fuehrer chose not to walk up the seventeen hundred and ten steps to the top.

On this spring morning, Elise stepped to the foot of her first, wide stairwell.

She looked about for any sign of something slithering or crawling. Nothing.

The nasty ants hadn't followed her.

She peeked back through the iron gate to be sure.

The sandy ocean of the Champs de Mars was alive with ants and sand slugs. The ants had spilled out of the hill she had opened, but they were also pouring out of the other hills as if they were all in communication.

Were they eating the slugs? It sure looked like it. Great blue rivers of ant crisscrossed the sand and at their intersections were roiling balls of ant that looked to be devouring the slimy creatures.

Better them than me, she thought.

There was an elevator, and she had a bit of fun punching its buttons, hoping for a response. A ride to the top would have been nice. The buttons just clicked, dead and cold. Oh well.

She began the climb. There was dust and sand here and there, but not as much as one might expect.

There were no footprints or sand slugs or ants she could see.

Her legs burned, and she hadn't even reached the first level. She looked out through the great iron beams at the city beyond as she climbed. There was the park, the dusty Seine, the 7th Arrondissement where the charming market of the Rue Cler once brought Parisians by the drove for fresh meats, fruit, antiques, and surprises. Some of the buildings were broken as if by bombs; others were just gone, buried in sand, or leveled.

Whatever had happened, it damaged all things it touched.

The singing continued high above, and now that she was getting closer, she could hear a guitar as well. She didn't recognize the song, but it sounded like the reggae songs that her Dad had listened to when they were at the beach.

She stepped up onto the platform of the first level that circled the base of the tower and into a fancy-dress ball where dozens of people dressed in the most unusual costumes danced and frolicked as if a disaster had never happened.

What? Elise took a sharp breath. What is this?

There was a man in a top hat and tails like she had seen in old movies with her Dad, and he was dancing with a woman wearing an outrageous costume of feathers and dazzling sequins. Another man wore a leotard of tiger fur, and he struck a pose like Hercules.

Three women made a dance circle around two children dressed as sailors, and they were having such fun, Elise couldn't help but laugh.

Dozens of them, colorful, strange, silly, and still as stone.

Mannequins posed and dressed for the party of the century.

Elise walked through the ball, her skin tingling from this weird mix of creepy and silly. Really? Storefront dummies in fancy dress? Who does this?

Someone had strung hundreds of string lights overhead from the ceiling of the level, and wires ran from these to car batteries that sat here and there. Nothing was lit now, but at night, it must have been quite a sight.

She had never seen the glow of light from the tower, but the nights were so thick with dust and sand that the tower had been more suggestion than reality once darkness fell.

There were punch bowls filled with colored sand.

There were wonderful posters taped everywhere, the sort of thing Elise imagined one might have seen back in the old days of the Paris nightlife. A full bar had been set up at one corner, twenty meters long, and stocked with liquor, beer, wine, soda, and water. Behind the bar was a mannequin dressed as a bartender from the 1920s. Next to the bar were cafe tables, and at one of these was an old-fashioned typewriter. A mannequin sat there, writing something, the paper as white as its skin.

Elise looked over the writer's shoulder at the paper sitting in the typewriter roller.

"Ma Vie Terne de Mannequin aux Galeries Lafayette."

Or,

"My Dull Life as a Dummy at Galleries Lafayette."

She read some of it, but it was naughty and rude, so she stopped herself.

Then she snuck another peek.

"Oh my," she said. Then giggled.

Her footsteps echoed as she walked, and that was when she noticed the singing had stopped.

What if they know I'm here?

Her experience with strangers had been mostly kind to this point, but that was no reason to let down her guard.

Oh. So, there's a cat.

It sat on a mannequin's lap and stared at Elise. It was a fat brown cat with a fat white belly.

There was a brown harness strapped around it, like a little costume

Elise reached out her hand.

"Here, puss."

It yawned and looked at her as if she had just been pooped out of a chicken.

"Nice puss."

The cat stretched, jumped down, and ran toward the stairwell that led to the next level.

Elise followed the cat up the stairs.

*

CHAPTER EIGHTEEN

The Lost Old Man

IT WAS A dizzying ascent.

Elise dashed up the metal stairs, and she could see through the ironwork, through the beams and struts at her feet and at her side.

It was a long way down.

The cat in the little costume had long since left Elise behind, but since she didn't see it come back down, she had to assume that it waited at the top.

The second platform, three hundred feet above the desert that had once been a park, wasn't as wildly bizarre or nearly as creepy as the fancy ball experience on the first level. There were a few tables set with plastic flowers and a massive sculpture of a long-horned bull that had somehow been brought to a position of authority atop a pile of sand. The bull had been painted every color of the rainbow, and it wore sunglasses. A cartoon word balloon, cut out of cardboard, hovered over its head.

"So, it's come to this," it said.

The hot-air balloon was there as well. It sat in the shadow of the west side of the tower.

Elise wouldn't have been able to see it from the street. The basket was tilted under the weight of the deflated gas bag. On close inspection, the bag was stitched together out of all kinds of blue sheets, blankets, and bags. The stitching was the gold she had seen, and it was copper wire that gleamed in the light of the red sun.

A sign on the side of the basket warned "Weight Limit 25 Kilos" in bold red letters.

That wasn't much weight, not even as much as Elise.

Who could be so tiny that they could ride in the balloon?

There was a fishing pole next to the balloon, and the line was tied to the basket.

Fishing for hot air balloons? What?

The singing had resumed, this time with an unfamiliar but pretty song. It was a man's voice, and it was accompanied by guitar. Two people and a fat cat at the top? Elise kept climbing.

Breathing was hard, and the backpack was heavy.

And then she was there, her head popping up out of the stairwell, onto the small top platform of the Eiffel Tower.

She smelled coffee, cat piss, and burning wood.

The singer was launching into another unfamiliar tune sung in something that sounded like Arabic when he stopped. The guitar jangled to a halt, and the note lingered in the air.

Elise stood in the silence of the morning and stared at the man who sat on a wooden stool holding the guitar.

He was lean, and his skin was the color of an old-fashioned diving helmet. He wore bell-bottom blue jeans, white deck shoes, and a red shirt. A dark blue watch cap topped his head, and long white dreadlocks spilled out from underneath.

The man's nose was bulbous, and his eyes were green as the sea and wide with the shock of seeing a little girl pop up out of the stairwell.

No, it couldn't be him.

"When you interrupt a singer, an angel in heaven dies of scabies," the man said, then returned to strumming his guitar.

Elise walked closer.

A little wood-burning stove was at the man's side, and next to that was a table holding a cup of coffee and a bottle of some kind of liquor.

A navy-blue pea coat hung from a rack.

A stack of wood was piled close, and the fat cat in the costume was lying next to it, sprawled on its back with legs akimbo and white belly exposed to the sky.

A dozen more cats, each wearing the little harness costume, idled about, lying here and there.

A mannequin, attractive as mannequins go, stood at the man's side. She was fashionably dressed in black and wore a charming little hat.

When the man resumed his song, he sang to the mannequin.

His voice was deep and good and rich with emotion.

If Elise were much older or wiser in the ways of country music, she would have recognized the tune as "Galveston."

The words were in Arabic, but that word kept repeating.

Elise stared at the man.

He was framed against the ochre sky and iron beams, the wind harder up here than below but still not bad, and he sang a love song to a plastic dummy.

"Who are you?"

The man stopped and glared at her.

"You, mademoiselle, are a killer of angels, an assassin of song. And go wash your face." Then, he brought a long brown finger to his lips and pantomimed "shush."

Elise felt her face. Dirty? She couldn't tell and didn't care.

"What's her name?"

Elise pointed at the mannequin.

The man raised a bushy right eyebrow.

"Who wants to know?"

"Elise St. Jacques."

He nodded.

"She is Tatienne, the profound and wondrous, premiere

diva of the Grand Opera and scandal of Antibes. Her mysteries have mysteries."

And with that, he began a song Elise recognized from her Dad's music collection.

"Beat on the Brat," by The Ramones. In French.

"Who are you?"

He stopped again, his eyes popping from his head with either surprise or anger.

"Monsieur Fancyboots, escort this Elise St. Whatever to the door."

The cat stayed sprawled, oblivious.

"Monsieur Fancyboots, you shame me. You are a presumptuous puss. Very well, ma fille, if what I say will silence you and allow me to continue sweet Tatienne's serenade, then so be it. I am the current owner of the Tour Eiffel. The restaurant is mine and still over-priced, the cafe is mine, if the damned electricity worked, the lift would be mine as well."

He set his guitar down and stood, arms out, voice rising, offering the view to Elise.

"I am, by virtue of that, also the owner of the finest, most awful, most heartbreaking view in the entire God-Damned world. I am the sole proprietor, and until a moment ago, sole tourist of this view of the city once called Paris. This pit, this hole to Hell, this wasteland. Paris is mine."

The man picked up his guitar and sat on the stool.

"I am Commander Jules Valiance of Les Scaphandriers, leader of the Astonishing Aquanauts and destroyer of worlds. Nice to meet you, Elise St. Blah Blah Blah. Now let me play in peace."

He began to sing again. "Guts and Teeth" by Old Man Markley in English this time, sung slow and warm, the sound carrying out through the breeze.

There were blankets scattered about. Elise picked one up, shook the cat fur out of it, and wrapped herself against the chill. She walked to the edge of the tower, delicately stepping around sleeping felines as she went.

All of Paris was there, and none of it.

The dry Seine, the sand-swept streets, the magnificent old buildings now shattered and broken. There was Notre Dame, still standing. There was the Montparnasse Tower, fallen and spread out across the 15th Arrondissement like a terrible deck of cards.

Something even more terrible could be seen off to the north.

There, the entire city was gone.

North of Paris was a pit, a crater as if the Earth had been scraped away. It looked like a wound.

In the distance, to the east, there was a dark red and black wall, a wave as tall as the sky, the oncoming storm of dust, lightning, and thunder that would strike when the sun went down. She could see it coming like you see a storm on the horizon.

Elise sat cross-legged and unstrapped her backpack. She reached into it and retrieved a bottle of cola.

She drank deep and sat watching the world beyond through the iron fence, a thousand feet in the air, less sand and dust up here, so she could open her eyes, really open her eyes and see.

This was a new, dead world. There were no colonies of people playing football or petanques.

There was no movement, no traffic, no bicycles. If there were people down there, they were hidden away, like Robert and Renny or the bungee man of Notre Dame. And this was certainly no world for a child.

Monsieur Fancyboots nuzzled up to her as if asking permission to join her in reverie. Elise opened her hand on her lap, and the fat old cat curled up on her, his weight a shock, and purred. She stroked him behind his ear.

They had never had a pet. Too much moving around, never in one place for long. Dad has always promised that, as soon as they settled, she could have a cat, or a dog, or a snake, or a gibbon if such things were sold in stores, although gibbons were known to fling poo, and that might have been problematic.

She liked the feel of Monsieur Fancyboots in her lap.

He was warm and squishy and fuzzy.

A perfect meal for a sand slug or shadow man.

Elise grew cold.

"I hate myself."

She hated the darkness in her, how she could turn a sweet moment sour with a thought.

There must have been something wrong with her.

But she wasn't a child that liked fooling herself, and this was no world for little furry cats, either.

For the second time in as many days, Elise cried.

This time, though, she cried in sadness, yes, at what she saw beyond, at what she knew to be the fate of the city, and the loss of innocence, and she cried for the horror that waits for cats and other small things in this awful new world.

But she cried tears of joy, too. Her heart was going to burst.

Of course, her Dad hadn't lied.

Of course, Jules Valiance was real.

Of course, he was real.

*

CHAPTER NINETEEN

Hunger

SCYNDA WAS THE color and texture of the sand all around, pale and rough with specks of red.

She was the Champs de Mar desert come to life.

The turquoise ant was vibrant in her fingers.

She held it by the thorax gently, so it wouldn't be alarmed.

The ant's antennae waved about, and its mandibles opened and closed, looking for something to bite.

Those steely sharp mandibles.

Scynda walked to the South Tower, carefully avoiding the lumps in the sand and the quivering, azure ant streams, thousands of them, seeking food.

You hungry little things. You've eaten all the human stuff that had been. The benches and the vessels of steel and the false trees that had once fruited strange lights.

You've eaten the human things, and now you are eating the slugs, and then you'll rest again in your castles until you have found or are given another meal.

I know you and your kind. You sleep when there is no food, and you can sleep for eons if that's the world you've found, a hungry world.

She held the ant over the iron at the foot of the tower, waving it, teasing it, then she brushed its mandibles over the iron.

Scynda's skin became dark bronze and sleek.

The ant opened its mandibles wide. The antennae became agitated. The mandibles clenched hard against the iron. Scynda released the ant so that it clung to the iron girder, biting, struggling to eat the iron.

Liquid squirted from the ant's mouth and thorax.

Wisps of smoke drifted up where the liquid, the acid, ate into the metal.

The mandibles sliced into the melted iron and the ant fed.

Scynda smiled.

The antennae on the head of the ant waved wildly, and the other ants somehow received that signal. They turned as one and streamed to the South Tower.

They came to feed on Gustav Eiffel's iron.

Somewhere in the infinite, Guy de Maupassant smiled.

*

CHAPTER TWENTY

The Silk Act

JULES VALIANCE FELL off his stool when the tower shuddered.

Elise pitched to her left, and Monsieur Fancyboots ran from her lap in surprise and indignation.

Jules lay sprawled with his guitar on his chest.

"Did the tower just move, or am I drunk?"

Elise looked down. There was a dark cloud of smoke rising up from below, covering the tower's foundation a thousand feet below.

"It's on fire."

Jules stood and ran to her side.

"Iron doesn't just burn, little dirty-faced idiot.

There can be no fire."

Then he looked down at the rising cloud.

"Ah yes. Strange times. The tower is on fire."

Jules moved fast, gathering a few things and dropping them into a sack. He strapped a gun belt laced with bullets around his chest, and there were two weapons in the holsters. This surprised Elise. In the stories her Dad told her of Jules Valiance, he hated guns.

He threw on the heavy coat. Elise turned and stood at the railing and watched the rising smoke or steam or whatever it was.

Jules put his fingers in his mouth and whistled.

"Puss! To me!"

Cats appeared from everywhere, popping their little heads up from behind boxes, from around corners. Three came running from the secret apartment that Gustave Eiffel had built for himself and that Jules now used as his own.

Elise felt the tower move again, just slightly, but when a thing like the tower moved, even just slightly, and you were at the top, fear hit you in the stomach like a shotgun blast.

She slipped on her backpack.

Jules had gathered at least a dozen cats, and they circled him as if awaiting instructions.

"You, idiot girl, take this." He threw her a cigarette lighter. It was gold and heavy.

"Take it quickly now, down to the next level, and spark the propane tank that will elevate the balloon. It is imperative that you do this. Go."

She didn't hesitate.

"We're going to ride in the balloon. Sweet," she thought.

Elise ran to the stairs and climbed down.

Jules went to each cat and manipulated something on their harness, something small on the back.

He pulled a tiny device from under his shirt, and it made a series of clicking sounds.

The cats all ran to the railing and climbed up, a well-trained feline infantry.

They sat on the edge of the railing, looking out over Paris.

Jules smiled.

"May there be a kind wind in this awful world, my little kitty dandelions. Au revoir."

He blew the whistle again.

A tiny propeller popped up from out of the back of the harnesses as if on cue.

The cats leaped from the railing into the sky above Paris.

Elise was almost halfway down to the second level when she looked out and, through the girders, saw a cat in a parachute drift slowly to the west.

She stopped, as you might expect, and pushed her face through to see better.

Cats in parachutes drifted off, gently sailing the soft afternoon wind into the red glow of the sun. Little propellers on their costumes gave them lift and some direction.

There was a golden tabby, then a white cat with black legs, then Monsieur Fancyboots himself. The parachute rotated, and she saw his face.

He looked right at her, and Monsieur Fancyboots seemed to smile.

"Idiot girl! You should be there by now!"

Jules Valiance came riding down the stairwell on a sheet of metal, his feet strapped into it like a snowboard. Tatienne was under one arm, her wig askew. Sparks and noise flew out behind him as he went.

Lightning quick, he snatched the lighter from her hand as he passed and continued on at speed. Elise ran to catch him.

She heard a loud screech of metal a moment later and, arriving at the second level, saw that he'd landed and kicked off the sheet metal. He was at the balloon, hoisting the bag through a series of ropes and levers. He had ignited the propane contraption that would fire up and give the bag lift, and it blazed white-hot.

Elise looked down over the railing.

The smoke was rising. It was hot and smelled harsh, like chemicals.

Steam?

There was a sound as well, like a thousand bunnies munching on carrots.

She looked closely and saw that there was something bright

blue rising from the steam clouds, and it completely covered the lower tower.

It was a blue wave, and it was surging up towards them.

It looked like it was alive.

"We need to hurry," she said.

She turned and saw that the balloon was up and inflating quickly. The basket was small, but they should both be able to fit. Their weight, though...the sign on the basket had said that it was rated for 25 kilos.

Jules dropped Tatienne into the basket. He gently straightened her wig and set her fashionable hat atop her white head.

"Adieu, mon amour coquine. You will find mannequins of extraordinary vigor and rough masculinity in the world beyond. Treat them well."

And with that, he pulled a lever on the propane tank.

The flame shot up, and then so did the basket. Jules cut the fishing line that had allowed him to sail her on Tatienne's little adventures. He gave the contraption a shove, and it sailed over the railing and into the west.

Tatienne, the mysterious, in her blue and gold balloon, floated out over the desert that had once been the Seine, slowly chasing a dozen little parachutes that drifted in the wind like dandelions.

Jules stood at the railing, watching the strange exodus through the growing curtain of dark steam. He pulled a cigarette out of his pocket and lit it.

"How do we get down?" Elise asked.

"We don't."

"You're joking."

"Two nuts walk through the park. One is a salted. That is a joke. This is not."

Elise hit him. He didn't even look at her.

"Stupid! You're supposed to do something!"

There was no time. The sound of the blue wave, the crawling

carpet that was eating the Eiffel Tower, was getting louder by the second. There was no time for any of this.

She ran along the rail, looking for a break in the oncoming wave. If she went down the stairwell, it would be certain death.

If only the elevator worked.

The elevator.

Without power, it couldn't go up, but maybe there was some sort of emergency switch inside that would let it descend. She dashed to the wide elevator doors and began frantically pushing buttons, looking for an emergency lever, desperate for anything that might get her inside.

Nothing.

The only way to buy more time, to give herself a chance at another few moments of life, was to go higher, then. So, Elise began running back up the stairs to the top.

Jules turned and watched her go. Smoke trailed from his lips. The sound was getting loud now. He leaned over and looked down at the crawling blue horror.

Ants. Millions of bright blue ants were eating their way up the tower.

"Ah. So there you have it. Ants."

It shifted again, hard this time, and Jules held fast to the railing, so he didn't fall. The sound of the ants dissolving, devouring the tower was loud now, a scream.

The tower shifted hard right. She was going to fall. Maybe fall before the ants got to the top.

He pulled long on the cigarette, then dropped it over the side.

"I don't want to die today."

He ran as fast as he could to the stairwell and went up.

When Jules Valiance emerged at the top of the tower, he found twelve-year-old Elise St. Jacques tying sheets together to make a rope.

"There are not enough sheets in Paris, girl."

She didn't look up.

Jules pulled the sheet from her hand.

"Follow me."

He went quickly into the tiny apartment that Gustav Eiffel had built as his little secret. Mannequins were there of Eiffel and Thomas Edison engaged in thoughtful conversation.

Jules went through a door in the back of the apartment into a dark little hallway. Elise followed. He held up a lighter to guide them, but he knew the space well.

They were in a larger room at the center of the tower, a room of machinery and huge cables. The place was clean and old.

"This will not be easy," he said.

He still carried the sheet, and he was wrapping it into a thick rope, then around his waist.

"You will hold on to my back and not let go."

Elise felt like her heart would pop out of her chest.

Was he serious?

"This is the old elevator spine of the tower. There are cables here that run the length of her to the antique motor room far below. We will need to be agile, and we will need to be strong, and there's a good chance that we will die a horrible death, pummeled by the fall or eaten by giant ants. Take this end of the rope."

He motioned for her to run around the cable mechanism, to wrap the sheet around it.

Done.

Jules wrapped the sheet around his waist and tightened it, pulling himself to the thick cable. He wrapped the sheet around his ankles, then his wrists and hands as Elise had seen acrobats in the circus do.

"Onboard idiot. We descend."

Elise hopped onto his back, Jules tightened the sheet with a mighty heave, and he jumped down into the heart of the Eiffel Tower.

They fell. Elise smelled grease and machine oil and the cigarette smoke that clung to Jules. Her stomach dropped.

Darkness, moments of light from outside peeking through the girders, then darkness because they were in the belly of the crawling mass of ants. He controlled their descent, and Elise could feel his muscles tighten when he did as he wrenched on the sheet. He was stronger than he looked.

They weren't in free fall, but they were moving fast.

Elise looked up and saw smoke coming from the tightly wrapped sheet from the friction. A squirming, writhing blue wall of hungry ants surrounded them, spitting acid and devouring metal.

Thud. They were on top of something.

Another machine room. They had made it down to the second level.

The tower shuddered and made a roaring, deafening noise.

Steam from the ants was leaking in all around them.

"It's going to fall," Elise whispered.

"Oui."

Jules unwrapped the sheet. It was smoldering, burning in spots. He opened a latched door at their feet.

A ladder led them down into another machine room.

Jules grabbed Elise by the hand and led her to a small set of doors.

"The old lifts. With luck, the pneumatics are still good."

He pushed the doors open and used his lighter to look at the series of old-fashioned buttons on the interior wall of the elevator.

"Voila."

He pulled Elise in with him and jammed a button.

Nothing.

"Merde."

The air was thick with fumes. Elise coughed and pulled her torn cloth bandana over her mouth to breathe.

The tower shook and didn't stop this time. It leaned hard to the left. It was going to collapse.

He flipped a little switch.

Nothing.

There was a little keyhole at the bottom of the door panel.

He produced a little metal pick from his dreadlocks and wiggled it in the keyhole.

There was an awful boom, and the floor beneath them dropped.

They were suspended in the air for a moment then fell hard. Elise scraped her knee and braced herself with her injured hand. It hurt.

Jules went back to work on the keyhole. Elise moved close to him. She had been scared in the past couple of days, but not like this.

The cabin was shaking, and the sound from outside was so loud that she couldn't think.

A click. Jules laughed and pushed the button again.

"Hold on."

They dropped.

The lift disengaged from everything above it and fell, a dead drop, gaining speed as it went.

Elise and Jules were airborne. Elise screamed. Jules laughed.

And then they hit the floor of the lift, and their descent slowed. The noise around them was deafening, the groans of the dying tower, the squeal of ancient hydraulics, the ants chewing on iron and spewing acid.

The lift stopped. Jules applauded.

"Note to self. Hydraulic fluid ages exceptionally well."

They were up in a flash. Jules shoved open the door.

It was pitch black. Jules sparked a lighter and revealed a large, red-brick room full of turn-of-the-century mechanisms of metal, rubber, and glass. It was a bit quieter here, the sound was muffled and deep, and there were no sickening fumes from the ants.

"Come with me."

Jules moved forward and found a thick old wooden door.

He stepped through, and Elise followed into more darkness. Echoes rattled off in the distance ahead.

"This is a tunnel to..." Jules began when he was interrupted by the sound of the earth coming apart.

*

CHAPTER TWENTY-ONE

The Death Tunnels

AS IT TURNS out, it takes twenty-eight minutes for a million acid-spewing blue razor ants to weaken the Eiffel Tower until it falls.

The crawling titian horror of razor mandibles and steaming corrosion enveloped Mr. Eiffel's wondrous creation in a frenzy of living destruction that frothed from base to radio antennae. The lower legs of the tower, each a city block wide, simply gave way under the pressure.

She leaned to the west and came down onto the park below.

The roar was the death of Paris, echoing through time.

The earth shook.

Below ground, in the hidden tunnels the military had used in the past and that Elise and Jules used now, it was as if a giant had pounded on the ceiling above them with a sledgehammer of the gods.

Elise covered her ears and dropped to her knees.

Through the dim glow of Jules' cigarette lighter, the ceiling spilled dust and small rocks.

The earthquake went on for several seconds, and then the tunnel fell silent.

A moment passed.

Elise watched as the light from the little flame moved off into the darkness. She followed.

"Where are we?" she asked.

There was no answer for a long time, just the echoed footsteps as they walked along the stone tunnel floor.

Finally, she heard Jules clear his voice. Elise thought he might have been crying, and that made her hate him a little bit more.

"Tunnels built with the tower. They run to a hidden basement, and then there are others that will take us into the city and beyond. We might be safe here for a while."

"Why did you save me?"

"I didn't save you. I saved myself. You were just there."

There was a red light in the near distance. As they made their way to it, Elise could see that the tunnel opened to the surface, and there was a concrete building with a steel door. Steps ran up to it, and others went up to the side, to the city above.

The lighter flame went out. Jules walked slowly, hugging the wall, so Elise walked quickly, angrily, and strode down the center of the tunnel toward the building.

She stopped at the door and waited for him, looking up at the crimson sky. Evening was coming, and so were the winds.

He shoved her aside and opened the door.

Elise watched him go for a moment, then followed.

*

The tunnel was not as dark as the other. There was a light blue glow in the distance. Jules was a silhouette against the dim phosphorescence. He didn't bother with his lighter.

Their footsteps made soft echoes. The floor here was uneven, just rough carved rock, and it descended with a gentle slope.

"Oh." Elise stared in wonder at the creature glowing softly on the wall of the tunnel.

It was a long feathery thing, like moss, and had a firefly glow. They were everywhere, growing thicker as they walked until the tunnel was bright with them.

She started to touch it.

"Don't, unless you want to be consumed screaming and alive by glow fungus babies."

"Glow fungus babies?"

"I found them; I am obliged to name them."

"Stupid name."

"You are stupid."

"You are."

"I know you are, but what am I?"

"That makes no sense."

"You make no sense."

"Where are Les Scaphandriers?"

Jules stopped and was silent for a moment.

"How do you know this name?"

It was Elise's turn to be quiet. She glared at him.

"How do you know this name?" His voice was low and angry, the words coming through teeth clenched tight.

"Where are they?"

Jules bent low, and his eyes burned into her, his face only an inch from hers.

"Who sent you? If you are one of them, I will kill you. If you are a wound, a madness in my mind, I will find a way to erase you. If you are a ghost, then damn you."

Elise just stared back at him, but inside, she was afraid.

He didn't look sane.

"Tell me," he said.

"I went to sleep, and when I woke up, the world had changed. It's been two days, and I've been trying to find help. Some people I met told me that ten years had gone by while I slept, but that can't be possible. They were crazy, like you. I'm telling you the truth. I went to sleep and woke up. Now it's this."

"How do you know this name? Answer me."

"My Dad told me stories. Bedtime stories. They were about you and Les Scaphandriers and how great and awesome and funny you were.

That's how. I thought they were just stories. That's how I know."

Jules stood slowly and reached into a pocket for a cigarette.

"You're a ghost, then."

He pulled hard on the smoke, and it drifted back out through his enormous nose.

"So, you're what I deserve. You are my curse, and I must find a proper way to send you back to Hell. Maybe with Holy Water. Who's to say?

Let's go."

They walked on, enveloped in the blue.

Elise could see that the glow fungus babies were covered in tiny tendrils, thin as thread, and these were waving about as if searching for something.

Am I a ghost? That would explain some things, but she was hungry and tired. Her body was sore, her knee and her hand hurt, her nose was dry and itchy with sand and dust. Her stomach growled, her heart ached, and she was furious. Not very ghosty.

No. I'm not a ghost, she thought. This is real, and this strange man, this funny story Dad told her, was going to kill her. I'll stay with him until we're out of the tunnel, and then I'll run as fast as I can to get away.

Jules Valiance, she decided, was not a hero. He was scary, he smelled bad, and he was out of his mind.

*

Scynda did not speak as a human does. She spoke through her skin, through her movement, through her eyes.

But if she had a voice, she would have said, "there you are."

The human man and girl were there just as she'd hoped, popping into view at the entrance to the glowing tunnel. It was the only place for them to go if they'd survived the fall of the tower.

She was not surprised that they had escaped the destruction, as surprise was foreign to her. She was impressed, though, because she hunted, and estimating her prey was how she survived.

Her Mistress had explained to her that this prey was foolish. She thought now, though, that it was soft, perhaps foolish, but clever with the instinct to fight for life.

This prey would not be underestimated.

The seven Men of Many Eyes waited in the darkness at the edge of the basement with Scynda, and they were hungry.

Her skin became a mottle of gray and black. She became the gloom.

She was hungry too.

She would eat the little human first. The Lurkers in Shadow, her Men, would feast on the one that smelled of smoke and dead flowers.

First, though, Scynda thought it might be wise to follow.

What secrets might be revealed?

Perhaps even more food was waiting down in the tunnels, soft and pink and vulnerable.

Yes, we will follow for a time, she thought. Then we will eat.

*

The loud thunder attracted it to the park.

There were ant things there, and it moved quickly to stay away from them. They had sharp pincers that might be able to cut its shell and get to the soft flesh beneath.

Its antennae waved about. They sensed bad smells of death and age. The ants made a smell that hurt. But through the noise of scent, it discerned the fresh, clean salt of the little hairless monkey and a new, different monkey smell.

Two hairless monkeys were here, and they had not been trapped in the giant metal thing that fell and was eaten by the ant things.

They were here somewhere, it could smell them with its antennae, and it would find them, and they would help it get home.

They would help the crab voyage back to its home in the deep beautiful ocean so that crab might bury its friend.

*

The tunnels of the glow fungus babies were bright and endless.

Elise and Jules had been walking at a fast pace for a long time.

Jules knew his way and would change tunnels quickly and decisively.

The air was thick with a dusty, ancient smell.

What did glow babies eat, Elise wondered. There were strange new life forms in the world she once knew, and they must have their own...what was it they called it in class...their own food chain.

Oh. She noticed little things crawling along the stone floor. They were like long cockroaches or crayfish. The repulsive creatures were everywhere but scurried away and disappeared at the sound or vibration from their footsteps.

Probably harmless, she thought, but definitely gross.

Jules and Elise had been silent, not a word shared since their walk began. Elise was stubborn and would not be the first to break the silence, but as time went on, she lost the edge of her anger and finally just felt the need to hear her own voice.

"Who used these tunnels?"

Jules said nothing for a moment then answered in a soft voice.

"The tunnels were empty and forgotten during times of peace. I am told they were used by The Resistance in the Second World War. After that, they were lost."

"Then how do you know where we're going?"

"I said mostly. My friends and I used these tunnels."

"Les Scaphandriers."

"Oui."

France had a long and proud history of ocean exploration.

She had sailed the surface and dived into the depths of the seven seas with courage and insatiable scientific yearning. The iconic copper helmets of the first deep divers, the modern bathyspheres, the first wooden diving bells, these and more ran deep in the blood of France. Les Scaphandriers was the name used to describe the men who traveled the depths for science, for fortune, to make a living, to construct, to detonate, to map, and to learn. It was also the name her Dad had given to the imaginary team of explorers led by Jules Valiance in his bizarre exploits with the countless wonders of the Worlds Below and Between.

Truth and lies, all mixed up, and now here was Jules Valiance.

Well, she thought, why not? I've lost my mind, so anything goes.

"What was your father's name?"

The question took Elise by surprise. Jules had been so quiet.

"Clark."

"I don't remember a Clark St. Jacques. How does he know of me?"

"This is my dream, so it doesn't need to make sense."

"Hmm. And you are my ghost, so your secrets are of the grave and will require extraction by paranormal instruments more complex than I now carry in my man pouch."

"Your what?"

"My man pouch. Shut up, idiot ghost."

Elise laughed out loud, and it felt good.

"Man pouch."

"Shut up."

"Whatever."

Jules held his hand up and stopped stone cold still.

Is he really going to hit me, she thought.

"We are being followed." His whisper was so low that she could barely hear.

Silence for a beat.

"I don't hear..."

"We are being followed. Run."

Jules pulled the two guns from under his coat and turned.

He fired one shot over Elise's head, back into the tunnel.

The noise was so loud that it hurt. Her ears hummed. Guns on television or in movies seem so cool and easy, but in person, when they explode near your head, they're scary beyond words.

"Run!"

She did. He fired again, following her at a sprint.

"Don't look back, idiot ghost."

And this time, Elise did as she was told. She ran as hard and as fast as she could.

If she had glanced back, she would have seen a shimmer, a glow that moved along the ceiling toward them as quickly as they could run.

Behind this glow was a wave of pure black, a dark that moved.

Elise was fast. She was surprised then when the old man passed her. She was going as hard as she could. Her legs ached. How long do we have to run?

Jules turned and fired once more as he ran. Elise's ears were numb, and her head was spinning, the noise playing games with her balance.

She fell.

She looked up, and Jules continued to run for a moment.

Then, he stopped and turned.

"Stay down, girl."

She glanced over her shoulder and saw the glow and the darkness coming toward them.

Jules fired again.

The things chasing them scattered and slowed, and she could see what they were.

Shadow men, the Men of Many Eyes. And something else. First glowing like the strange fungus on the walls, then the color and texture of the stone floor, then standing at a crouch and becoming dark red.

She was beautiful and weird and horrible, and her skin was like a separate, living thing. A skin painting, always changing.

"Now, let's go."

Jules picked her up and swatted her on the back of the head.

He ran, and so did Elise, as fast as they could.

*

Yes, Scynda knew now with certainty that the man was dangerous. She pursued, but with caution. The Men of Many Eyes followed her, followed them. The human's weapon had not found its target, but it was a deadly thing and would be respected.

*

The tunnel split off into four directions, and a ten-meter ladder led up to the stone ceiling. Elise and Jules stared up the ladder into the light from the glow fungus babies. There was an iron wheel, a porthole, above their heads.

Fungus clung to the ladder, and Jules pulled the stuff away.

It burned and clutched at him, and he was quick to toss it far to the side. The fungus left red marks where it had stung him.

Jules climbed the ladder, clamped his hands on the iron wheel, and tried to turn.

Nothing.

He strained again, hard this time. There was the slightest groan of metal on metal.

Elise stood at the bottom of the ladder, looking off into the glow of the tunnel. She scanned for any sign of those weird, scary things that were chasing them.

There. Something moved, black against the glow. The things were coming.

"Hurry."

She climbed the ladder to below Jules. He was straining hard against the wheel, and it was moving inch by inch but ever so slowly.

"Hurry."

"Say that again, and I will kick you off the ladder with great violence."

Jules twisted the wheel again, his knuckles turning white.

It moved, but not much. This would take time that they didn't have.

He swung around to the other side of the ladder.

"Girl. Climb up as high as you can."

Elise climbed until her head was just below the iron wheel.

She was on one side of the ladder, Jules on the opposite.

Twenty feet below them, the shadows of the Men of Many Eyes moved from all directions to the base of the ladder.

Scynda, glowing like the fungus babies, stood right below them.

Elise could see her clearly for the first time, the skin rippling with changing colors and textures, her nakedness, her eyes as big as saucers with lashes that moved like feelers. A mouth both human and fish with tiny, sharp teeth. She was beautiful, feminine, and horrifying.

She sang. That weird mouth opened, and out came a sound like a high wail. It was musical in moments, discordant in others, a song, a moan, then ending in a hiss.

Jules was paying no attention. He had the wheel moving now, slowly but moving. Iron rust like sand drifted down into his sweaty red face.

The woman creature reached up with a slender glowing hand

and wrapped her six fingers around the ladder. She climbed and sang as she came.

Elise drew her feet up as high as they would go.

The dark men climbed.

"Hey," Elise said.

Jules said nothing. His focus was on the wheel. It groaned and shrieked as he turned.

"Help."

And then the wheel made a sound like a gasp and lifted up.

"Into the porthole," he said.

Jules pulled one of his guns and fired down. Elise scrambled up into the hole where the wheel had been, her fingers numb with panic, terrified that she would slip and fall.

The slug hit one of the dark men square between the hideous red eyes. Dark liquid sprayed out, and the Man of Many Eyes dropped.

Jules took a deep breath and aimed. The female creature had been swaying left and right.

He shot center-left, and the bullet passed through her shoulder, a molten arrow, and blood followed it.

Scynda sang a discordant cry and released the ladder.

She dropped to the ground, the lurkers following, and dashed off into the tunnel's blue glow.

Jules slipped the revolver back into the holster. He took a heavy breath and climbed up through the porthole.

The heavy iron wheel shut with a thunderous clang behind them.

There was no light. Elise could hear Jules next to her, could smell his funk, but the darkness was absolute.

A shrieking metallic sound slammed the floor near her feet.

A lock on the porthole.

A rustling of cloth. A click. Jules had his lighter in hand, and the glow of the flame revealed dark wood and brick.

They were in a narrow little room. There was a brick wall directly behind the porthole on the floor.

An ornate Turkish carpet led down the narrow, wood-lined hall to something lighter. They walked closer, and Elise saw it was a white door.

The flame of the lighter went out. Elise could hear Jules shake it and try to spark it to life again.

Nothing.

Jules led her to the door in the blackness.

He knocked three times, then twice, then once, then three times again.

There was a long moment, and then an answering knock from the other side repeated the pattern.

Jules knocked "shave and a haircut."

The door responded with "two bits."

It opened inwards.

*

CHAPTER TWENTY-TWO

Dinner Bell

THERE WAS NOBODY there.

Who had answered his knock?

There were ships in the shadows. Elise felt as if she'd stepped into a lost ocean of boats, ships, nautical gear of all kinds. The room was vast, lit through the windows by the red glow of the sandstorm moon outside.

A museum?

Yes. This was definitely a museum, one so large that just stepping into it felt like leaping off of a building into space. There was a full-sized warship, a glass case with a model submarine, a sailboat hanging from the ceiling. Windows as tall as a three-story building lined the walls, some of them cracked and some shattered. The cold wind whipped through the breaks, bringing sand and noise.

Elise followed Jules. He looked left and right, scanning as if looking for those horrible things that had been chasing them.

Who had answered his knock?

Were there ghosts here?

She was tired and cold. Her stomach rumbled. She had been too busy with murderous shadow creatures, metal-eating ants, and collapsing world landmarks to worry about food, but now she realized that she was really hungry. She reached into a side pocket of her backpack and pulled out a candy bar.

Elise considered giving Jules a bite. She didn't.

"What is this place?" she asked.

"Musée national de la Marine. The National Navy Museum. Be quiet."

"Who answered the knock? Where are they?"

"You are a child, so I must remember that your brain isn't properly formed yet. Be quiet."

"No."

"Fine. It's a code to an automated system that opens the security door into the museum. It recognizes the knocking pattern and replies with two knocks of its own and opens the door. Or maybe it was Jorge, the tiny mime who lives under the replica of the Trieste and who has been pining for my return. Maybe it was a trick of the wind. Perhaps this is a plot to capture a little idiot girl. Now be quiet."

Elise munched on her candy bar.

The museum was a wonder. She knew this, even in the gloom. The space was a hall of glorious treasures, memories of exploration, and sea-going adventure. This was the kind of place that Jules Valiance, her Dad's version of Jules Valiance, would have loved.

Elise wandered over to a massive collection of shining ship bells. There were dozens of bronze and brass bells, different sizes and designs, artfully displayed with little plaques that told of their ships and their histories.

She couldn't resist. Elise tugged on one of the little ropes, and a bronze bell rang out.

The sound made her smile.

Jules grabbed her hand and stopped the bell. His grip was so tight it hurt.

"Hey," she said.

"How stupid can you be?"

Elise pulled her hand away. She was too angry to speak, but she knew that he was right.

What was she thinking? It had been a stupid move, but she wasn't about to admit it.

"You didn't have to freak out."

Jules stopped and turned. He raised his right eyebrow and glared at her, the glare an opossum might give a hornet that wouldn't stop stinging its nose.

He started to speak but was interrupted by the sound of the entire three-story glass window to their right imploding and showering glass in a hurricane of knife blades.

Elise didn't know how, but it was as if Jules was faster than the explosion. She was swept up in his arms and protected before she could think, before she could stop chewing the candy. They landed with a hard thump, and she lost her breath as they rolled under a huge model ship. She gasped.

She'd never had her breath knocked out.

It was a horrible feeling. Elise thought she was dying. The sound of a thousand shards of glass cascading around them was a wall of white noise. Her eyes were closed tight. She couldn't breathe. She couldn't think.

Jules was holding her close, his coat covering them both.

The glass stopped falling, and her breath mercifully came back with a rush. She looked out from under the protection of his smelly coat.

An avocado green nightmare was coming through the emptiness where the window had once been. This nightmare was as big as a bus, sickly green, with tentacles thick as telephone poles and yellow eyes that were...those eyes...those awful eyes. As harsh and as hateful as the sun burning down on a dying man.

It was a squid, a giant squid, and it was a horror.

Elise started to scream, and Jules placed his hand over her mouth.

The squid slithered into the vast hall of the museum.

How? Squids live underwater. This dissonance, this incongruence, made it even more frightening. The tentacles reached out, searching, touching everything.

The eyes searched.

It moved across the floor; the mantle held high. A roving arm rimmed with tire-sized, tooth-lined suction cups clasped a full-scale replica of an 18th-century warship. The thing moved, lightning-fast, and attacked the model. All eight arms and the two tentacles whipped around the ship in a heartbeat, in a frenzy. The wooden ship shattered and splintered under the awful pressure of the beast.

There was a sound, a sound like chopping wood, and Elise realized that it must be the creature's beak tearing into the ship, slicing and rendering in a frenzy.

Jules pushed them further back under the model and into the darkness, trying to hide them. They bumped into something. Elise looked over her shoulder and saw a dark red shell.

They had bumped into a giant crab.

Jules panicked and went for his revolver. Elise grabbed his arm, holding him, stopping him.

It was her crab. The one that saved her. It was hiding under the big model, it had been there first, and the dead sea monkey was still on its back.

"He's nice," she said through a whisper.

Jules's eyes were like saucers.

"It is a huge crab carrying a dead monkey."

"Yes."

The crab moved slightly, turning, and its antennae moved towards them. They were like stalks, and at the end of the stalks were eyes.

The crab looked at them. First at Jules, then at Elise.

The sound of the wooden ship being destroyed lessened. The squid was finishing its work.

"Hi," said Elise.

The crab didn't respond, as one would expect, as it didn't have vocal chords and whatnot, but it continued staring at Elise with those tiny eyes.

The thing reached out a massive razor-sharp claw.

Elise had seen that claw destroy one of the Men of Many Eyes. It slowly touched her face, gently brushed her hair.

Elise patted its shell.

"Mon Dieu," said Jules.

The noise of the squid had stopped. Elise and Jules peeked out and saw that the massive creature was moving quickly through the hall, the viridian tentacles searching, reaching into every nook and cranny as if each arm had its own intelligence. It made a deafening slap sound as it went.

"Idiot crab girl, we need to get to the diving bell.

There." He indicated a wooden and brass diving bell the size of a small car that was on display. It was on the other side of the hall, with a raging green land squid between them.

Elise pushed up against the crab, squeezing further under the display and against the wall. No way.

Jules shrugged.

"Bon chance."

He was gone before she could say a word. Jules shot out from under the display and hit the floor at a sprint.

It was at least fifty meters to the diving bell.

Jules picked up a small litter bin as he ran and tossed it hard to his left. The bin hit the floor with a loud crash. The noise attracted the squid, and the colossal thing rushed towards it, arms thundering across the wooden floor. Jules dashed past it and kept going, not looking back.

Elise watched in terror as he climbed into the diving bell, slammed its little observation hatch, and disappeared.

The crab was still as stone; even its strange eye stalks froze as it watched the squid.

Breath deep and stay quiet.

Don't move.

There was no clever way out, nothing to do. She didn't even pull out her blade. The machete would be of no use against something so huge, so monstrous.

Elise touched the crab shell and shut her eyes.

The squid would eat the crab, and she didn't want that.

Disappear. Just breath and pretend it all away. She thought about her Dad and other good things, the way she would when the girls at the Garden had been cruel. Elise was quiet and still as she was the first night alone after her Dad's death.

Just be calm.

The wooden floor beneath her was cold, and now it shook with the movement of the giant squid as the beast came closer. The suction cups stuck to the floor as it went, and they made a loud popping sound. Pock pock pock.

A single tentacle as thick as her leg hovered a meter away from Elise. Did it sense she was there?

It came closer, and the crab scuttled out, coming between the disgusting green arm and Elise.

She could see the suction cups that lined the tentacle.

Each of them was circled with tiny teeth, and the fear hit Elise then. This would be a horrible death. Her blood became ice, and she couldn't breathe.

The air exploded with a sound like a heavy metal guitar chord. A wave of air slammed into them, so hard that she felt it in her bones. Her ears popped as if she were on a plane.

Again, that noise and that pressure. Again.

The squid arm retreated, writhing and flopping. Elise looked out from under the display table.

The giant squid was rolling on the floor in agony, tentacles flailing and smashing everything they struck.

Again, the noise and the pressure.

Jules Valiance was standing at the diving bell. He was wearing a massive backpack and aiming a gun the size of a tree limb at the Kraken. The bizarre weapon was of shiny metal and shaped vaguely like a torpedo.

He fired again, and there was the noise and the slamming thud of pressure.

The giant squid exploded.

A ghastly shower of cephalopod pulp and blue blood rained over the museum hall, painting everything in gore. Even Elise, under the table, was sprayed with the stuff.

Huge chunks of it plopped down like nasty squid hail for a few moments.

Quiet.

Elise ran to Jules. He shed the backpack and gun.

"What was that?"

"I will call it The Landopus. No. The Terra Squid. Yes. An unknown species. This new, weird nature reveals another of her infernal secrets."

"No. That gun."

"Ah. Do you know how a sperm whale hunts the formidable Architeuthis Dux or giant squid?"

She giggled.

"You said sperm."

"Sound waves. Not even leviathan wants to dance with tentacles of death, so the sperm whale emits a stunning bolt of sound created in its massive cranial cavity. This atomic echo location incapacitates the colossal squid, making it easy prey."

He patted the gun.

"This, I developed for much the same reason. Stun the colossal squid, tag it, track it for research and amusement. Today, I adjusted the dial to eleven. The results speak for themselves."

He indicated the hall of squid gore.

"Calamari. Bon appetit."

"I thought you left me."

"I did. Then I remembered the sonic gun and was afflicted with guilt. You are an idiot, but an interesting one."

The crab sidled to them, antennae waving. It had a chunk of squid in its pincers and was eating.

"You have a friend who is a crab the size of a cafe table, and there is a dead sea monkey on its back. Do you not find this peculiar?"

"Absolutely. I think he's been following me."

Jules kneeled down in front of the crab.

"What are your secrets, monsieur crab? Why do you follow this idiot? Who is the monkey?"

The crab continued to munch on pulpy squid.

Jules began a strange movement, swaying back and forth while slowly waving his hands. He looked like he was doing a squatting hula dance.

The crab's eye stalks tracked him. Then, the crab began to mimic the dance.

Jules knees made a loud cracking, popping sound.

"Merde."

He toppled over backwards. The crab stopped dancing.

Elise leaned over Jules. He held his knees and sat up.

"Are you okay?"

"Betrayed by age. The dance of the Polynesian whisper crab is for the young."

He stood carefully.

"But now we know that it does not see us as food. It sees us as kindred spirits. Why? Who can say? This is the mystery."

He motioned for Elise to follow him into the diving bell.

There was barely room for the three of them, and they made quite a spectacle.

Jules punched a button on the bronze interior of the bell.

"If the emergency power systems have survived, we descend now far below the Maritime Museum. We will be safe there, I think."

The diving bell began a smooth descent down into the floor.

The mechanism was as quiet as an elevator. Blackness enveloped them except for little lights at the control buttons.

"Good. The roof is a field of solar cells. Obviously not terribly damaged by the storms and the sand. There will be light below."

And then there was a soft amber glow that showed their destination.

Elise stepped out into a dream.

*

CHAPTER TWENTY-THREE

The Hall

"WHAT IS THIS place?"

"A joke. A graveyard of clowns. Welcome, little idiot, to the Hall of Les Scaphandriers."

Jules flipped a switch on the wall, and incandescent light bulbs hummed to life.

Here was an expanse of impossibilities, a room as vast as the museum above, and in so many ways, it was exactly as Elise's Dad had described in his bedtime stories to her, just as thrilling and strange and surprising.

If the League of Astonishing Aquanauts was real, this would have been the perfect place from which to launch adventures into the ocean's most improbable mysteries, an underground academy dedicated to weird science and exploration. Elise stared with wide eyes, not breathing, and had a sickening moment when she doubted her own sanity or consciousness.

This isn't real. I'm lying in a pit somewhere, alive but dying, hallucinating. Or I'm dead, and this is what happens, and I'm not cool with that. Or this is a dream.

There were tubes of glass as tall as sailing masts.

Great cables of copper and rubber stretched the length of the golden vaulted ceiling, attached to gadgets as small as her hand and as big as a house. The hall stretched on for dozens of meters, and there were displays of marine life, globes, maps, couches, desks, and flags of every nation.

Elise turned and was face to face with an old-fashioned diving suit, the three-window copper helmet of intricate and artful design, lead boots, soft rubber skin that spoke of mysterious missions to the depths of the South Seas.

Here was an aquarium without water, and it was as big as a car. Inside of it was a diorama of the sea, with plastic sea creatures and divers and submarines in a riot of color and exploration. What possible purpose could this have served?

Then there was a globe where the land receded, and the ocean basin was the surface, the skin of the globe created in relief so that the great canyons and mountains of the Earth's ocean were raised up and rough to the touch.

She tried on a set of mesh metal gloves that were too big for her hands and were labeled "For Shark Feeding Only."

She skimmed the titles on the bindings of the library of books.

"My Oceanic Life."

"The Living Deep."

"On Cephalopod Intelligence."

"The Wlodarski Study on Cetacean Ecotypes."

"Doc Savage and The Bubbles of Fear."

"The Snorkeling Manifesto."

"A Confounding History of Weird Sciences."

She studied the devices of exploration that ran the length of one wall. There were grappling devices with suction cups instead of hooks. There were nets, cradles, and bins of all colors and shapes.

Snorkeling and scuba and diving gear galore. Brass widgets, iron weights, wooden buoys, glass bells.

There had always been an amazing vessel in her Dad's stories of Les Scaphandriers, the proud and bizarre ship of the Aquanauts that seemed to have a life of its own and could journey into the darkest depths or even fly above the clouds like an airplane. When death or worse was knocking on the door of Jules Valiance and his mighty team, this miraculous submersible would always find a way to bring them home, and usually, it was an unlikely way indeed.

Their ship was named The Aquaboggin, and there, at the far end of the hall, Elise discovered a sleek vessel, a submarine resting in a tall metal cradle. She was a beautiful thing, ten meters long and maybe more, sleek with golden metal and clear glass, dressed in dark blue and bright green paint. Elise could look down below the cradle that held the sub.

The floor disappeared beneath the web of armatures and lashings. The submarine was suspended over a hole in the floor, and the darkness there seemed to go on forever.

This ship was just as her Dad had described, and there, on the bow, was inscribed her name.

Elise sat on the cold floor and stared up at the ship for a long time.

So many strange and amazing things to see.

Elise had never seen an old-fashioned phonograph before, but it wasn't hard to figure out what it was and how it worked. She rifled through a stack of old vinyl albums with wonderful, evocative covers. A platter of black went onto the phonograph, and in a tick, she was dancing to a lovely steel drum calypso sound that filled the hall.

Jules was lying on a couch. Areas around the hall were set up as little lounges with furniture and conveniences. He was smoking, his eyes closed.

"Why?" asked Elise.

"Why what?"

"Oh, maybe just a few things. Like, maybe, why were you on top of the Eiffel Tower when you could be here?"

He was quiet and didn't even open his eyes.

"Why do you smoke? It's wicked bad for you."

"What's up with the guns? You hated guns in the stories Dad told me."

Nothing. Elise kept dancing as she spoke.

"This was a secret, right? I mean, I never heard of Les Scaphandriers, except in stories from Dad. So, why was this place so secret? What did you guys really do? Where are the rest of them? What's next?"

Jules cleared his throat.

"I went there to get away from here. I smoke because it makes me feel good, and these are not tobacco cigarettes; they are the medicinal seaweed reefers of Les Scaphandriers." He took a deep drag of the weed and exhaled.

"I found the guns on a dead soldier, and they did today what they were made to do. This place was a secret, yes, and it was a secret because that was our tradition. We preferred it that way."

He looked straight at her with cold eyes.

"We did many things, and the last of them was terrible. Les Scaphandriers and everything we stood for died because of this last thing, and this last thing killed the world too."

He shoved a finger into her chest.

"Shut up and let me sleep because, next? There is nothing next."

He closed his eyes and turned away.

The record skipped. Elise stopped dancing. She moved the needle away from the record and sat down on a soft velvet couch as far away from Jules as she could. She didn't think he wanted to talk anymore, and she didn't want to hear anything else he had to say, not for a while at least.

The last thing she saw before she fell fast asleep was the crab settling in on the floor next to her.

*

There were showers and toilets but no water. There was the amber glow of the solar lights, but there was no warmth. When Elise woke up, she found the shower room and cleaned up as best she could with one of her bottles of water, using as little as possible.

She found metal lockers in the shower area, and on each of these were names in copper plate. She chose one labeled "Splatter" because she thought it was a funny name and unloaded weight from her backpack.

She smelled something cooking. Her stomach practically jumped out and started searching around on its own.

Elise found Jules in a small kitchen frying meat in a skillet. There was blue flame from a propane tank. The sizzling meat looked suspiciously like dog food but smelled delicious.

"Can I have some?" asked Elise.

"It is tinned meat. Canard. Duck. We will share."

There was an open bottle of white wine at his elbow.

He took a swig then offered the bottle to Elise. She waved it off.

Breakfast was at an ornately carved dining table set with unusual nautical ornaments, flowers ten years gone, and a few candles. Elise sat at one end of the long table, and Jules sat at the other.

He had created quite a feast out of a Les Scaphandriers survival kit. There was the fried confit de canard sautéed in olive oil, canned apples drenched in syrup, a dark, mysterious broth that tasted of onion, and another bottle of wine. Jules had drained the first bottle while cooking and was now well into the second.

His nose and cheeks were bright red.

Elise devoured the food. It wasn't bad, and it was the first warm meal she'd had since waking up to this new world.

The crab was still nibbling the massive chunk of squid pulp it had scavenged in the museum. It stayed close to Elise and had followed her as she explored the hall that morning.

Jules wasn't speaking. Elise didn't like the awkward silence.

"This is great," she said.

Nothing.

"I slept like a rock. How about you?"

Nothing.

"Is it okay if I stay here for a while? It seems safe here."

"You need to go. You and the crab with the dead sea monkey on its back. You both will leave this place today."

"Why?"

"This word. Why. It is your favorite, no?"

"Yes."

"It is a dangerous word. A curse. If it had an opposite, the world would be a better place. An antonym of why. What is the antonym of why? Perhaps content? Perhaps zen? Perhaps you should stop using that damned word."

Elise pushed back from the table and went as far away from him as she could go.

She was reading one of the thousands of books from the library, an illustrated little book that smelled of age and spoke in French of prehistoric creatures when she heard a loud metal sound from the other end of the hall.

She noticed that the crab was no longer at her side.

Curious, Elise walked to the sound and found Jules and the crab standing by a carved wooden box the shape and size of a coffin. Wait.

It was a coffin.

The sea monkey was lying in the little coffin on a pretty yellow quilt, its hands at rest on its pale white chest.

The crab's eye stalks hovered over the coffin, and Jules stood with his head bowed.

Elise joined them, and they stood silently for a few moments.

Then, Jules gently placed a wooden door atop the coffin and latched it into place with bronze latches.

He motioned for Elise to grab the end of the coffin, and they lifted. It was light enough for the two of them to carry, and Jules led them through the hall.

The crab followed.

There was a room of white stone with a curved archway entrance that was set off to the southern end of the hall. Inside, there was a room lit by the soft glow of the solar lights that was rounded and bare, except for a trio of wooden benches set like church pews. They faced an altar of dead flowers.

The walls were bronze busts of men and women long dead.

There were plaques with names, and there were remembrances of all kinds. It was a mausoleum for Les Scaphandriers, and that's where the monkey was placed in his little coffin, in a metal and marble slot in the wall.

"When I die, if indeed I do, I will not be buried here," Jules said.

"Why not?"

"It is so cold in here. Lifeless. My corpse would appreciate the warm touch of earth, I think."

The trio sat quietly for a long time, Jules and Elise on a bench and the crab at the feet of the girl.

"What was it?"

"A sea monkey, I suppose," said Jules.

"There's no such thing."

Jules was silent for a moment.

"No, I did not think so. But here we are."

"I wonder if it had a name," said Elise.

She reached down and touched the shell of the giant crab.

"You need a name. But it needs to be a good one. I haven't thought of one yet, but I will."

After a time, Jules stood and said, "You need to go."

*

CHAPTER TWENTY-FOUR

Exile

AND THAT'S HOW Elise found herself back out on the streets of dead Paris.

She was so nervous and scared that her stomach hurt.

Angry too, and perhaps most that, mostly furious.

Jules escorted her and the crab to the promenade at the foot of the Musée national de la Marine. It was early morning, and the winds blowing across the Trocadero were dying down, but it was still cold.

He gave her a bright blue jacket that almost fit. It was a garment of many pockets and thick lining, warm and waterproof. He had replaced her little, worn backpack with a sturdy bit of gear that could hold more and was just as lightweight. It had been stuffed with as much food and water as she could carry.

Little bits of survival gear were in there too, matches and fishing line and pills that were supposed to help if she became sick.

She wore goggles that would keep the sand from her eyes, and her old handkerchief was now a nylon mountaineering mask. A flashlight helmet that was a little too big for her protected Elise's head. She had her machete, but she also carried a steel dive knife on a strap at her thigh. There was a sturdy metal watch on her wrist that gave time, direction, and much more.

He had offered one of the guns, but she had said no.

They scared her.

Jules pointed to the south.

"There is nothing to the north but wasteland. Everything there is gone. East and west are like what you've seen. South, it looks like south might be better. I cannot say. Perhaps you should go there."

Elise didn't say anything. She just started walking, and the crab followed.

Jules watched them go.

He stood for a long time in the cold breeze of the morning.

He watched until Elise and her strange companion had disappeared from view. And then, he dropped to his knees, and his shoulders lurched as he cried, the kind of overwhelming and uncontrollable sobbing you might have as a child when it feels as if the world was out to destroy you.

This crying went on for some time before he stood and returned to the museum and then into the hall.

*

She followed the compass on her watch south into the 16th Arrondissement along Rue Benjamin Franklin. She kept to the side of the avenue and ducked into side streets at every other turn.

The red sandstorm winds were light. Dunes were piled everywhere, and she realized that she should probably watch for tracks. The sand was smooth like fresh snow.

The buildings along the avenue were damaged like the rest of the city. Crumbling facades, stone burned black, windows shattered.

The winds built through the day and into the afternoon.

Elise made good time, but to where she had no idea. The sun began to drop over the horizon, so she and the crab worked their way into the battered black wreck of a car and tucked down into the floorboards, hidden from the world.

Night fell. She slept in fits. She nibbled on her food and sipped water.

Day came, and she went on the move again. South.

This became her routine for three days. Her legs were tired at first, but she was building strength.

She was careful with her food and drink and made sure to stay in the shadows. She gave bits of food to the crab as well, but he didn't seem interested.

What would he eat, she wondered.

There were no strange surprises, no life at all, just sand and concrete and dead trees and cold.

How a twelve-year-old could make it through that wasteland might be a mystery to some, to those who have no children or have no experience with their unexpected strength and their capacity to adapt. Of course, she wasn't alone, and when your sidekick is a crab the size of a German Shepherd with claws like scythes, then you find more courage than you might otherwise.

But still, kids are tough.

She passed by the scorched and dead Parc St. Perine and on towards the Boulevard Peripherique, the ring road that had circled the great city. The city was less congested here, less a maze of destruction and more open.

Something moved behind a large hole in a street-facing wall, something brown and quick.

Elise ducked behind the wreck of a car. The crab stayed with her and settled into a low sand dune; a trick that made him almost disappear.

Yes, something was moving in the darkness of the building across the street. Several somethings. She heard voices.

Men dressed in dirty brown shrouds stepped out of the building and into the light. There were five of them, and they were wearing dark sheets that wrapped and covered them head to foot like she had seen some of the Arab people wear on her trips into the city.

The men carried large bags. What were they doing? Stealing?

Elise thought about that for an instant. It's not really stealing if there's no one alive, right?

Scavenging? Yes, that was the word. They were scavenging.

The five stayed tight together and walked south, looking this way and that.

The man in front and the man in back were carrying clubs and axes.

Elise didn't like the look of the men. They looked dangerous. She started to wish that she had taken Jules up on his offer of the gun.

She stayed quiet and still until the men disappeared from view.

"I think we should take a different path, don't you?" she asked the crab.

Elise carefully moved off down a parallel road that ran south, and she kept a sharp watch for the men. They might have been helpful, but something about them didn't look right.

Something about those men frightened her.

Hours passed. Elise walked slowly, cautiously, staying in the shadows.

So many old homes, so many empty shops. In one burnt-out storefront, she spotted an unopened bottle of beer. She grabbed it and slid it into her new backpack. Her Dad had let her take a sip of beer once, and she hated it, but any kind of liquid might be useful in this new world. Dad would have approved, she thought.

Voices screamed and shouted nearby. To her right, from where those men had gone.

Elise froze.

Stay right here, she thought. Do not go over there. That doesn't sound good, not at all.

Curiosity is a tough thing to beat.

She ran down a side street and towards the Rue de Curry.

Towards the shouts.

Elise turned a corner that let out to the wide boulevard Murat.

There was a giant creature floating just above the street, purple, blue, and red and in some places as clear as glass. Hundreds of thin tentacles writhed from beneath its bell-shaped body. It was an enormous, flying jellyfish, a man-of-war the size of a car.

Elise felt her blood frost over in her veins. She was so terrified that she couldn't breathe.

The crab nestled down into the sand and was completely hidden.

Two of the men were wrapped up in the creature's tentacles.

They weren't moving, and they were being pulled up to the body of the thing. The other three men were dancing around the jelly, trying to strike it with rocks and debris, shouting at it as if doing so would force it to release their friends.

One of the men had a long metal rod, and he threw it like a javelin. It bounced off the jelly's glistening skin. A tentacle no thicker than a rose stem shot out and wrapped around the man's neck.

He screamed and seized up as if his entire body had been shot through with poison. The jelly pulled him into the nest of its other arms and began to rise.

So, this was what Robert and Renny had told her about, this horrific jellyfish that killed and floated away.

The remaining two men ran off screaming, dropping their bags as they went.

The massive Air Jelly lifted higher and higher until it was above the rooftops, a grotesque hot air balloon that carried the dead bodies of three men.

"Sick, right? Now turn around slow."

The voice made Elise jump. She turned.

Three filthy kids, maybe her age, maybe a bit younger, stood just behind her. They each had chunks of wood that were embedded with razor blades.

Elise placed her hand hard on the sand that covered the crab, her way of trying to tell it to stay down.

She stood and raised her hands in the air.

The boy in the middle was taller and looked tougher than the other two. His dark face was covered in black grease, and he was dressed in torn old leather and denim.

He poked the razor club at Elise. He spoke in French.

"Give us all your stuff, or we'll slice you till you're dead."

Elise didn't move. The boy's voice was trembling.

"Who are you?" she asked.

"We'll cut you. I swear it."

"She's so clean, Hemmi," said one of the others, "how did she get so clean?"

Silence for a beat while they stared at each other.

"Right. How'd you get so clean?"

Elise didn't know what to say. She wasn't going to tell them about the Hall of Les Scaphandriers.

So she said nothing.

"Do you speak English? My French is crap," she said.

"Give us your things," the tall, dark one said in English with a thick accent.

Elise wasn't going to do that, and she didn't want the crab to hurt them or get hurt trying. She wanted this entire situation to go in a different direction, but she wasn't sure how to get there. They were kids, like her, so there must be grown-ups. Maybe there's some help.

"I'm Elise. Were those men, those men who got killed by that thing, were they your friends?"

"Hell no. They'd kill us if they saw us. Probably eat us too. They're the worst round here. Friends? Hell no."

"Well, there's only two left to worry about now. Why were you following them?"

"More where that came from. We call them Sheets, but I don't know their proper name. They run the neighborhood and stay at PSG. We follow the bastards 'cause they know where to scavenge stuff. We go in after them and sometimes find some things. Mostly not. Now shut up and give us your bag."

"You didn't tell me your name."

"What are you, stupid?" The tall one, the one the other had called Hemmi, lifted the razor club as if to swing it at Elise.

The crab rose from the sand, and its massive claws came up as well. Elise took a step between the crab and the boys.

She dropped her hand back, motioning to the crab "stay" like you would a dog.

The boys moved back, eyes wide at the sight of the huge creature.

"What the Hell is that?"

"He won't hurt you if you'll just leave us alone."

"Hell, that's food, that's what that is."

Hemmi took a step forward.

"Stop. He'll kill you. I've seen him do it. He will absolutely kill you."

Hemmi hesitated.

Elise moved back, and the crab went with her.

"Wait." Hemmi lowered his razor club.

"You on your own? Just you and that thing?"

The crab's eyestalks waved back and forth.

Elise nodded "yes."

"How old are you?"

"Twelve."

"Damn. You ought to be dead. How do you do it?"

"I'm not by myself. I've got him, and he protects me."

"Yeah, but where did you come from?"

"My name is Elise, and that's all you need to know. Now, who are you?"

"I'm Hemmi, and this here's Zola and Flaubert. You want to come back to The Nursery with us, you can."

Elise looked closely at the three. Yes, they were her age, perhaps younger, but it was hard to tell through all the dirt and ragged clothing. Hemmi was black, with dark brown eyes and unruly hair. Zola was a small blonde boy who looked like he hadn't eaten in forever. Flaubert, now that Elise was looking hard, was a girl. She was thin and pale under the crust of filth, and she had no hair peeking out from under the baseball cap. Shaved head? Maybe.

She was a girl, though, and that made Elise feel a little more comfortable with them, with the thought of going along.

"The Nursery? What's that?"

"It's where we live. Come on, ain't got much time out here."

He was right. The wind was picking up, and the crimson wall of the night storm was building in the distance.

She would need a place for the night, and maybe this would do. "Okay."

*

Rats in a maze. That's what it felt like to Elise. She followed, and Hemmi led as they dashed and scrambled through the dark hallways of deserted buildings, into alleys, and then again into forgotten storefronts and back into side streets, meandering and reversing direction. At first, she tried to keep track on her compass but quickly gave up. Hemmi and the other two seemed to know exactly where they were going.

They spilled out of an alley into a broad plaza and ran towards a tall, fat building of broken glass that had obviously once been taller. The top of the structure was gone as if something had removed it with a scythe.

There were mountains of rubble all around, debris of steel and shattered glass.

The storm was on them now, and the sun was almost down.

The wind pelted them with sand, and the spark flies were starting. A vicious bolt of lightning struck a metal pole near them, and they ducked. Elise's ears rang, and her skin tingled.

They ran.

A fire-damaged sign out front read "Hospital."

Hemmi stopped Elise and pointed to the crab.

"That thing. It's one of them, ain't it?"

"He's okay. Really."

"If it makes a wrong move, I'll kill it."

"You'll have to kill me first."

"I can do that," he said and turned toward the building.

Elise and the crab followed.

They entered through broken glass doors of the old Emergency Entrance underneath a big red cross.

*

CHAPTER TWENTY-FIVE

Curious?

JULES VALIANCE SAT in a soft leather chair facing a video monitor on a brick wall in the Hall of Les Scaphandriers, his face lit by the glow of the screen and by the burning cigarette in his lips.

He thought about one word.

"Curious?"

That word, written in every language known and unknown, languages dead a thousand years, that word glowing in elegant filigree script everywhere and on everything ten years ago in the cathedral at the bottom of the sea.

The last room before the end of the world.

"Curious?"

That simple word.

He hadn't been certain that the solar batteries of the place would be enough to bring the video screen to life, and so he'd ignored it for a day or two.

He couldn't help himself, of course. He never could, and that was the problem, obviously. So, by killing the lights and other contraptions, he found that there was enough power to turn on the screen and play a video.

There was no sound, and that didn't matter. This was unedited footage, the helmet cams of the team as they descended.

They explored. That's what they did. They explored, no matter what, no matter the risk, because humanity was meant to explore.

Les Scaphandriers had been formed, some say by Jules Verne himself, as a secret arm of the French Navy, a small team of scientists, naval officers, and adventurers who were assigned the task of exploring the unknown 70% of the planet. They sought new life in a mysterious world hidden from the eyes of mankind, they fought clandestine battles against organizations that would bring down the country, they studied and mapped and celebrated their brilliance for a hundred years. They were unknown to the public, heralded by only themselves and a few souls fortunate enough to call them friends. Celebrities, mostly, chefs and actresses and writers and musicians. They were the secret party, the hidden celebration, just another impossible thing in a fantastic world.

They explored, no matter the cost, and usually with plenty of wine at their side.

So that bright morning ten years ago, they had descended in their spectacular Aquaboggin into the depths of the Atlantic Ocean toward a strange blue glow that the U.S. Navy had discovered by chance in the Bay of Biscay.

It was a bright blue object shining up from the ocean floor in seven thousand feet of water, and there was no logical explanation for the thing.

They were the last and best of Les Scaphandriers, jammed tightly with their gear into their unparalleled submersible, descending to explore what might be a strange volcano, a rift in the earth, a Russian mistake. Who knew?

They had wine and smokes and elaborate gadgets. They had science and patriotism and ego, so what else would they need?

The video switched between helmet cams and would be hard to follow for someone who hadn't been there that morning.

There was the interior of the sub. Fast forward. There was Lt. LeBuche, laughing and joking with the estimable and inscrutable

Guyanese malacologist Three John. Zuzu, the beautiful but deadly. Private Splatter and his fiery red hair. The Asian elder North McAllister. So many good sailors. Fast forward.

The glow through the porthole of the sub, a bright cobalt in the blackness of the abyss, growing larger until it filled the screen.

Fast forward.

The glow is revealed. Light pouring out from blue and golden towers. A structure of light and metal at the bottom of the Atlantic Ocean.

A cathedral.

Jules felt his heart racing as he watched, just as it had that morning when Les Scaphandriers discovered a blue and gold replica of the Cathedral of Notre Dame in the heart of the sea.

Make no mistake. The Atlantic Abyssal plain is the blackest of black. So, the fiery light of this strange cathedral was blinding at first. It took the cameras a moment to adjust.

Impossible. Jules piloted the submersible closer and around the spires and chimeras. On closer inspection, it wasn't exactly Notre Dame de Paris, but it was shockingly similar, a gothic cathedral of stained glass and stone, and the glow came from within it with the force of the sun.

Just impossible.

The excited murmur and current of fear in the sub were so strong that it was almost overwhelming. Jules could remember that feeling as if it had only been a moment ago.

Fast forward.

Hovering at the tall metal doors of the cathedral structure, lighting spilling out from cracks and seams and glass. Words carved roughly into the metal of the portal in letters a meter high.

"Keep Out."

They had joked. They had argued. They had a brief but intense discussion. Should we go inside? We mustn't.

We must.

We can't.

We are Les Scaphandriers, and we are at the bottom of the sea staring at a man-made structure that's a complete anomaly, an impossibility, a curiosity beyond anything ever seen in the history of our world.

This will re-write history. This will change everything we know. This is what we do. This is what we did.

We will.

We did.

God help, me, thought Jules as he stared at the video.

We did.

The sub had forward and aft robotic "hands" that pulled the portal doors wide. The light was blinding. They moved forward and into the abyssal cathedral at a snail's pace.

A rush of water stirred particulates and shook the sub as the massive doors slammed behind them.

Roaring, rushing, chaos as the water inside of the vast cathedral was drained by force, drained in a heartbeat, countless liters of cold, deep ocean water drained so quickly that the submersible dropped to the stone floor with a painful thud and rolled onto its side.

He remembered the taste of fear and blood as they piled out of the submersible hatch into cool, fresh air. Impossible. Fresh air at the bottom of the ocean. Staring up at the flying buttress and gothic vaulted ceiling as the others gathered around, cameras rolling, words blending into a chaos of excitement and discovery.

Great statues of strange creatures, like men but not, perhaps men of the sea or gods of the ocean or some fevered imagining of a mad sculptor. A tiled floor of many colors, clean and shining under the overwhelming cobalt light from an enormous globe at the center of the cathedral. The globe was a full ten meters around, pure blue light coruscating with energy so that tendrils of power constantly writhed along its surface.

This blue orb of awesome energy hovered in a bracing structure of pure gold and looked like a porthole or a massive lock.

Fast forward.

The team scattering about the place, studying every detail, the excitement, the thrill. Then, the realization that there were words carved and etched and written on surfaces all around them and the words began to glow a soft blue light the globe and the words were shown as only one.

"Curious?"

Jules at the base of the globe, the camera focused on a tiny doll-like sculpture, a merman cherub holding a violin no bigger than your hand.

Had it moved?

Inscribed in shifting languages at the base of the little sculpture was "Don't Touch."

Jules reached out with his aqua-gloved hand and poked it with a finger.

The cherub began to play the violin.

The sound then, the thunderous painful sound. Behind them, just as in the Great Lady of Paris, a towering pipe organ, but this one crusted with coral of all colors and alive with tiny creatures like crabs. The organ came to life with such power that Jules remembered being afraid that the stained glass would shatter and send the depths of the ocean roaring into the place, drowning them all like rats.

The organ played a song he didn't recognize as the little sculpture fell backwards and revealed a red button at its base.

A brass plaque next to the button had tiny lettering inscribed on its surface. Jules leaned in to read it. The thunder of the organ grew louder and louder. He remembered the pain in his ears, the pounding of the low frequency moan in his heart. Watching, ten years gone, in the cold of the Hall of Les Scaphandriers, he felt sick as he looked again on what the little plaque said, carved in English. Wait, in French. No, it was Arabic. Spanish.

Hindi. Ancient Mayan.

He remembered shaking his head. The inscription was all languages at once, and it said,

"Curious?"

Madness. This was madness.

And of course, the great Jules Valiance, the leader of Les Scaphandriers, the Commander of the Society of Astonishing Aquarists, the man who lived for the thrill of exploration, for the visceral pull of discovery, did exactly what they wanted him to do.

Jules pressed the button.

The porthole erupted in blue energy, and the thundering, whirling, overwhelming sound of the organ became a cascade that overwhelmed them.

Tendrils of that energy reaching out, capturing Zuzu as she cursed and pulling her into the seething energy pit. McAllister, then, pulled along, clutching desperately at the tiled floor. A section of stone ripped from a wall flying like a missile, striking LeBuche as it went, cutting him nearly in half.

Holding the jacket of Three John as both of them were being sucked toward the portal, fighting the pull, making it to the sub.

"No man left behind!" his voice screaming these words but drowned by the roar of the energy cascade. Three John wrenched away by the growing force of the energy pool.

Screaming. That's my voice screaming, he thought.

All of his friends disappearing into the pit.

The camera shaking madly as he somehow made his way back into the sub, climbing in through the top hatch, desperate to get away from that noise.

The hatch closing just as the walls and glass of the cathedral imploded around them and swept the submersible up and around and into a vortex of rushing water.

Jules at the controls, jamming buttons and bringing the sub to life, full power to escape the maelstrom and get to the surface.

The ocean around him...the ocean...my God.

Jules escaped the pull of the titanic rip current. The others, Three John, Zuzu, and the rest, were sucked into the torrent. The rear camera showed the bright cobalt light where the cathedral of Notre Dame at the bottom of the sea had been, and it showed something so horrifying that it still gave him nightmares, night terrors that sent him screaming out of bed.

The ocean was collapsing into the cobalt energy, the writhing tentacles of some unknown power. The seafloor, the water, everything was being pulled into that awful light.

These miles wide energy portholes opened up in the deepest canyons in all the basins of the world's ocean simultaneously. Thousands of them. In the space of four hours, the ocean, the one body of water that covered seventy percent of the Earth, the precious thing that gives life, was gone.

That was the day that the world ended, the day when the ocean was pulled into the seafloor to who knows where and the skies became red as blood with hurricane sandstorm winds and things from Hell came to kill everything he knew.

That was the day Jules Valiance killed his friends and destroyed the world.

The video went black.

That word, that question, stabbing again and again into his heart.

"Curious?"

*

CHAPTER TWENTY-SIX

The Nursery

TWO DAYS INTO her stay at The Nursery and Elise still didn't feel comfortable.

There were eight kids in total, and they were all the same age. Ten years old. Hemmi looked older, and Zola looked younger, but they were all born on the same day ten years before, born on the day the world ended.

Getting into The Nursery was no easy task. The lower levels of the hospital had been completely burned out and stripped. Hemmi couldn't tell Elise how that had happened for sure, but the tales were of panicked Parisians ransacking the place for medicine and then somehow setting it on fire. There was also a scary story, one that Hemmi would tell the kids in the dark just to keep things interesting, about monsters that roamed the halls on the day the world ended and how the things hunted and killed anything that moved.

Once you climbed the rickety burnt-out stairwell and slithered through the countless piles of debris that made a maze of the place, you had to tightrope walk a series of wooden planks set out over a five-story drop into darkness. Elise had declined to follow them at first glance, afraid that the crab couldn't make it, but he was more agile than most crabs and lighter than you'd think, and he skittered across the make-shift bridges with little effort.

The Nursery was on the top floor. Someone had done some decorating, making the wide rooms and halls as pleasing and homey as possible in impossible circumstances. There were plastic flowers and paper ribbons, and plush toys scattered about the place.

Hemmi explained to Elise on their first night that Ms. Dodd had been with them since they were born, but she had been killed two years ago.

She went out to look for supplies and came back to them with horrible wounds that wouldn't heal.

Ms. Dodd had taken care of them since that first day.

She concealed and protected them from the things that came to kill. She was a nurse, and they were newborns.

Eight kids.

Elise walked into the newborn's room on that first night and counted the little cribs, all set up in rows. There were twenty places. Twenty places for twenty babies.

Hemmi pointed her to a corner of the reception room.

There was a mattress and some blankets, and that's where Elise slept. He also gave her a book. It was fat with handwritten pages.

"Ms. Dodd's diary. She taught us our letters and a bit of reading, but I can't make much sense of it because the writing is all scribbly."

Elise opened the book. The English script was cursive.

She was tired, but she stayed up late the first night, reading by the light of her twist torch.

Ms. Dodd's diary told of those first days and weeks after the world changed. The horror she felt, then the determination to save the babies. Everyone else had run or been killed. Things, and then people, had stormed the lower levels, stripping everything. She had defended and barricaded The Nursery as the babies wailed and cried. Ms. Dodd was an English nurse from Banbury who was engaged to marry a Frenchman named Marc who worked at the zoo. She dreamed of better things, but Marc never came, and better things became impossible.

Elise grew cold as she read of Ms. Dodd's ordeal and terrible choices. Newborn babies are needy things, and she had done the best that she could, but there was only so much food and so much medicine and so much time. So, there could only be so many babies.

Some of the white pages were stained with tears, and some were stained with blood.

Elise stopped reading. She understood what had happened, enough to know that a brave woman had done everything in her power to save twenty little lives and that only eight were left. That in itself was something of a miracle.

*

Elise spent time evaluating her situation on the second afternoon at The Nursery.

She found Hemmi playing a version of basketball with two of the other kids. The children of The Nursery were thin and frail but energetic and had scavenged a fair amount of food and drink that was stashed into lockers in a locked room.

Only Hemmi had the key.

The smell in The Nursery was pungent, a rank mix of filthy toilets and filthy kids. Elise didn't think she would get used to the stench.

The noise was constant even at night. The kids subscribed to no particular sleep pattern, so Elise was cranky from constantly being awakened.

They were decent enough, as Ms. Dodd had apparently been quite the disciplinarian, but without her, the politics of children had begun to assert itself, so manners were there one moment and gone the next.

Elise found the place stifling. More than that, she didn't feel any safer here than she did out in the street.

Hemmi was about to take a shot when Elise interrupted.

"You have a second?" she asked.

He tossed a ball of stripped rubber and tape to one of the other boys and joined her. They walked to the Reception desk and sat.

"What's up?"

"Did you ever think about getting out of here? Finding a better place?"

Hemmi spit.

"You been out there. Better? What's better?"

"You can't stay here forever. It stinks, and it's dark, and it's just crap. You're going to clean out the stuff right around here, round this block, and you'll need to scavenge further and further away. You can't stay here forever."

"Yes, I can."

"What if there's something better just a mile down the avenue? You'll never know."

"There isn't. Don't be stupid. You want to go, go."

Hemmi returned to the game.

*

That night, Elise was awakened by a scream.

She was tucked in a pile of blankets under the reception desk with the crab at her side. Her first instinct was to curl up into a ball and stay still, hiding.

Another scream. Angry voices.

Elise shook off the blankets and ran to the sound, around the corridor corner and near to one of the old restrooms.

Flaubert, covered in blood, was standing over one of the other kids, a dark little girl named Gwynne. Elise had noticed the girl before, that she was different. Her speech was thick and hard to understand, and Elise thought that she might have been born with some sort of condition.

She was sweet but simple, and now Gwynne was screaming

and bleeding from a cut on her head. Her face was red with blood. Hemmi and two of the boys were standing around the two in a little circle.

"Kill her." It was little Zola. He was pointing at Gwynne. "Kill her."

Flaubert kicked the girl hard in the side.

The crab raised its claws and started to move toward them.

Elise grabbed his shell like you would a dog collar and pulled him back.

"What is this?" she asked.

All eyes turned to Elise. Flaubert threw a rock at Elise. It hit her in the chest, and she dropped to her knees.

The crab moved then, and Elise grabbed one of its back legs and yanked hard. It stopped, but the claws were raised high and were waving quickly back and forth.

Hemmi pushed Flaubert.

"Why'd you do that? Elise didn't do anything."

Flaubert went to kick Gwynne again.

"Stop!" Elise said.

She noticed, then, the shining metal blade in Flaubert's right hand. A razor.

Gwynne was crying and holding her head in her hands.

Blood was pouring from her face.

She curled up into a tight ball.

"You needn't have come out here, Elise. This is our business." Hemmi pushed Flaubert hard and away. Flaubert tucked the blade into her belt, under her shirt, and stepped back.

Hemmi said something quietly to Flaubert, something that Elise couldn't hear. Flaubert shrugged and walked away.

"Next time, I'll take her tongue," she said as she went.

The little circle of boys stepped back as well.

Hemmi came to Elise and knelt down next to her.

"You needn't have come out here," he said again.

The crab moved between them and knocked him back on his butt.

"Hey!"

Elise moved to Gwynne. There was a nasty straight slice in the girl's scalp just below her eyebrows.

Elise was terrified. Her heart raced. The cut didn't look too deep, but there was so much blood. Elise thought for a moment that she was going to be sick.

Elise put her arms around Gwynne.

"It's okay. It's okay."

Hemmi stood up and came to them. The crab only let him get so close.

Elise glared up at him.

"She needs a bandage. She's bleeding really badly."

"Let her get her own. Little freak. Hell with her."

"What did she do?"

"That's between the freak and Flaubert. That's how we handle things."

"Please. She needs a bandage."

"We don't have any."

"Fine."

Elise spent the next hour taking care of Gwynne. She used the beer that she had scavenged to clean the cut and the blood. She then tore strips from an old sheet to wrap the girl's head. Elise sat with her arm around Gwynne for a while, the two of them tucked under the reception desk with the giant crab curled up in front of them like a dog.

Elise asked, but Gwynne at first wouldn't say what had caused the fight. The crab fascinated the child. Gwynne stroked the creature's bumpy red shell. The two eyestalks swiveled and leaned in, looking closely at her.

"What's his name?"

"I haven't named him yet. He's amazing, though."

"All things must have a name. Especially amazing things."

Elise smiled. True.

"Charlie. His name is Charlie the Crab."

Gwynne nodded approval and adopted a solemn look.

"Good name. Charlie."

The three rested quietly in the darkness for quite some time.

Then, just as they were drifting off to sleep, Gwynne said,

"Ms. Dodd always said that she liked my singing. I like to sing. Flaubert cut me cause of it. Flaubert told me to stop, but I like to sing. I don't want to stop."

"You can sing to me if you want. Sing to Charlie and me."

Gwynne was quiet at first, and then she began to hum, and then she began to sing in a shy little voice. She sang softly, lullabies that had probably been sung to her by Ms. Dodd.

Elise drifted off.

And then Gwynne fell asleep at Elise's shoulder on the last night of her short life.

*

CHAPTER TWENTY-SEVEN

Monstrous

SCYNDA'S SKIN SHIVERED.

A wave of color and texture swept over her, from her toes to the top of her head.

The Razor was coming. There wouldn't be much time.

The bullet wound had sealed, but it was painful, and the skin around the wound was injured and didn't speak, didn't change, just stayed a dull slate gray. There was something still inside her, an object from the man's weapon, and it burned.

The howling night winds lashed her with sand, but they were dying away bit by bit.

Morning was near. The Razor would come with the morning, then. This place would be erased from the world.

Much to do and no time.

Her Men of Many Eyes were flanked around Scynda. She caressed the brick face of the hospital, and her skin became it.

The human child was here.

Scynda didn't have time, but she could taste the blood of the child. Her skin could sense her oils and scents and fear. The male human who had wounded her with the hot weapon was not here, so there would be no revenge on him. Not today.

But Scynda would have the child, and she would need to hurry.

*

Elise woke up, and Gwynne was gone.

She thought nothing of it and gathered her things.

Elise kept her kit with her wherever she went. She felt safer that way.

Charlie the crab followed her as she went to a stairwell, stepping over a sleeping child as they went. His legs clicked and ticked on the tile.

They climbed the stairwell and lifted the bracing that secured the door at the top. She popped out into the morning sun.

The top floors of the hospital had been destroyed, sliced away by who knows what, so the stairwell led to the new roof, a tangle of metal and stone that had once been a hospital floor. Now, it was a wide rooftop terrace where the kids could get fresh air, where they could see the city around them, always careful not to show too much of themselves. Careful not to make themselves a target.

Elise stretched as she made her way across the terrace.

The wind was light, and the air was cold.

She could see her breath. She pulled a water bottle out of her backpack and a nutrition bar.

She walked to the edge and looked out to the west, over what remained of Paris. The crab stayed back from the ledge as if nervous, but Elise didn't mind heights, so she sat down and let her legs dangle over the side.

The nutrition bar was good but had a funny taste that she couldn't place. Chicken?

She read the label.

"Concentrated Coq au Vin."

Chicken and wine mushed together into a bar. Well, Jules had been a jerk, but Les Scaphandriers knew how to eat.

She offered a bite to Charlie, but the crab's feelers waved wildly, and it tucked its face down.

"You don't like this stuff, do you? We need to get you something to eat."

Something rustled behind her. Her head whipped around. It was Hemmi.

"Hey."

"Hey."

He sat next to her but didn't dangle his legs.

"Je deteste hauteurs," he said, "I don't like heights."

They sat quietly for a moment. Elise considered giving him a bite of her food but then decided not to give him any. She wasn't sure that she liked Hemmi.

"You shouldn't be so mean to Gwynne. She can't help that she's different."

"Different gets you killed. And she's annoying, singing those stupid songs."

"The songs mean something to her. Maybe it helps her to think about the lady who protected you, Ms. Dodd."

"Yeah, well, Dodd is dead, right? She's dead, and we've got to be strong and, you know, forget those kid songs and move on."

Elise finished her Coq au Vin.

"If Ms. Dodd wasn't dead, would you be so mean to Gwynne?"

Hemmi didn't say anything.

Elise thought about the diary of Ms. Dodd. It had contained handwritten charts and schedules.

The nurse had raised the babies in a structured environment, or as best you could imagine under the circumstances.

There had been daily prayer and song and chores and classes in French and English and math and everything else.

For the first eight years of their lives, these kids had suffered, but they had some sort of order. Then, Dodd was dead. Where had the structure, the order, the environment that she had built, where had it gone?

"Are you in charge?"

Hemmi looked at Elise as if she were kidding.

"Seriously. Who's in charge?"

"Pas moi," Hemmi said. Not me.

"Then, who?"

"Nobody."

Elise was about to say something but stopped herself.

There was something off to the west.

A dark cloud. Too early in the day for the big sandstorms, but maybe this was something different.

"Hey," she said and pointed off in the direction of the black mass on the horizon.

"Storm."

They watched it as it grew. The storm was coming towards them, but as it got closer, they saw that it didn't span the entire horizon as a proper storm would. Then there was a sound, a vibration.

That's a weird storm, Elise thought. It's shaking the ground.

A scream erupted from the stairwell.

Elise and Hemmi turned around just as Zola came running up onto the rooftop.

They saw the fear in Zola's dirty little face, and then they saw something else, something dark and slender and awful rising up behind him.

"Hemmi!" he screamed just as a Man of Many Eyes reached out from the doorway and grabbed him by the leg. Zola went down and was dragged back, his screams becoming liquid and shrill.

Elise and Hemmi had no time to think, no time to react, they were frozen, and they watched in horror as the Man of Many Eyes tore at Zola, ripping him, slicing him.

There were more screams now from down below, shouts and pleading from the other kids of The Nursery.

The rumbling vibration from the coming storm was getting louder, more intense.

Elise felt as if her heart was going to explode from her chest. She glanced back over her shoulder.

That wasn't a storm. It was an ebony ship, as big as a city block or bigger, and it looked like a plow or a razor, and it was tearing and slicing and ripping the city. Debris and smoke churned up from its massive blade and were sucked back into the mass of the thing.

The coming black storm was a monstrous machine, and it was excavating Paris.

A hiss.

Elise turned back and heard Hemmi gasp.

Scynda the Assassin stepped out of the stairwell and onto the terrace, her skin red as blood and her teeth shining like needles.

She hissed again, and Elise saw that her eyelashes were tentacles that writhed and twisted around her face.

Charlie the crab scuttled toward Scynda. Elise grabbed Hemmi by the wrist and pulled him, running, frantic to get away.

But to where?

The rooftop was a tangle of debris, stone, wood, and metal rods. Places to duck down and hide for a moment but was there another door, another hole they could drop into, another escape?

Elise and Hemmi ran, not looking back, the entire hospital beginning to shudder under their feet.

"Is there another door down?"

Hemmi shook his head "no," his eyes wide.

They stopped hard at the other side of the rooftop, their feet practically at the edge of a five-story drop to the street below.

Elise turned back and saw the ebony ship in a hideous cloud of flying debris and destruction, a metallic tornado devastating everything in its path, now less than a mile away, and it was so huge that it dwarfed the skyline.

There too, was Scynda. She had tried to pursue the two of them, but Charlie cut her off and was standing, claws raised, between the kids and Scynda.

Scynda was still smiling. How could something so terrible be so beautiful? She was sleek, her color shifting and shimmering from red to granite gray, her skin changing as well, her eyes piercing and hypnotic.

Elise could see the wound in her shoulder, a place where the skin didn't change, where her flesh was dead. But those pointed teeth, those awful, pointed teeth, and claws.

She didn't seem eager to move closer, not willing to do battle with the crab. Elise saw why. Scynda was waiting. The Men of Many Eyes, her companions, emerged from the stairwell and slinked out onto the rooftop at her flanks. There were five of them.

"No," Elise said and made to run toward them.

They would kill Charlie. Hemmi grabbed her and pulled her back.

The crab stood its ground. The hospital was shaking now, and Elise could see dust rising as if the entire structure was about to fall apart. The roaring, sucking, overwhelming sound of the giant black ship was so loud now that it hurt her ears. The ship was a half-mile away, and already it became the horizon, an ebony wall devouring Paris.

One of the Men of Many Eyes lunged for the crab and received a slashing from a claw. Blood sprayed. Two of the others leapt in and went for its legs. Charlie pivoted and slashed again. Scynda stayed back, swaying and moving as if somehow directing these assassin pawns. They went for the crab again, and one of them got a leg and tried to flip it. A claw struck, and the Man of Many Eyes lost a hand.

It wailed.

Elise had the dive knife out and was running towards them without even thinking. Hemmi couldn't hold her back.

Not her crab. Charlie was her only friend in this world.

She fell as the building shook under her feet. Scrambled up and ran again.

They had the crab now, three of them.

Scynda moved in, grabbed a leg, and wrenched, flipped Charlie. The dark red crustacean was swinging its huge claws, but it was on its back now. The eyestalks waved back and forth, desperate and frenzied.

Elise couldn't get there fast enough; her feet were clumsy, she fell again and scraped her face, and Hemmi was next to her, and this time he was with her, trying to help.

Scynda smiled and plunged one of her clawed hands into the armored chest of her crab.

"No!"

The men of many eyes began striking at the crab, evading the flailing claws and legs, the blackness of the enormous ship swallowing the sky behind them, a coming storm of absolute death and destruction.

Scynda struck Charlie in the chest again and again.

The first strike hadn't pierced the shell, but the second and third did; Elise could see the crab shudder and kick wildly.

She screamed.

It didn't matter anyway because they were all dead in seconds. The black death ship, as tall as a mountain, was on them, and there was no stopping it.

"What's that?" Hemmi asked, pointing.

Elise looked up to the east.

The submarine of Jules Valiance could fly, and apparently, it had guns because it was firing bullets with deadly efficiency.

*

CHAPTER TWENTY-EIGHT

To the West

THE SUBMARINE OF Les Scaphandriers soared out of the east, a shining blue and gold missile as big as a small bus, and tracers blazed white-hot streams from its gun turrets.

The bullets hit the targets as if radar guided.

The Men of Many Eyes erupted in a dark explosion of mist.

Scynda looked up at the coming submarine, and her eyes grew wide. The tentacles of her lashes writhed.

Her skin, the talking skin, became as white as clean paper in the instant before a dozen heavy lead slugs hit. Scynda, the great assassin, the chameleon, the thing that haunted the dreams of the living, died instantly.

The sub, propeller blades spinning from the port, top, and starboard, swooped to Elise and Hemmi and hovered a couple of feet from the debris-covered terrace. The blades kicked up dust, but Elise couldn't even hear them over the roar of the coming black ship.

A porthole opened on the side of the sub, and a little staircase dropped down.

"I can't leave them," Hemmi said. He was crying, and before Elise could say anything, he was off to the stairwell and down into the hospital.

Elise ran to Charlie the crab.

Her friend lay on its back in a wide pool of blood and tissue that was the only thing left of the Men of Many Eyes. His eyestalks moved slowly right and left and then found her, focused on her. His armored legs were still.

Elise could see the wound in his chest, and she started to sob.

She embraced him, and the eyestalks followed her. She didn't know if she should move him or flip him, and the black ship was almost there, and she didn't want to leave him.

"Idiot girl, we must go."

It was Jules. He was beside her.

"No. He's my friend."

"Ah, then he must come as well. Never leave a friend. Grab him."

Elise lifted one side of the crab, Jules got the other, and they ran back to the hovering sub.

The cabin of the sub was like that of a small plane, with a narrow aisle and seats on either side. They set Charlie on the floor. Jules moved to the pilot seat and strapped in. His finger jabbed a button on the control panel.

The porthole door began to close.

"The kids down below. We can't leave them."

Jules looked back at her, and there was sadness in his eyes.

"There is no time."

He was right. Beyond the thick glass forward window of the sub, there was nothing but a hurricane of flying debris and a wall of complete, utter blackness.

The destroying ship was on them. If they didn't fly away now, they would die.

"This will be terrifying," Jules said.

The door shut, and the sub shot up so fast that Elise hit the top of the cabin with her head and then plummeted back to the floor, dazed and in pain.

Jules Valiance had the sub in a steep climb.

He looked out of the port glass, down at the city below.

The hospital was moments from being bulldozed under the mile-wide swath of the black machine and consumed like everything else around.

Jules turned back to the task of flying the sub. The air was turbulent, and he was concerned about dust clogging the vents, debris striking the propellers. The vessel shuddered as he went into a sharp turn back over the hospital.

"Mon Dieu. The little fellow."

There was a tiny figure on the rooftop. It was waving at them.

Jules dropped the nose of the craft and spun down like a dart, the throttle shoved hard, the engines straining. Elise was thrown backward and grabbed onto a seat as she went to stop herself.

"Perhaps you should obey traffic regulations and avail yourself of the safety belt."

Elise was dizzy and scared, but she found the strap and clicked it at her waist and shoulders as the sub roller coasted down to within a few feet of the terrace.

Jules popped the port hatch.

Hemmi scrambled inside.

"Strap in," Jules said, and he throttled down and pulled back, and the sub shot up almost vertically just as the mountainous black machine turned the hospital into so much dust.

The terrifying sound of the black machine faded behind them as the three propellers strained and the submarine bucked.

Elise felt wetness on her face. Her head was cut, and she was bleeding. Hemmi sat stone silent, his eyes closed and mud streaks on his cheeks where his tears had carved dark paths. His breath was ragged. She looked to the floor of the narrow aisle between the two rows of eight leather and chrome seats and saw her crab there, legs slowly moving and eye stalks limp.

"What can we do for him? How can we help him?"

Jules spoke without looking back, his eyes locked on the sky ahead.

"He is a crab. His lower carapace has been damaged, and I have nothing with which to treat him. I'm afraid that..." he stopped. "Wait. Oui. There is something. Hold on. Might get bumpy."

He pushed a button and twisted a knob at the controls, and autopilot engaged with a kick and a drop.

Jules was at the crab in a flash. He stared into its eyestalks.

"Rest, monsieur chariot, you will not face heaven's butter sauce today."

He lifted the creature gently but with effort, the floor lifting and shifting under him because of the turbulence and moved him aft.

There, Jules hit a switch, and a floor hatch slid upwards. He disappeared below for a few moments.

Elise watched anxiously. Seconds went by, and her hands went to the buckle on her harness. She couldn't just sit there.

Jules popped up out of the floor, sealed the hatch, and scrambled back to the pilot seat.

"Where is he?"

"The outrageous missions of Les Scaphandriers presented great danger, and there was always a risk of swift, surprising, violent, sometimes ridiculous death. The brave victim of such fatal doings would be put in cold storage, down in the bay of the Aquaboggin, until a suitable time came for burial at sea with honors. This cold unit was also a wonderful way to chill our beverages, as you can imagine. Your crab is there now, cooled so that his metabolism slows, and perhaps, the grip of death can be delayed. This is the way of the oceanic crab. Perhaps your big fellow is no different."

"He's on ice?"

"Oui."

Jules pulled hard on the rudder, and the flying sub shuddered and dropped hard to the right. Elise looked out of the starboard window and saw the mountainous black machine getting closer below them.

"What are you doing? Let's go," she said.

Jules said nothing as he swooped down closer and closer to the wall of metal that was chewing up the city below.

Jules had to see. He had to see what it was that was eating his beloved Paris.

The sub flew until it was perhaps a hundred meters from the roaring cataclysm of dust that billowed up from beneath the thing.

Black metal plates with spiked rivets. Rust and dirt on the surface, but it was smooth and went on forever. Great rotating blades, like fat wheels, slicing and grinding and cutting the earth below as the great metal wall moved forward. Elise could see debris getting sucked up beneath the mountain of metal as if being vacuumed.

It was a great black machine as big as a mountain that chewed up the earth and devoured what it wanted.

The flying sub tilted up and around, and they were over it again, flying just along the ridge of the thing.

There was a rectangle of black, a control tower with stout metal rails that ran for dozens of meters along the top of the machine.

Elise saw them then, people dressed in rags and chained to levers and wheels, and next to them, men with guns and whips. But they weren't men. They were something more.

"Of course," said Jules, "there are strange creatures aboard that Hell ship. These are things that are not of our world."

The men looked strong and thick. Their skin was white and black, and there were tall fins that ran from their heads along their naked backs, like fish or lizards. The men weren't human at all; they were something awful.

The flying sub motors whined then roared as Jules accelerated.

"We must go," he said quietly.

They flew into the west, then, as quickly as the propellers would allow, into the setting sun.

The cabin was quiet; only the soft rhythm of the chopper blades could be heard. The rising winds of the coming night storm made the Aquaboggin shake, rise, and drop as it fought the currents and eddies in the sky.

Hemmi slept.

Elise stared out of the little window at her side.

The desert of broken buildings and torn earth that had once been the great city of Paris passed below them.

They were thousands of feet in the air and moving fast.

"Where are we going?"

Jules pointed vaguely into the distance.

"Into a world gone mad, little idiot."

All that was left of Paris receded behind them.

*

CHAPTER TWENTY-NINE

Praetor Agrunctus

CHROMATOPHORES ARE THE tiny cells in the skin of some creatures that enable color change, texture shifting, and bizarre visual communication. Cuttlefish and other cephalopods are the masters and can flash every color of the rainbow in displays that would shame a chameleon.

A wide wall in the control room of thundering mountain of black metal known as The Razor was dressed in a sheet of skin, flesh that was rich with chromatophore and so much more vibrant and liquid than the crude glass and wire that humans called television.

The tiny organic cells were elegant, with every color and shade and tone, able to shift and change in the wink of a gnat's eye.

The skin wall communicated with plump insects the size of apples that flew about Paris, observing curious activity and scouting for valuables.

One of the flying spies had been circling the hospital when a minor war had erupted above its roof.

Praetor Agrunctus sat in his control throne and watched the death of Scynda the Mirror and her Men of Many Eyes on the skin wall, where it played out in real-time, in life-size, in all of its surprising suddenness.

A human flying a weapon over the city? Impossible.

The Shock Tide at the first moment of the invasion had been overwhelming and decisive. The ocean was drained without much fuss. The Earth defenses fell in hours, and the world was cleared of meaningful resistance, allowing the fleet of Razors known as The Rolling Deep to begin work. This much Praetor Agrunctus knew for certain. Otherwise, he never would have been commissioned to do his work.

Now here was the strange man again, the one who had sent the signal to their forces in the first place, in a tiny flying vehicle, and this fool had killed one of their most valuable assets.

Agrunctus spit, and the stuff hit the floor with a splashy thud. The phlegm wad sprouted legs and scuttled away into a dark corner of the control chamber.

The chamber was a black bubble of a room that sat atop the center of the mile-wide Razor, the monolithic destruction engine that was consuming the 16th of Paris.

From here, the Praetor of a Razor could monitor the progress and track quotas. It was an important job, and Agrunctus took it seriously. There were twelve Razors on planet Earth, and that meant he was one of the twelve most important creatures on this world, a fact that he was quick to point out when he started to feel small. Why, without him and without his expertise in the demolition and extraction of detritus, where would they be? Somebody needed to sort through the garbage for gold.

Being the Commanding Praetor of a Razor was sedentary work. Agrunctus sat in the control throne, monitoring the work at all times. His food was delivered by human slaves, his waste sucked through tubes in the seat of the throne, his vile amusements periodically stimulated through a series of skin screens and privacy funnels. This sedentary life meant, of course, that his dull mass flopped over the arms of the throne in fatty folds; his limbs so swollen and corpulent that it was difficult to tell where one leg ended, and the other began. Agrunctus, like most of The Rolling Deep, was essentially humanoid in shape, but his head was like an overstuffed yellow rubbish bag atop a pile of greasy fat.

He could move, but not much and not often. If you were in the control tower to smell him, you would gag and run screaming at the stench.

"Human," he said in a voice thick with phlegm, "come here."

A skinny man dressed in rags moved out of the shadows and came to the throne. He was filthy and starved, and he dropped to a knee before Agrunctus.

"Do something funny, then watch the skin screen."

The human flapped his arms and quacked like a duck.

Agrunctus chuckled until yellow sputum coated his rubbery lips.

"Enough. Now, watch."

The visuals on the skin screen reversed and then played out the massacre at the hospital. The flying camera bug hovered as the submarine of Jules Valiance flew down and killed Scynda and the Men of Many Eyes. The visuals froze on the Aquaboggin as it began its flight to safety.

"Do you know that vessel?"

"No, Praetor," said the frail man.

"Why should I believe you?"

The man's face was lean and haunted. He pointed off into the corner of the control tower. A cage was hanging from the ceiling, and in the cage were a small child and a woman, both half-clothed and starving.

Agrunctus smiled.

"Yes, your family. That's why I should believe you, right?" The Praetor laughed again as if it was the funniest joke he knew, funnier even than a starving man mimicking a bird.

The man bowed his head as Praetor Agrunctus laughed.

"Well, no matter. Back to work."

The frail man nodded and walked, head bowed, out of the

control tower, down a tunnel, up a ladder, and back onto the broad, wide deck of The Razor.

The sandstorms were a full blow now, and the cold, harsh winds whipped the man's naked skin. He clutched his arms against himself to ward off the chill as best he could.

Lightning cascaded above and around while the spark-flies buzzed and ignited. The deck was calm amid the chaos, always a smooth ride as it plowed through the earth, so the man made his way to one of the observation towers.

A guard, huge with black and white skin and fins like a shark, stood at the entrance to the small tower. He allowed the man into the little stairwell that led a few meters up to the top. There, the man joined another, and the two donned goggles and stared out through clouds of smoke and debris billowing up from The Razor's countless rotating blades.

It was hard to see at night during a sandstorm, but the goggles used a light, like night-vision, that helped to cut through the chaos so that the men could help the Praetor plot the most lucrative course through the city once known as Paris.

Praetor Agrunctus didn't know where the richest troves of human-made technology might be found, but the humans certainly did, and it was their job to guide The Razor to the televisions, cars, refrigerators, toys, vacuums, computers, and electric toothbrushes.

There was a little control panel in front of the two men in the tower. They both knew the city well after so many years, so they both punched a button and the same time and pointed off in the direction of The Galleries Lafayette.

The Razor, a mile wide bulldozer, turned to the east and made its way to the mall, grinding and sucking up our detritus as treasure while it went.

*

CHAPTER THIRTY

Night Flight

BRIGHT LIGHT, THEN an immediate, loud bang.

Elise straightened and focused, her eyes gummy from sleep. The cabin of the Aquaboggin was dim, and there was no light coming through the windows.

She looked outside, into the night, and saw nothing but blackness. Then, another lightning strike, a frightening boom of thunder. Her eyes hurt from the flash. They were flying through the night storm, and there was lightning all around them.

She unbuckled and made her way up front, the floor falling and rising below her feet, and strapped into the co-pilot seat next to Jules Valiance.

The large viewing window before them was black with streaks of white-hot light erupting near and close.

The cabin was cool, but she saw sweat on Jules's face.

He smiled.

"Ah yes. We fly in a tiny metal tube through a hurricane of lightning. Not an enviable position."

"Will lightning hit this thing?"

"It is a possibility. One strike can kill us all. But look." He pointed off to the left.

The moon. It was a sliver, just a slice of silver in the black, but it was there. And stars too, beautiful stars twinkling in the darkness.

"Mr. Moon and his stars. I have not seen them in ten years. The storms come every night and hide their beauty. Aren't they wonderful?"

Elise smiled. She loved the moon. Her Dad used to tell her stories about the moon and the stars, silly funny stories where anything was possible.

"I flew up, over the sandstorm. Otherwise, the winds and the sand would have destroyed us. The storm is so tall I feared that we would never get out of her grip. At an altitude of ten thousand feet, it was as if we entered a new world. The sand pounding the ship went silent, and we were here, in this wonderful place where there's a moon, and there are stars, and there is peace."

A bolt of lightning struck.

"And deadly lightning, of course. There's that. But look at the sky."

Elise did; she looked out into a night that might have been a night from ten years before when the world was right, and none of this had ever happened.

"So, little idiot, if we are to die, then we die with a view of our world as it should be."

"That's cool and all, but I'd rather not die."

"Point well taken."

Elise watched the lightning strikes, strange tentacles of white light appearing and then disappearing all around them, lighting the red mass of sandstorm below them, so bright that it hurt her eyes. The bolts were coming from above, from a thin haze of dust high above their ship, and reaching down into the storm, everywhere and unpredictable. It was only a matter of time until they were hit.

"A strange tableau, is it not? But of course, you are correct. It would be folly to die tonight because we were taking in the view," he said. He looked back and included Hemmi in the conversation.

"So, to your left under the seat, you will find a little paper bag in which to deposit your vomit. Please remove the bag and hold it near your mouth. Do you children like the roller coast rides?"

Hemmi's eyes were closed. He didn't answer, and if he had, he would not have known what to say as he'd never heard the word rollercoaster in his life.

Elise grabbed the little bag and held it to her chest.

"I hate rollercoasters," said Elise.

"I love them. We shall call this rollercoaster "The Escape from the Lightning of Painful Death." Hold on."

Jules pushed on the little wheel in his hands and began to emit a piercing scream, something that he had learned from Bedouin tribes of the Wadi Rum, but of course, Elise did not know this, nor would she have cared at that moment, because the nose of the Aquaboggin dropped into a completely vertical position below them and they plummeted.

Her stomach went up to her forehead, and her food bar shot out of her throat and into the bag like a circus performer out of a cannon.

The engines were at full throttle, the propellers rotated into the proper pitch to send them into a spinning descent. The lightning-lit sandstorm ceiling below them approached through the forward glass, closer and closer, until they were in it.

That's when things got really bad. They were at full throttle drop, and when they hit the sandstorm and punctured the ceiling, it felt as if a giant hand had swatted the Aquaboggin.

The powerful wind and lashing sand slammed them, and the sub went from straight vertical to an upside-down position, flying, dropping, spinning so wildly that Elise didn't know which way was up.

Jules fought the controls and stabilized her, bringing her back into the steep descent. The noise of the engines and the sandstorm was deafening, but Elise thought she heard him scream, "Sand might clog her engines!" right before sand clogged her engines.

The cabin went dark. The power was out. Hemmi screamed. The sub was no longer flying; she was dropping.

Jules was jabbing at the controls and pulling at the wheel, but nothing was happening.

He cursed and wrenched at a yellow handle near his seat.

There was a loud pop, and the sub seemed to slam into a wall of air. Elise was pushed so hard into her seat belt that she thought it would snap, and her eyes felt like they were going to shoot out of her head. Then, they began to descend again, slowly this time, still shuddering and dipping but in much more control.

"Parachutes," Jules said.

The sub's conical nose raised up, and they were back into a more or less normal position, but she still twisted with the winds as they caught the chutes.

"Not out of the woods yet, girl. If you were in prayer, I would continue," he said.

Soft amber emergency lights illuminated the cabin. Elise saw that Hemmi was sitting with his mouth wide open, vomit on his lips, eyes wide with terror.

Jules pulled another handle in the cockpit, and there was a sharp hissing sound, like steam escaping, that lasted for several seconds.

"Canisters of gas in the engines," he said as he started trying once more to bring the sub to life. "Designed to fight fire and to dislodge seaweed or tiny fish from the impellers. Perhaps they can clean out this infernal sand."

Elise couldn't see out of her window, couldn't tell whether or not they were close to the ground, or a mountain, or a building.

A barking cough, then a straining of rotors. The lights in the cabin began to flicker.

Jules cursed and struck the control panel with his hand.

Another cough, and the engines fired up. Jules pulled down on the throttle and cut the parachutes.

They were flying again but almost blind, the forward beams of light not enough to cut more than a dozen yards ahead through the storm.

"I will land now," Jules said, "and we can hope that God's lottery sets us down next to a pleasant cafe with pretty waitresses and acceptable wine."

The altimeter on the sub was practically worthless in the storm. Jules didn't trust the readings. The descent was so bumpy that the nose of the ship kept dropping and falling, making it impossible to track the horizon for objects, for the ground.

A thump, a slide, and they were no longer bouncing through the storm. The cabin leaned to the right, and everything was still.

They had landed, and they were alive.

Elise looked out of the window. Just blackness and lashing sand.

Jules dimmed the cabin lights and brought up the ship's side beams.

Light spilled out on either side of her from a half dozen high beam light projectors designed to cut through the blackness of the deepest realms of the ocean but useless in the sandstorm.

He killed the lights, then the engines and all but emergency power, opening vents for air.

"Hours until sunup," he said.

He tended to their injuries. He smeared some cold glop on the cut on Elise's forehead that was supposed to seal it and heal it, in his words. Hemmi's ankle was swollen, so Jules wrapped it in gauze and gave him a couple of pills for the pain.

"This is called bourbon. An anesthetic of sorts, but with an American attitude."

Hemmi took a shot of dark brown liquor, gagged, coughed, and sat back into his seat, eyes closed.

"That was awful," he said, the first words he'd spoken since Paris.

Jules shrugged and took a swig.

Elise looked through a tiny glass pane into the cold chamber where Charlie was lying. His feelers and legs moved slowly, so he was alive, but the color of his shell wasn't the dark, rich red. It was gray in spots and pale. Jules had sealed the wound in his shell with some paste that was supposed to work on people, but they had no idea if it would help a giant land crab with a hole in its chest.

Charlie was dying, she was sure of it, and he was her only friend in the world.

She sat in the co-pilot seat next to Jules for an hour or more during the storm. They talked.

"Where do you think we are?"

"Brittany. The coast. Or, what was the coast when there was an ocean."

"How did you find me, you know, at the hospital?"

"The watch that I gave you to use. It has a geo-tracking device. And a corkscrew, but you are too young for such things."

"What was that thing that was in Paris, that bulldozer There were people on it, like slaves, and those other things that weren't people. What were they?"

"I suspect that it was, as you say, a bulldozer. Who is driving and why, a mystery."

"I met some people in Paris, nice people. Two men named Robert and Renny. I think that the bulldozer was going in the direction of their little apartment. I hope not, but I think it was. I think they must be dead, too."

Elise was quiet for a moment. She thought about the two nice men and their little place, the plastic flowers and the marks on the wall of the days since the end of the world.

It made her sad, so she started talking again.

"I think those things killed the kids in the hospital. I think Hemmi saw it. I don't think he's doing so well."

"I suspect that you are correct," Jules said.

"Is there a toilet in this thing?"

Jules pointed aft.

"The little yellow door to the port side. Do not open the red door on the right. You will flood the cabin with radiation, and we will all die, withering away like salted slugs."

"Really?"

"No, it is a closet."

And it went like that for some time as they waited.

Hemmi just sat quietly, sometimes sleeping, sometimes staring out into the darkness.

Then, the harsh winds grew soft, the sound of sand rattling against the ship disappeared, and a scarlet light began to flood into the cabin.

The sun came up over the horizon, and they saw where they had landed.

*

CHAPTER THIRTY-ONE

The Sheep and The Oyster

THEY WERE IN a wide desert, smooth sand as far as they could see to the port side, but to their right was the single white cottage, its sides piled with dunes as high as Elise.

The little cottage of stone sat only yards away, framed in faded wood and sand scoured white.

A charming old sign hung from a frame that extended from the black slate roof.

"Le Mouton et L'Huître."

The Sheep and the Oyster.

There, outside of the sub, was a lonely little restaurant in the middle of a desert, and they were sitting in the parking lot of sand as if they were on holiday and had just arrived for breakfast.

"Perhaps they have fresh croissant and hot coffee. Let us see."

Cold air rushed in when Jules opened the hatch. Elise hesitated near the cold storage space.

She wanted to see what was outside, but she didn't want to leave her friend. Jules touched her shoulder lightly.

"The emergency power will keep the crab cold. There is nothing you can do for your friend at this moment, Elise." It was the first time that she had heard him use her name.

Her heart felt like it was going to break, but she followed Jules to the exit hatch. He was right.

There was nothing she could do.

They stepped out onto the sand and sank to their ankles.

Elise looked for lumps, wary of those awful sand slugs and who knows what else.

The desert stretched on as far as the eye could see, but now, out of the sub, it became apparent that they were on a plateau that looked out over even more deserts and mountains beyond that.

"What is this place?" Elise asked.

Jules smiled and patted the side of the Aquaboggin.

"She is still true. I targeted a pre-programmed point on the mapping system. The tiny island of Ouessant, the westernmost shore of France and home to the ubiquitous Stiff Lighthouse."

He looked around.

Except for the little cottage, the island was almost perfectly flat.

"Ah. Correction. Once home to the ubiquitous Stiff Lighthouse. It has gone the way of the dodo bird."

"Why are we here?"

"This was a fuel depot and way station for Les Scaphandriers," Jules said, "our bistro at the Atlantic's edge."

Elise looked off into the west, at the mountains and ridges and desert.

Hemmi stood next to her.

"Is that where the ocean used to be?"

Jules joined them and stared off at the vast, arid horizon that had once been the Atlantic Basin.

He was silent for a moment and then spoke quietly.

"There once were many seabirds. Beautiful seabirds," he said, "and sheep. Wonderful, delicious, tiny black sheep. And so much green grass."

They heard no birdsong, just the soft whisper of the wind.

So still. Nothing moved on the sand, no living things that they could see.

Jules turned and wandered off towards the cottage.

Elise and Hemmi followed. She could see that there were solar panels on the slate roof. An enormous stack of wooden boards and beams was piled high behind the place, spilling out to either side in a tumble of dusty debris.

Jules knocked on the wooden front door.

"You think somebody still lives here?" Hemmi asked.

The door popped open. Elise and Hemmi jumped back, startled.

Madame de Laclos glared at Jules Valiance with bushy white eyebrows that wiggled like cat tails.

"If you've come to save the world, you are too late. We're closed," she said.

What does a restaurant owner at The End of The World look like?

She was tall and lean, with large eyes and freckled, smooth white skin. There was no telling her age had her hair not been a shocking white, and even then, she could be forty or seventy. Her thin ankles were wrapped in socks of many colors; her dress was of denim and leather, her apron a matted curtain of sheep's wool. Elise thought she smelled like lavender soap and cigarettes.

"Gracie," Jules said.

Madame de Laclos stared at Jules and her attitude changed from "get out of my place" to "my dreams have come true" to "I'm going to kill you with an axe" in the space of a blink.

"Jules," she answered. Then she hit him in the nose with her fist.

Jules rocked back, gathered himself, wiped the blood from his nose, and smiled.

"My Gracie," he said.

She considered him for a moment, her lips puckered up into a bow. She looked down at Elise and Hemmi.

"For the children," he said.

Jules gestured to the two kids and smiled again.

Madame de Laclos grimaced.

"I despise you, Jules Valiance. For the children, we are open for breakfast. Bienvenue. And wipe your stinking feet."

They did as they were told and stepped across the threshold into the cottage restaurant.

The Madame muttered under her breath as she stalked into the dim room.

Elise smelled damp wool, flowers, and burning wood.

The restaurant was beamed with dark wood, and warm light shone from a cast-ironed pot-bellied cooking stove.

More light spilled in from the clean glass windows. Piles of sheep's wool in the far corner of the room. One small wooden table with place settings and a decorative candle, unlit.

There were fishing nets hung from a wall like so many curtains. Wooden casks were stacked in the back of the room, where there was a tiny kitchen with a sink and a brick bread stove built into the wall. There were doors also in the back of the place that were closed. A bathroom, perhaps a bedroom.

Most wonderful of all, though, there was green. So much green and even little bursts of color from flowers here and there. Elise didn't think it was possible for anything green to grow in this dry new world, but here, in this little cottage, there were small plants as green as emeralds.

Little flowers, potted herbs, patches of grass in trays.

The Madame stoked the fire in the iron stove as she went and then began making preparations with a thick skillet and chopping blades.

Elise was curious. What could she possibly be cooking?

Jules and Hemmi sat at the table. Elise carefully stepped over lush piles of wool and stacks of books and made her way back to where The Madame was cooking.

The woman's thin, wiry hands gripped the chopping blade tightly and chopped at strange things on a cutting board. Little bits of the things flew into the air as she went "whack whack whack."

Bugs? Ewww.

She was chopping up bugs?

Elise looked more closely. Shrimp. They were like fat shrimp with wings. Madame de Laclos worked fast. She pulled off the wings, ripped away shells, and chopped the yellow and translucent meat into chunks. The meat went into the skillet with a handful of green herbs, and within moments there was a pile of the stuff.

The Madame glanced over to Elise and regarded her some disdain.

"Are those bugs?"

"What if they were?"

"Do they taste good, for bugs?"

The Madame smiled slightly.

"Well said. Not bugs." She walked the skillet over to the stove and dropped it on top. The meat began to sizzle, and it smelled delicious.

"These are flying shrimp," the Madame said as she cooked, "they come in swarms just before sunset every day. Flying east, towards the mainland. I catch them with those nets."

She motioned to the fishing nets on the wall.

The yellow fat of the shrimps melted under the heat, and the clear, slimy meat began to turn white, then pink.

Hemmi and Jules popped up next to Elise, and all three stared into the blazing skillet with wide eyes.

"That smells good," said Hemmi.

"I dreamt a dream of shrimp sauté, and voila, it is true," Jules said.

"Go fill your cups with water from the sink," the Madame said. They did as they were told. Clear, cold water shot from the faucet.

"This place has water," Elise said to Jules.

"Yes, there is a deep well. A spring beneath. Thank God, there is still water in the sacred belly of our world."

Elise drank deeply of the spring water, and it was the best thing she had ever tasted, until, moments later, she took a bite of the sautéed flying shrimp, and she thought that her heart was going to explode through her chest with happiness. She had been so hungry, they all had, and they devoured a skillet's worth of the shrimp like jackals at a carcass. The Madame had another skillet ready in a flash, then another, and another, until they were as full as they had ever been of anything in their lives.

Hemmi wandered off into a corner and rolled up in some blankets of soft sheep's wool. Elise thought about sleeping as well but instead sat at the table with Jules and the Madame. She was quiet, listening, as they spoke over cigarettes and cups of water.

"Where were you?"

"Away. In Paris."

"Ah. Are there people there?"

"Not many, no. Not many at all."

"I am the only one here on the island. At The Turn, the things..."

Jules interrupted her.

"The Turn? Is that what you call it?"

"What else? Do you have a better name?"

"No."

"Well, then, shut up. The things came from where the ocean had been only moments before. I hid in the shelter below the restaurant. It is well protected, as you know. I stayed for a long time, then came up and found a sandstorm had smothered the village. I went house to house. Nothing. No one. Just, those things every now and then, but I had my rifle, and I know how to use it. This you know as well, yes?"

"Yes, I know."

"As time went by, I pulled the houses apart for wood and scavenged as I could. The big things rarely come anymore, just the flying shrimp and other harmless creatures. I pay them no mind unless I'm hungry."

"They are delicious. A treat for the senses. Like you, Madame."

She snorted, and that made Elise laugh. They both looked over at her as if they'd forgotten that she was still sitting at the table.

"And what is your story, ma fille?" asked the Madame.

"My name is Elise St. Jacques. I was in Paris."

"Where is your family?"

Elise shook her head no.

"I am sorry, Elise," the Madame said, and they sat for a while in silence.

"What about him?"

"Hemmi? He came from a hospital in Paris. There were kids there, but he's the only one left, we think."

"Jules, I did not know you were so parental."

"I am not. Nor do I pretend to be so. I find these children offensive but harmless mostly, and they might prove useful as bait."

Elise punched him in the arm, and Jules feigned agony.

"Something tells me that you are not joking, Jules Valiance," the Madame said. She took a deep drag on the cigarette.

"Why now? Why have you come here?"

He just stared at her. Elise thought that it was awkward.

"Ah, you have come for fuel," she said, "so that you can go on your grand adventure and set this world right again. Les Scaphandriers. The League of Astonishing Aquanauts. The secret soldiers of the sea."

Jules was quiet.

"So, how do you know each other?" Elise asked.

The Madame laughed.

"I am Scaphandrier," she said, "retired to guard our little way station on the coast. The Sheep and the Oyster is a restaurant, yes, but it is also a fuel depot and way station. We were quite the state secret, Elise. Mums the word." Madame put her finger to her lips and smiled.

"Did you know a man named Clark St. Jacques?"

Madame thought for a moment.

"No. I don't know this name. Why?"

"He was my Dad. He told me stories about Les Scaphandriers, but he never mentioned this place. I think his stories were made up."

"Sometimes," the Madame said, "I think our stories are made up as well."

She pointed a bony finger at Jules.

"So, have you come for fuel? If not, then what do you want? I won't have you stay here, there's not enough of anything, and this is a restaurant, not a hostel."

"Yes, I need fuel for the submarine."

"Of course. There are things I need as well, Jules Valiance."

She stood and slapped her hands together.

"The boy has gone to sleep, Elise, so you will clean up the kitchen. If you do it well, there will be a fine breakfast in the morning before I kick you out. Quickly now."

Elise did as she was told, gathering the dishes and rinsing them in the cold water of the sink. The water felt good on her hands, and she was glad to do the work. She listened to the conversation between the Madame and Jules under the clatter of the dishes and the whisper of the faucet.

"Valiance, is the world, the whole world, like this?"

"I know only Paris, but the ocean is gone, the basins are dry, and the sandstorms are everywhere. There might be lakes that survived, inland waters, but without the ocean, the world's cycles are broken. The air is surely leaking away. So yes, I must assume that the world as we knew it is gone."

"And these creatures, these things that come up from the canyons or fly in on the wind, are they from another world? They must be."

"I do not know, but I assume we deal with otherworldly beasts."

"You were alone in Paris?"

Jules went quiet then.

"Where were the others? Why were you alone?"

Silence.

"What did you do, Jules Valiance? What do you know?"

"I will be on my way tomorrow morning. Please keep the children here."

"You did this, didn't you? You and your great explorers? You did this?"

"The little idiot girl is kind, but watch the boy. He is like a feral thing."

"Oh, Jules."

Again, silence.

Elise looked back from the sink and saw that the Madame was holding his hand in hers.

When Jules Valiance spoke, his voice trembled. He sounded old.

"Gracie, I leave in the morning. Do you need ammunition for your guns?"

"No. There is plenty below."

"I have little medicine. Little food. What is it that you need?"

Madame de Laclos stood and walked to a little table.

There was a plastic box on the table, a music player of some sort. She flipped a switch, and little lights came on.

"I don't use the electricity often. The old solar cells are good for just a few hours a week."

She pushed a button on the box, and it began to play a song.

Elise recognized the music, a lovely country track by someone named Patti Griffin.

Madame de Laclos took Jules by the hand and brought him to her. She leaned into him and spoke softly, just loudly enough so that Elise could hear.

"I need you to find yourself. You are lost in there somewhere," she said, pointing at his chest.

Jules took her in his arms. They began to sway with the music, dancing cheek to cheek.

The Madame kissed Jules on the cheek.

"I need my hero, Jules Valiance, to slay a monster," she said.

Elise was embarrassed. She shuffled off to the pile of wool and snuggled into it, and soon she drifted off to sleep as the music played softly and Jules Valiance and the Madame danced.

*

CHAPTER THIRTY-TWO

Our Last Restaurateur

HEMMI SCREAMED IN the night.

It was a horrible sound, the scream of a terrified child. Elise came awake and saw that the boy was sitting straight up in the pile of wool, eyes wide, shouting as if chased by the devil.

Madame de Laclos was there in an instant and wrapped the boy in her arms. The screams stopped, and he nestled into her, sobbing. Elise watched as the woman comforted Hemmi, then tucked him back into the blankets and wandered off into the gloom of the restaurant. Elise crawled over to Hemmi.

"Are you okay?"

Hemmi muttered something rude and profane.

"Some of them might be alive," she said, "maybe some of the kids are alright."

The words felt false as soon as they left her lips, and Elise regretted them.

"No," Hemmi said, "they're all dead. I saw them. Those things killed them all like they was nothing. I don't know what kind of things those were, but they killed all my friends dead."

Elise didn't know what to say, so she didn't say anything.

They lay in the dark and soon fell sound asleep.

*

Morning came with the smell of sizzling herbed shrimp.

Elise and Hemmi woke to that wonderful aroma and the sounds of the food cooking. The two were nestled in heaps of warm sheep's wool. Elise saw that Hemmi's eyes were gummy with sleep and tears.

They ate, devouring heaps of the shrimp and guzzling cold water, then took turns at the bath. There was a porcelain clawfoot tub in the little bathroom. The Madame heated water on the stove, and Elise simmered in the warm water until her skin puckered and the bath grew cold. The Madame explained that all the bath soap had been used up years before, but a drop from a big jug of lavender-scented laundry detergent would do the trick. There were little flowers growing in pots on the windowsill, and they, along with the detergent, gave the room a lovely scent. Hemmi came next. He was filthy, as there had been no water for bathing at The Nursery, and The Madame spent time adding and replacing the water in Hemmi's tub until he was as clean as could be. Then there was Jules, and for his bath, Elise was most grateful. Jules Valiance was a stinker and in need of a good soak.

When the sun was up full, Jules escorted Elise to the submersible to check in on Charlie.

Elise peered into the cold chamber through the little glass porthole in the floor.

The crab was still, its shell nearly white except in places under its claws and belly where there were still spots of dark red. The eyes on talks were receded back into its shell.

The feelers waved so slowly that Elise had to look hard to see the movement.

He was alive, but not for long, she thought.

"Do you think he's in pain?"

"No, girl, I do not. And I am Jules Valiance of Les Scaphandriers, and if anyone would know such things, it is I. So, he is as peaceful as can be, and he dreams of eating little fish. Of this, you can be sure."

Elise didn't really believe Jules, but it felt good to pretend, so she did.

*

The Madame stood at the doorway to her restaurant. The red sun was high, and the breeze was light. Jules, Elise, and Hemmi stood there as well, and it was time to go.

"Merci, Madame, for your hospitality. There is much for me to do, and I must be on my way," Jules said. He turned to the children.

"You will stay here. You will earn your keep by catching flying shrimp and turning this foul soil into a garden for Madame. I will return and feast, but in the meantime, you will obey her, or she will throw you into a chasm to be devoured by slimy things."

"Where are you going?" asked Elise.

Jules knelt down and took her hands.

"You are a brave little idiot girl. I thank you for your courage. I will tend as best I can to your crab friend, and perhaps you will see him dance when I return."

"Where?"

He pointed off to the west.

"I made a mistake. Many years ago. I go west now to correct things."

"Your hands are shaking. Are you scared?"

Jules smiled.

"I, the great Jules Valiance, am wetting myself."

He thought she would laugh, but she didn't.

"Well, you can't go by yourself. I'm going with you."

"No, you are not."

"Yes, I am." She held her hand out flat. It didn't tremble at all.

"Steady as a rock," she said.

He quickly stood and moved to The Madame. They stared at each other for a long moment, then embraced.

"I will return, Gracie," he said, "and slay more of your monsters."

She kissed him on the cheek.

"As you were born to do. Bon voyage, Jules Valiance of Les Scaphandriers. God speed."

Jules turned and walked quickly to the Aquaboggin. He looked down to his right, and Elise was there.

"I said I'm going with you."

Jules looked hard into the wide eyes of twelve-year-old Elise St. Jacques.

"Where we go, idiot, we might not come back."

"I know."

Jules looked back to Hemmi.

The boy turned without a word and went back into the restaurant.

"He's staying," Elise said, "I think he needs to stay."

With that, Jules turned and saluted The Madame. She made a rude gesture.

"You'd best be on your way, old man," she said and pointed at the sky.

Jules and Elise looked up and saw that there were dozens of massive, floating jellyfish drifting in from the west. The electric blue of their skins glistened in the rising sun, and tentacles curled and uncurled, searching for food.

Jules smiled slightly.

"Of course," he said. Then he slapped Elise on the back and ran to their flying sub.

In moments the engines of the Aquaboggin were rumbling, the propeller blades began to spin, and Elise was strapped into the co-pilot seat with Jules at the helm.

The blades whirred to life, and they lifted up and to the west. Jules circled back once, a final salute to the great and wonderful Madame de Laclos, the lady of the island, the last restaurateur on Earth.

"We have fuel now, and we must evade those disgusting jellies, so hold on."

Jules jabbed a button on the console, and twin wings flipped out from either side of the Aquaboggin. The autogyro propellers stopped spinning and dropped back into their homes while jet engines ignited.

"I hope you like to go fast."

Elise gave him a thumbs up.

The ship blasted ahead, a rocket accelerating with such speed that Elise was jammed back into her seat and her eyes slammed shut.

The jellies were a blue and purple blur as they shot safely past them and beyond.

To Madame de Laclos, they were a shooting star with a bright orange tail. She watched Jules and Elise go and then went back inside. Once the jellies had passed by, it would be safe to harvest food. The flying shrimp would be coming soon, and now there was another mouth to feed.

As the years passed, Hemmi would become the greatest gardener that the island of Ouessant would ever know, but that's another story.

*

CHAPTER THIRTY-THREE

The Little Ship We've Seen

THE MEMORY SCENE of the little flying ship played out across the skin screen once again.

There it was, a flying metal tube with propellers and weapons, swooping and firing and killing their most skilled assassins.

Agrunctus had played it several times now, back-to-back, without commentary, as the Razor continued its dissection of the city.

"As you can see, Goddess, it is a speck of a vessel but carries a deadly sting. Scynda and her Men of Many Eyes fell like infants to a sword."

If Agrunctus expected a reply to his commentary, he was mistaken.

Silence, then the skin screen rippled, and the video of the little flying ship was replaced in a blinding snowfall flash of pulsing chromatophores by a figure too dark to see, swathed in shadow and static.

"Are you full?" came a voice soft and gentle.

"Not yet, but almost, only ten percent to go. This city, this Paris, was rich soil and you will be pleased."

The face on the screen came into focus. Thin and feminine, scalp covered in a glowing shroud tapestry, skin a masterpiece of organic and inorganic elements wedded in flowing and sensual patterns, eyes wide and vibrant and golden. She smiled, and her teeth were perfect white gems that sparkled with arcing electricity.

"Such a lush place, so deserving of respect, and it's being harvested by another grotesque abomination that sits in his own filth and ponders nothing except the next pretty thing to torment. You are perfectly suited for your role, Agrunctus, you and the others who pilot the Razor Ships on what was once Earth. You disgust me, and I love you for it."

Praetor Agrunctus was silent as he considered how to respond. Her royal eyes were pleasant, and her royal voice was a soft, slinky thing that tickled the fun parts of his belly. Her words, though, confused him. Was that an insult or a compliment?

He chose to gurgle something inarticulate and bow.

The feminine creature on the skin screen raised an eyebrow then spoke again, more loudly, with more force. It was a command.

"When your ship is satiated, return at once to Orcanum for release. This world is almost done, and we will go on to the next."

"What of the little flying ship, Goddess?"

"You're already hideous, Agrunctus, don't add stupidity to the mix. What's it going to do, bite me?"

The skin screen shuddered in waves of black and white, then went dark.

Agrunctus sank back into his control throne with a loud, wet, slippery sound. He let out a sigh of relief. He was glad that the conversation was over. He liked to torture; he didn't like to be on the receiving end of the whip.

*

CHAPTER THIRTY-FOUR

The Great Lady at The Bottom of The Empty Sea

ELISE THOUGHT THAT she might get used to the bouncing and the rattling of the submersible as it was buffeted by the winds, but she didn't.

The red glow of the sun was ahead. They flew above the storm and below the haze of dust and sand that choked the atmosphere above, slicing through the relatively clear space between.

The dry desert of the ocean basin was obscured below them, but now and then, a mountainous peak was visible, a plateau, a dark canyon.

Elise thought about all the wonderful animals that had lived there, the dolphins and the whales and the sea birds.

All gone. All dead, like most of the world.

Her Dad loved the ocean and the creatures that live in the depths. They would visit aquariums and marvel at strange fish, octopuses with their intelligent eyes and clever ways, even the sharks and rays so beautiful and fast.

She could hear his voice now, in her thoughts, excited about playing in the surf or watching a television show about whales or reading a magazine about the sea and dreaming of having their own boat to sail.

Her Dad's voice was many things to Elise, now. It was a

comfort, an unwanted ghost, a reminder, and a wound. At that moment, she hated his voice because she knew that he would be hurt by the death of the ocean and its animals, but he had hurt her by dying and leaving her alone.

Part of her wanted to hurt him, hear the pain in his voice because she loved him, and he had left her alone. That thought made her ashamed, and that shame just made her angrier.

She wanted her Dad's voice to shut up.

*

They flew for hours.

Elise nodded off and was awakened by a loud beeping sound.

A light was flashing on the cockpit flight console.

Jules put the ship into a steep descent. There was no storm below them now, just canyons and mountains, like photographs of the Grand Canyon that she had once seen, but far more vast, stretching on beyond the horizon.

The ship passed below the cliffs of the tallest of the mountains and the turbulence lessened, their flight became smooth, and the ship leveled out.

This had been an ocean.

Elise found it hard to imagine at first, but then there was a shipwreck half-covered in sand. Another, lying on a shelf that then dropped another thousand feet straight down into the canyon.

Was that something alive?

Yes, she thought. Yes, it was. They were dropping fast, but she could see creatures like centipedes squirming and crawling along the canyon walls. Swarms of flying shrimp passed them by, going up to the sun as they were on the descent, and she heard a soft pelting as the things spattered on the exterior of the sub.

They flew deeper now and out of the sun, so the light became dimmer and dimmer.

Jules piloted them toward towers, tall outcroppings of rock, sentinels that had been carved by ocean currents for millions of years and now stood on wide plateaus.

Elise heard Jules take a sharp breath as they got closer.

He said something low that she couldn't hear.

She looked closer at the towers as they approached and saw that there were carvings on them, strange faces and figures dancing and monsters she could not have imagined.

He flipped switches, and the autogyro propellers popped and dropped and took over their flight, the jet engine falling silent.

They moved more slowly now but in control and hovering like a dragonfly.

"Our years of exploring her depths and we knew so little," Jules said, "we thought she had given up her secrets but look, idiot girl. We are four thousand feet below the surface, and those petroglyphs speak of a civilization older by far than ours. Who did this? Where did they go?"

He switched on the exterior floodlights and circled the towers as they descended. The faces carved into the rock were of creatures more fish than man, and chiseled tentacles seemed to wrap the entire monument, writhing and overlapping. They were close enough now that Elise could see little things like cockroaches climbing all over the stone. There were small crabs as well, with legs like spiders.

Had something like this carved spire been found by explorers in the deserts of Egypt or in the jungles of Peru, they would have been considered wonders of the world. The artwork was primitive, crude, but clearly defined, and there were things on the pillars, rituals of violence, that more than troubled Elise. Elise was fascinated by the towers but disturbed by them as well, in some primal way that she didn't understand.

"If these were under the ocean, they were carved before the ocean was even there, right?" she asked.

"Perhaps, or they were carved under the ocean a million years ago by creatures beyond our imagination."

Elise thought about the people they had seen atop the massive black bulldozer in Paris, the humans in chains and the other things, the things that looked like they were alien, with fins and strange skin.

Those things looked like the carved faces on the tower.

"Maybe these are new," she said.

"No. Some of the rock is worn away by tides and now by wind. These are older than time as we know it."

A little beep and a flashing blue light.

"Ah. We are nearly there."

"Where? Where are we going?"

"There," Jules said. He pointed forward at the flat plateau below them, at the bottom of the Atlantic basic, a thousand miles from the coast of France, from the restaurant of Madame de Laclos, from dead Paris and the things that devour it.

They flew slowly toward a gothic cathedral sitting amid a plain of boulder and sand, a cathedral carved of ocean rock and coral and shells.

There were flying buttresses, some broken and some not.

There were broken glass windows, huge and round. It was spectacular, beautiful, and yet horrifying because Elise knew that it was impossible, a cathedral so much like Notre Dame here at the bottom of an empty sea.

She looked at Jules. His eyes were wide, and she could see that he was sweating and pale, even in the dim light of the cabin.

He's scared, she thought.

Maybe I should be scared too.

The rotating blades of the sub echoed in the canyon as Jules brought the Aquaboggin to a soft landing at the mouth of the cathedral.

The bright floodlights all rotated aft.

Thousands of tiny roaches and crabs scuttled and scurried away from the light, revealing the stone and coral surface of the magnificent, horrifying building.

It was the cathedral of Notre Dame, but it was not. It was a bit of this and a bit of that, the whole a representation of gothic cathedrals and churches across Europe but fashioned out of rock and reef and detritus. And it was at the bottom of the ocean.

Jules set the Aquaboggin down a few yards away from the entrance to the cathedral. The vessel settled softly into thick sand, landing gear popping out port and aft to stabilize. The propellers slowed then stopped.

The exit hatch opened with a hiss, and the ladder slid down.

Jules stepped out, and Elise followed.

She noticed that he had a gun in his hand and she didn't know how she felt about that. A flashlight in the other hand, and one on his helmet, pierced the gloom. Elise wore her helmet as well, so she switched on her lamp.

The sand was white, the canyon walls dark.

Sound was strange this deep in the trench. The canyon twisted their slightest whispers into echoes that went on and on.

Elise looked up, and the sky was a slender, crooked red sliver cutting between the canyon walls far above them.

There was a sudden sound like a bird's wings in flight.

A swarm of flying shrimp blasted past and around and over them. They covered their eyes and mouths as the creatures passed into the gloom.

Jules walked to the central portal of the cathedral.

There were little crustaceans all over the tall metal portal doors, a dark swarm.

"Clap your hands," he said. Elise clapped and the roach things scattered with a sound like a blanket of shells being dragged across glass.

Jules reached out and grabbed one, quick as a wink, and

popped it into his mouth. His cheeks turned purple, and he spit it out.

"Ack," he said, wiping his lips. "It tastes of baby poop and despair. I am appalled."

"That's so gross," she said.

Jules led the way through the metal doors into the cathedral.

His lights were twin beams that helped them see a bit, but not much. The light from the jagged edge of the sun far above was almost useless.

Stone benches, overturned and broken. Sand and debris on a colorful floor of rough tile. The soft scuttle here and there of unseen small creatures. Jules trained the flashlights behind them, and Elise could see a huge pipe organ covered in a squirming mat of sea roaches.

At the center of the cathedral was a pile of debris, as tall as Jules, broken coral and rock in a jagged tumble. Jules stood quietly before the pile for a long moment then walked around it as if searching for something, perhaps searching for a way in or for what had been covered.

Elise felt something crawl on her neck. She yipped and swatted at it, and it squished under her hand. One of the sea roaches. She shivered and swatted herself all over.

"This is it," Jules said aloud but to himself. "This is it."

"What? It's a pile of rocks."

"No. This is where the world ended. Maybe if we know more, this can be where the world is reborn. Who's to say?"

There was a sound then, a big thunderous thump, followed by another. It came from behind them.

Elise and Jules turned and were face to face with an elephant ten meters high with eyes like a goldfish and teeth like a shark. There were toothed suction cups on its long trunk.

The thing's skin shimmered and changed colors like a cuttle-fish, and it walked on legs as thick as telephone poles.

The elephant made an angry hissing sound and rose up on its back legs, exposing a belly covered with scaly armored plates.

"This is unexpected," Jules whispered, "an angry, territorial alien elephant has staked its claim to the naked cherub with the violin. Strange days."

Before Elise had time to even begin to absorb what Jules had said, he grabbed her by the arm and was carrying her back toward the Aquaboggin at full sprint.

The elephant dropped back to all fours and began thundering towards them. Jules shoved Elise up into the hatch and shut the door. He moved to the pilot's seat and switched on the engines.

"Hello," he said. The elephant was in front of the sub and staring into the forward viewing glass. The eyes were freakishly huge, bulging, and appeared to be extremely angry.

Elise buckled into the co-pilot seat just as the elephant's undulating trunk reached out and shoved the glass.

The Aquaboggin rocked backwards.

"She is strong and annoyed," Jules said, "but I do not want to harm her."

The elephant opened its huge, toothy mouth and bellowed.

The sound was so loud, even in the sub, that it hurt their ears and rattled the ship.

The sound died down, and the elephant regarded them for a long moment. With a loud grunt, it turned and walked back to the rock pile.

They watched it as it began piling loose rubble onto the pyramid of rock. Bit by bit, it grew the pile, carefully and surprisingly gently lifting rocks and adding them on.

"Is that its nest?" Elise asked.

"Perhaps. There is only one way to know for sure."

"How?"

"We must talk to the elephant to learn its secrets."

"No," she said, "that would be a bad idea. Maybe we should just go."

"Not an option."

Jules opened the hatch, dropped the ladder, and stepped back out into the cathedral. Elise poked her head out of the hatch but didn't follow him. She just watched as the old explorer stepped towards the enormous creature, his hands raised in the air and his knees bent in a slightly silly way.

Jules whistled.

The elephant turned. The saucer-sized eyes flashed anger, then squinted as if looking at Jules, considering, thinking.

It bellowed and began walking towards Jules. He kept his hands in the air and dipped his stance a bit.

Elise thought it might have been the least threatening pose that a person could strike, but then she was proved wrong when Jules dropped to his back and lay there, legs akimbo, potbelly exposed.

She wanted to shout to him, to tell him to stop acting like a fool, but she was afraid that the sound would startle the beast.

I don't even know how to fly this thing, she thought.

I'm going to be stuck down here.

The elephant towered over Jules Valiance. He lay there like a dog waiting for its belly to be scratched.

The glistening, constantly color-shifting trunk reached out tentatively and pushed on Jules's stomach. He made a high-pitched sound but didn't move much.

The elephant cocked its head and considered Jules.

Elise thought that it looked curious.

It roared. Jules wiggled his arms and legs back and forth like a dying cockroach.

The elephant made a throaty, weird, gurgling noise and stood up on its back legs.

Was that a laugh? No, it's going to crush him, she thought.

It trumpeted. Then it went back to all fours and turned away, back to gathering rocks to add to its pile.

Jules stood up. Elise joined him.

"Really?" she asked him.

He dusted sand from his back and shoulders.

"It was an opportunity. We live, or we die. Best to take the path unexpected."

He motioned for her to sit down next to him on the sand.

They watched the elephant go about its odd task of building its mound.

The sound of rocks falling woke Elise up. Jules was already standing. Time had passed. The elephant was gone but to where she didn't know. It had walked away while she slept, and now there was an avalanche coming down one of the cliff sides at the bottom of the ocean.

Jules motioned for her to follow him. They walked quickly back and into the Aquaboggin.

The hatch was shut, and they were in their seats.

Through the forward viewing glass, they watched little stones, chunks of coral, and waves of sand tumble down into the valley.

"There's someone coming," said Elise.

The cause of the avalanche came sliding down the side of the valley on his back, under control like a snowboarder.

He was a big man with skin that was sharp patterns of black and white, and he had a fin that ran alongside his back.

This was the kind of man they had seen riding atop the machine that had been destroying Paris.

The man stepped out from the avalanche and onto the seafloor.

He was tall and powerful, with thick limbs. There was some kind of armor around his waist, like a kilt made of fat scales.

"A merman," Jules said.

Yes, I think you're right, thought Elise.

Something in the distance caught her eye.

"Uh, Jules, I think there are more of them."

Several more figures were running out of the gloom along the valley floor toward the cathedral.

Click.

"What was that?"

"I locked the door."

*

CHAPTER THIRTY-FIVE

Into the World Below

THE MERMEN WERE dressed for battle.

They had armor that covered part of their bodies, and the blade weapons that they carried came in several forms, an axe, a sword, a spear.

Jules activated the engines, and the propellers began to spin.

"We're leaving, right?" Elise asked.

"Fish men and a sealephant creature have arrived on the scene. Delights beyond imagination. We are not leaving. But you stay in the ship. If they attack, fly out of here as quickly as you can."

"I don't know how to fly this thing."

"Yes, life is fat with lessons. Next time pay attention."

Jules was out of the sub before Elise had a chance to complain.

"Bonjour, my friends, who wants a cigarette?" Jules said, his hands open and at his sides.

The four soldiers flanked him. They were close enough now that Elise could see the thick, almost leathery nature of their skin. Their muscles rippled like pythons beneath the black and white skin. Any one of these brutes would break Jules in half.

She glanced over at the control panel.

Pull back on the throttle and the stick, step on something at her feet, maybe she could fly it up and out. Or maybe you're being stupid, she thought.

The soldiers, if that's what they were, had Jules surrounded. Elise saw that his hand was near the pistol on his hip. This is not going to end well, she thought.

"Parlez-vouz Francais? English? I have a smattering of Esperanto, if that will do?"

The tallest of the merman stepped up to Jules. He towered over the old man.

"Ah," Jules said, "you must be in command, with such height and vigorous muscularity. I am Commander Jules Valiance, of Les Scaphandriers. I represent Earth and her ocean. What's left of it. Who are you, and why do you carry large pointy weapons?"

The merman made a low clicking sound and glared at Jules.

A whistling sound came from a blowhole on the back of his neck.

The others moved closer and raised their weapons.

"Yes. Elise," Jules said loudly enough for her to hear, "there is a green button below the yoke of the vessel. Push it, please. Quickly, before I am disemboweled."

Elise stared at the control console. There were a dozen green buttons, and she didn't know what a yoke was, except in an egg.

"Elise, all due speed, please."

The merman leader leaned down to Jules and glared at him, only an inch away from the old man's face. It made another clicking sound, low and guttural. The sound from the blowhole was a wet fart.

Elise wanted to push all of the green buttons, but what if something blew up?

The ground shook. There was a bellow, a roar, a thundering sound, and the ground was rattling so hard that the entire Aquaboggin shifted left and right.

Jules dropped and rolled away from the mermen, scrambling on his hands and knees, looking back at the enormous alien elephant that was rumbling toward them, eyes blazing and trunk held high.

The mermen brought their weapons up, but the elephant was on them so quickly that they didn't have a chance to form a flank or run away.

The enraged beast swatted them with its trunk, and the mermen went flying. One of the warriors was sent as far as the cathedral's inner wall, where he struck the stone with wet smacks and slid back down, perfectly and completely dead.

A blade cut the elephant's thick hide.

It roared again and kept roaring, bringing its legs down as weapons, as bludgeons, the three mermen scrambling to get out of the way.

Elephant blood sprayed as a sword ripped into the skin on the back of one of those massive legs. The elephant's trunk grabbed one of the mermen and lifted him, the toothed suction cups ripping and tearing at the merman's flesh.

Jules was back in the Aquaboggin. He pushed Elise out of the way and dove into the pilot's seat.

"The green button, you idiot."

He pushed a button under the yoke, and Elise heard a loud hiss from the exterior of the sub.

Heavily pressurized gas sprayed out in clouds from all sides of the Aquaboggin.

Elise watched in horror as the elephant, bleeding from its wounds, shuddered and swayed.

There were two mermen still alive and moving. They stopped and dropped to their knees and fell face down into the sand.

The elephant slowly knelt.

"What did you do?"

"Gas," Jules said, "an anesthetic created from the leaves of the coca plant. We used it to temporarily paralyze fish so that they might be studied. It was also employed once to incapacitate a prehistoric gill-man in the sultry darkness of the Amazon, a relic from a lost time, but that is another story entirely and one you are unlikely to believe."

The elephant creature was down on its knees but not unconscious. There were several bloody cuts along its skin, and it was touching the wounds with its trunk.

Jules grabbed a little medical kit and began climbing back up out of the hatch.

"Where are you going?"

"There is a creature in need, little idiot."

The elephant turned at Jules's approach, its eyes blazing.

He held up his hands. Jules then reached out and gently touched the creature's trunk.

Elise couldn't hear what he said, but Jules spoke for several moments. Then, he reached into the kit and produced a tube, like paint or glue, and applied something sticky and yellow to the many bloody wounds.

He offered up a bit of something.

The elephant ate it.

Is that a chocolate?

Yes, Elise thought, he just gave the thing a chocolate.

Jules patted the beast on the side and made his way back to the sub.

"You have chocolate?" asked Elise.

"Chocolate flavored antibiotic. You never know," he said.

Jules and Elise sat in the Aquaboggin and watched the huge beast as it rested in the gloom of the cathedral on the bottom of the sea.

"Will it live?"

"Of course," said Jules, "the wounds are superficial. She is just tired and, how do the English say, shagged out."

A few moments passed, and then the creature stood.

While its legs were shaking and it swayed as it walked, the

sealephant made a soft trumpeting noise and staggered out of the cathedral and into the darkness of the valley beyond.

The merman began to stir.

Jules hit them with another dose of the coca gas, and they fell again.

"We don't have much time. That was the last of the gas. Let's go."

Jules and Elise rushed out of the Aquaboggin and raced to the rock pile.

He pulled rocks away from the pile. Elise helped him. They worked hard, tossing aside smaller bits of rubble then dragging bigger chunks out of the way.

"This is terrible. The poor thing spent all that time building the pile, and now we're wrecking it again," said Elise.

"Consider it exercise for the beast's physical rehabilitation."

There was a glow, a blue glow coming from under the mountain of rocks. They worked harder and harder, and the light grew brighter as they did. It was cold in the deep trench, but Elise and Jules were sweating from the effort. Minutes passed, then an hour, and then they had moved enough of the rock on one side that the other side crumbled in a mini avalanche and blue light flooded the cathedral.

Elise's skin tingled, and there was a copper smell in the still air, the smell of ozone after a lightning strike.

A pedestal, and on the pedestal was a little sculpture of a cherub holding a violin. The light was rising from beneath the pedestal, softly illuminating the tiled floor at their feet.

Jules walked swiftly to the cherub and struck it with his hand. He cursed.

Elise didn't understand. He cursed again and struck it with his fist, and it must have hurt, but he did it again and again.

Jules screamed. Elise was afraid, and she stepped away from him.

With a final curse, he reached out, his hand bloody from striking the stone cherub, and grabbed it.

The touch of his palm against the stone of the sculpture was what it had been waiting for, just that simple touch.

The pedestal turned to dust. Elise could hear a hum growing louder and louder from beneath their feet. The light became intense, and Jules backed away as a tiny circle of energy where the pedestal had been erupted and expanded.

The glow was a spinning pool of white and cobalt energy in the floor of the cathedral, a shimmering circle as wide as a dinner plate, then a dinner table, then ten meters across. The mirrored surface spun slowly, rotating eddies of quicksilver, and the edges of this strange pool were eating the floor as it expanded.

Jules and Elise stood at the edge of the energy pool.

The expansion stopped. It was thirty feet across, and the bright blue light was blinding.

Elise picked up a rock and threw it at the glowing pool.

The rock hit the surface and disappeared without a sound. The shimmer rippled like the surface of the liquid metal pond, then returned to its slow, hypnotic rotation.

"The mermen are waking up. We need to make haste away," Jules said.

"Go where?"

"Under there. To the world below. Or perhaps between. Who's to say?"

And that's what Elise was waiting to hear.

The Aquaboggin thundered to life with Jules in the pilot seat and Elise next to him. The propellers spun faster and faster until they were a blur and then until they were practically invisible. The ship lifted a meter or so off of the cathedral floor, then hovered over to the lip of the cobalt blue portal. Its diameter wasn't wide enough for the ship to simply descend. Elise held tight as Jules angled the vessel port side up, starboard side down, until they were looking through the view glass directly into the silvery rainbow sheen of the hole to another world.

The rim of the portal and the tendrils of coruscating blue light reached out, enveloped the nose of the sub. The light was bright but not blinding, constantly in motion, hypnotic. There was no sound. They were moving forward, but Elise couldn't tell; there was no way to judge movement, just the swirling of the strange liquid light.

Jules studied the altimeter, the sonar, and the radar.

Everything was dead. The light had a mass, a watery thickness that blocked the instruments.

"We enter an ocean of light," he said.

Elise's skin and the cabin of the sub was a shifting palette of blue and white, reflecting the liquid sea. With nothing to guide him, Jules simply steered the vessel dead ahead at a slow pace, bringing the propellers in and letting the impellers of the jet engines do their work. He considered attempting to take a sample of the liquid light, but he wasn't sure how to operate the controls that would obtain it. That was something the science team had always tended to, led by North McAllister, the archeologist and reefer head.

I should have paid more attention, he thought, then dismissed the regret as beneath him and piloted on.

Seconds went by, then minutes. The Aquaboggin continued to dive for an hour. Then more.

The light from the liquid sea was steady, always shifting colors, but the brightness remained constant. Elise went from terrified to exhilarated to fascinated to bored fairly quickly. A part of her hoped that a vicious merman would "jump scare" to the side of the view glass, just to break the beautiful monotony of the cobalt sea.

She had just begun to doze off when the ship shuddered, and she felt a tilt to port.

"You are still buckled in tightly, yes?"

"Yes," she said.

The swirling light in the view glass was changing, becoming darker, bluer. The cobalt became a deep, rich, saturated aquamarine with strokes of green, like an impressionist painting of the ocean's depths.

The Aquaboggin shook slightly, and Elise could feel it move up and down, then side to side as if she were in a strong current.

There was a sound now, distant, but she could hear it, a rumble below a high soft static, getting louder and louder.

Bubbles.

Elise saw bubbles in the aquamarine, and the swirling chaos of color became just a single sheet of roaring, deafening bubbles; then she saw nothing but dark blue-green, and the sub bucked. Jules fought at the controls as the instruments came to life. There was the ping of the sonar, the ticking of altimeter and depth finder, the whir of a strange little device that whirred, and who knows what else.

She gripped the sides of her leather seat.

They were in the ocean. She could see silvery fish darting about, particulates in the water, and they were spinning downward like a top toward a massive whirlpool, an undersea tornado. They were in a powerful current going down into an oceanic storm.

Jules stopped fighting the controls and let the current take them. They were moving fast, spinning around the tides of the maelstrom and then into the surging power of the whirlpool.

"Do you have your sickness bag for vomiting?" he asked.

"All used up."

"That is unfortunate."

They entered the maelstrom, and the sub spun around and around, rotating to the left with the power of the sea storm. The centrifugal force jammed Elise and Jules against their seats. Elise thought that her face felt like drippy melted rubber and her ears popped hard.

She couldn't keep her eyes open against the strain. She wasn't sick yet, but it hurt, her muscles pulling against the G forces. The noise was so loud that she couldn't think.

And then they were through.

The violent spinning stopped.

The sub drifted calmly, silently, and Elise opened her eyes to see a crystal-clear ocean through the view glass. The seafloor was just below them, and she could see the waves rolling softly above. Somehow, they were in a shallow sea.

An ocean. Maybe our ocean?

Elise felt a shadow to her starboard and turned to the glass just as a massive great white shark, jaws wide, bumped the sub inches from her face.

She jumped. The shark's dark eyes seemed to consider her for a moment, and then it swam away into the clear water trailed by dozens of tiny scavenger fish.

Elise wasn't frightened of the shark. She felt such overwhelming happiness. Maybe this really was their ocean with sharks and whales and dolphins. Maybe there was a way to make things right again.

Jules piloted the sub upwards to the surface.

*

CHAPTER THIRTY-SIX

Wandering Haven

THE OCEAN WAS clear and full of life, just as it had been and perhaps just as it would be again someday.

The submersible, the Aquaboggin, carved through the waters at good speed, rising as it went, shedding bubbles.

Jules and Elise smiled as the vessel reached the surface, and the water dropped away from the forward view glass.

There were two suns, one large and golden, the other small and blindingly white, and they were gloriously bright in a sky as blue as the mind could allow. Jules flipped a switch and the forward glass popped up with a hydraulic whoosh.

The air was warm and fresh and smelled of the sea.

There were structures that rose from the surrounding ocean. Towers, buildings, monuments, but just the peaks and tops jutting out from the water.

The ocean had flooded a great city here, and they were floating above the flood.

Dolphins jumped off in the distance, breaching up and out of the water, playing or hunting. Baitfish, mullet perhaps, skittered here and there, chasing schools of flying shrimp.

The sun felt wonderful on Elise's face.

Jules guided the vessel slowly along, past great stone buildings carved out of rock and stone that glistened with quartz lines and was the color of Georgia clay.

"Idiot girl, in the unfortunate case that you had not deduced this for yourself," he said, "we have somehow found ourselves in a new world."

"There was a flood."

"Yes, apparently so."

He checked the instruments on the control panel of the Aquaboggin.

"The sea here is shallow. Fifty meters according to the instruments. We are looking at the top of a primitive city, and there is much more beneath us."

Something moved along the surface of the stone building to their port side.

Elise squinted. She couldn't see it at first, then it moved again.

A big red crab, the size of a dog, was clinging to the side of the building. Its eyes were on stalks, and they considered Elise for a moment, then the crab shimmied down the side of the building and into the sea.

Charlie had come from this world. She had brought him home.

"Do you hear that?" Jules asked.

Elsie heard nothing at first, only the soft splash of water against the hull of their sub. Then, off in the distance, she heard the sound of laughter and music.

It sounded like a party or a concert or a circus.

Her Dad had taken her to a carnival once, a wonderland of Ferris wheels and games and wooden coasters and people with unique talents doing strange things. What she heard now reminded her of that night.

The sub cruised toward the sound, and in just a few moments, they passed between stone pillars, and a floating city was revealed, a village adrift on a bed of wood and rubber and trash all tied together to create an island.

Seagulls swooped down over them as they stared in wonder at the carnival.

*

There's a circus, then there's a fair, then there's a carnival. A circus is a tidy thing, wild but controlled, sensory overload contained in a space where your focus is directed, and a joyous story is told. A fair billows out beyond your reach, but it's yours, a child of your community, and it tells the story of your town's tastes and smells and attitudes. At a circus, you become a child. At the fair, you become a teen in love. But darker amusements can be had when the train rolls into town at midnight and madness sprouts on the town field like strange mushrooms. At the carnival, you become the stranger. A carnival invades and shocks, its dark story spills out as if dumped onto a field by dark authors, and comfort is a wink and a nod. The carnival is where you see and taste things you shouldn't, where the thrill is streaked with fear, where the tent might be the last place you'd take your child. The circus is a clown with a rubber nose and a smile. The carnival is a man who eats living chickens with a leer.

At night, after the story is told, you want to run away to the circus. You want to run away from the carnival.

Under the two suns of this new, flooded world, Elise and Jules stepped out of the sub and onto the solid footing of the docks of a vast floating island. The carnival, if that's what it was, and it certainly felt like one, was an eruption of life and color and music along the docks and into the crowded jumble of streets that had been fashioned out of wooden planks, sheet metal, and other debris.

There was a tall wooden stage and on the stage was a quintet of musicians playing instruments of all kinds, percussion and string and brass. The musicians were a strange mix. A beautiful human woman with bright red hair worked the bow of a violin while a black and white merman pounded a massive set of skin-covered drums, and a thin child dressed in colorful rags blew a gleaming trumpet.

The crowd was mixed as well. The merpeople danced and partied with humans. A trio of sea monkeys dashed past them, chattering and clapping. A small flock of penguins waddled along and made chirping sounds as they went.

The music was contagiously energetic, wildly rhythmic, joyous. Elise was horribly embarrassed to see that Jules was moving to the music, his elbows to his side and his head bobbing back and forth.

"Cut it out," she said.

Jules snapped an eyebrow up and danced even more.

Food smells drifted on the wind, and Elise felt her belly rumble. Something smelled really good. They walked on, through the crowd of revelers, toward the smell of whatever was cooking. Tall billboards were splashed on the sides of rough tents, lurid artwork promising to introduce the curious to strange visions. Here was a human from exotic lands dressed as a pigeon who could contort in the most unusual ways. There was a half-man, half beaver that seemed to be able to remove his tail at will.

Elise stopped at a plank of wood that was hammered to another to form a wall. Upside down and sideways on the plank was nailed a faded, water-stained, and hand-drawn poster of a strange-looking elephant. She turned her head upside down so that she could read, but the words were in a language she didn't understand. The elephant was wearing armor and carrying a spear in its trunk.

"Jules, look," Elise said.

Jules studied the poster for a moment.

"A story unfolds. I suspect that this is a 'lost sealephant' poster.

Clearly, the poor creature came to our world in the event they call The Turn but must have escaped from its owners before the flood. If I am to guess, based on its habit of piling rocks atop the portal, this sealephant does not want to return."

"But what if somebody misses it."

"No, the poster hints to me that she is a beast used for battle. Perhaps she is done fighting. The strange men who fought with her in the valley must be four that were also lost. Warriors, trying to reclaim their beast of war. This explains much."

"I hope she gets away from them."

"So do I, little one."

They stumbled, danced, were half-shoved by the crowd into the island's food court. It was a narrow alley and on either side were food vendors grilling, sizzling, steaming, chopping, and baking a dizzying array of foods.

"My tongue explodes in anticipation," Jules said.

"Can you speak normally for once? Your tongue explodes? What?"

Jules shrugged, the classic French gesture for, among other things, "what are you gonna do?"

Street chefs barked and beckoned to them at every step, offering things that were batter fried and other things that were wrapped in dark breads and others that were still alive and skewered. The chefs were human and merman both, working and competing for attention side by side.

They stopped at a tidy little stall where a chubby woman was deep-frying fish. It smelled glorious.

Jules leaned down to Elise and whispered, "Do you have any money?"

Elise gave him an "are you kidding" look.

Jules grimaced. He was wearing dark jeans and a striped shirt with his Scaphandrier outer vest. He began rifling through the various pockets. A whistle, a single bullet, an anesthetic bulb, chewing gum, a laser pointer, a dissolvable fishhook, a grenade, a rubber duck. No money.

"Bonjour, Madame," he said to the woman frying the fish.

She turned and smiled so widely that her head might have split.

"Bonjour!" she replied in French.

The two began speaking excitedly in French so quickly that Elise couldn't keep up. She caught bits of phrases, a word here and there.

"Wandering Haven. Edith. Ten years.

From the Vendee. Crazy world, right? Thieving sea monkeys. What happened, who's to say? Husband catches, and I cook."

She dropped sizzling fish chunks into little tins and handed them to Elise and Jules.

"Merci," Jules said, shaking her hand.

She made a "not a problem" gesture and bent down to Elise with a warm smile.

"Bonjour, ma fille, and welcome to Wandering Haven of the world called Orcanum. I am Edith. There's no money here, just trade. So give me a grin, and we'll call it even for the fish."

Elise grinned.

The fish was a delicious, crispy delight.

"Edith, I am Jules, and this is Elise," he said in English, "we come from Paris."

"Yes," Edith said, "my English is not so good, but yes, I understand. But Paris is still there?"

"Just a ghost of the city, I'm afraid," said Jules, "and we fled even as the ghost was fading."

"Ah. So sad.

I am sure my Cholet, my town, is no more."

"What do you remember of the day, what some call The Turn?"

"What does the fly remember at the end of a swatter? We are the lucky, and there are few of us. Just here on Wandering Haven. The survivors live here and here alone."

"How many?"

"Perhaps a few hundred," she said in French.

"These strange beings, these black and white men with fins like sharks, are they new to this world as well?"

"Oh no, monsieur, this is their home. They are the Orcanum. Not bad, but some of them are brutes, so be cautious. Took some doing, but we can understand each other a bit. We must get along because their world was turned as well, all of us at the same time. Flooded. This is a world of two seas, so we make do together."

"Two seas?" Elise asked.

"The Earth's ocean didn't just disappear, my dear. It was brought to this world at The Turn. Our entire ocean dumped into theirs. Can you imagine? Well, of course, you can."

"This place, Wandering Haven. You built it?"

"Yes, out of flotsam and jetsam from the flood. Our village isn't much to look at, but we love her. Big place too and growing all the time."

"How did you arrive here?"

"We were at the beach, my family and me, and a hole opened on the shore. My husband Fernand and I were pulled in, but not...I was pulled into the waves but not..." and she stopped there because Elise could see that she was going to cry if she continued.

Jules put his hand on Edith's.

"Not my children," she said, "just us. Ten years ago. I dream that they are alright, back home in Cholet, playing. That's what I dream. Who's to say?"

"Perhaps they are," he said. They thanked her for the fish and walked back into the noisy musical chaos of the carnival.

The thin Asian man dressed in an old wetsuit had been listening, concealed behind planks of wood near the food stall where Edith served her fish. He was an old string of a thing smoking a thin reefer, his long silver hair fashioned into a tangle of dreadlocks. He discreetly followed Jules and Elise as they explored.

You could barely read the faded logo on the front of the tattered wetsuit.

Les Scaphandriers.

*

CHAPTER THIRTY-SEVEN

A Shotgun Blast to The Face

ELISE WALKED WITH eyes wide at the side of Jules Valiance through the din of the carnival.

The ground at their feet was sandy plywood and other lumber all tied and nailed together. Here and there, water sloshed up through cracks. It might have been her imagination, but she would feel the whole thing shift slightly now and then as if they were walking on the deck of a giant ship.

Neither Elise nor Jules noticed the skinny old man that was following them. He was good, popping in and out of alleys and huts and scrambling under and between and over to stay hidden.

The people of Wandering Haven were of all ages and nationalities, a melting pot of languages and cultures. The Orcanum were also more diverse than Elise thought possible, with big ones and little ones, some working at food stalls or little shops, others, the big ones, wearing thick armor and carrying blunt weapons crudely fashioned out of debris. They didn't speak words she could understand but chattered in a strangely musical language of clicks, whistles, and song. She got close enough to one of the big ones to see that the skin was smooth, the black-and-white pattern a bit different on each one, the fins along the back of the arms and legs and head of various sizes and attitudes. The face was almost human but with dark eyes buried deep under a thick brow, a bump where the nose should have been, and a large mouth full of sharp teeth. They weren't sharks, she thought; they were more like the orcas she had seen at the Aquarium with her Dad.

You could see Orcanum in the water as well, surfacing to breathe through holes in the back of their necks and then diving back down into the clear water off the docks of the island. They were fast, so fast that they could leap out of the water and onto the wooden planks of without seeming to exert any effort at all.

Jules tugged at Elise, and they approached a filthy tent where a crowd had gathered, a mix of people and Orcanum. A young man stood on a box and shouted to the crowd, barking for them to come in and experience the concert of the Octo-Thing, the wonder of the centuries, nature's conundrum, a puzzlement of the sea. The curious were filing in, handing the man little items as payment for entry.

Jules couldn't contain himself. He paid with a button and a single bullet, and so the two of them found their way into the tent.

Sunlight bled through little rips in the fabric, but it was mostly dark. A single candle on a small stage offered a strange sight, a lump of wriggling tentacled flesh that glistened. Elise had seen octopus before, but never one like this.

There was a little foot, like a baby's foot, at the end of one of the writhing arms. Other tentacles were tipped with what looked like tiny hands. With a soft suction noise, the creature pushed itself up and stood.

The head was a bulbous amalgam of octopus and human, with wide eyes and a mouth hidden below the mantle.

"Oh," Elise said, pointing at the little hand reaching out from the tip of a fat tentacle.

The Octo-Thing picked up a violin and began to play a tune.

The gathered crowd gasped, laughed, applauded.

The eyes of the thing seemed sad, even as it played a happy melody, and Elise felt uncomfortable.

She looked up at Jules, and his face was stone.

"Let us go, Elise," he said. They walked back out into the sun.

"That was weird, but I felt sad for it," Elise said as they wandered back into the streets.

"A tent is no home for that beautiful creature. Laughter and applause do not soothe its soul. The Octo-Thing will someday swim free. So pledges Jules Valiance."

"Can we go check on Charlie? Maybe it will help him to be back home."

"Of course. And there is something else that I would like to see back at the vessel. Curse me as a fool, but I have neglected the obvious."

*

The warm sun had heated the interior of the Aquaboggin, but her batteries were solar-powered, and they kept the cooler at just above freezing.

Elise stared through the little glass portal, through crystal etchings of frost, at the gray body of the crab.

Nothing moved, not the feelers, not the antennae, not the eyes on long stalks.

She had expected this. Elise didn't really believe in miracles anymore. Charlie was dead, and he was always going to die, just like everything else.

There were soft beeping sounds from the cockpit. Elise traced a heart shape on the fogged surface of the glass and kissed.

"Goodbye," she said, "you were my friend, and I'll never forget you for saving my life. Thank you."

She walked up to where Jules sat in the pilot seat. He was staring at a round screen that had little glowing blue dots. The beeps came from the screen.

"This is the Aquaboggin," he said, tracing the outline of the sub on the screen. Elise could see it clearly. There were two flashing blue dots in the front of the ship.

"That's us?"

"Oui, the tracers built into our watches."

"So, what are those other blue dots?"

There was a tight grouping of the dots to the northwest of their ship.

"Those are testament to how far my astounding faculties have fallen. They are beeping shameful obscenities at my own stupidity."

"Excuse me?"

Jules was out of his seat fast and strapping on diving gear.

"One hundred meters over there, in fifty feet of water, are Les Scaphandriers."

Elise watched in wonder as the old man geared up. He was moving so quickly that she couldn't follow.

A vest, fins, regulator, small silver tank, headpiece with goggles, dive knife, and oddly, a rubber duck.

Jules popped up out of the top hatch tower of the Aquaboggin and shouted something extremely rude in French. Elise heard a splash and ran up the little ladder to see what had happened.

She watched a trail of bubbles move away from the ship's port side.

He was fast for an old man.

*

The water was clear and blue, a gorgeous aquamarine dressed in sheets of soft sunlight.

Jules Valiance swam as quickly as he could, and that was fast indeed. His heart began to pound, and he silently berated himself for his reefers and wine before using a calming technique he had gleaned from Indian fakirs that allowed him to slow the rate of his pulse. There was a time when he could feign death, or at the very least, extreme ennui, but now it was all he could do just to keep from having a coronary incident.

He could taste dust in his mouthpiece. It had sat for ten years, just like he had. He hoped that the rubber hadn't dried out.

Something large and dark swam up from beneath and surged past him.

One of the beastly Orcanum, an adult male. The creature swam off, then stopped, turned, and watched Jules.

Jules swam on. He would cross the Orcanum problem if it became one.

A flooded stone village lay below him. The flood caused by the arrival of Earth's ocean had devastated this place. It was deep here, several hundred feet, but the rooftops of the flooded city were of all heights. He swam over a tall monument, a statue, a hut half-buried in silt.

The Orcanum kept pace and distance, watching.

There. Jules saw a hilltop into which were carved stone dwellings. The crest of the hill was a ruined temple, bone-white in the crystalline waters. The beeping transmitters of Les Scaphandriers were there, fifty feet below the surface.

The merman was in his path without warning.

"You are quick for such a big fellow," thought Jules.

Jules tried to swim around, but the Orcanum male put its massive hands out to stop him.

Jules treaded water for a moment. They stared at each other. Jules tried sign language. The Orcanum didn't move.

Jules pulled his dive knife out and showed it threateningly to the creature. The Orcanum opened its mouth wide and displayed a set of teeth that made the knife look positively puny.

"Fine," thought Jules.

He whipped the rubber duck out of his vest and gave it a squeeze. The duck squeaked loudly, farted bubbles, and shot up to the surface.

The Orcanum chased after the duck.

Jules swam as hard and as fast as he could toward the transponders. The rubber duck ploy almost always worked, but it never worked for very long unless the creature in question was particularly dim.

The beeps grew louder in his helmet. He looked about, scanning the sandy floor of the hilltop temple.

There. A rusted metal lockbox. He swooped down, grabbed the box, and made for the surface.

Or, he would have made for the surface if the Orcanum hadn't appeared above him. The thing grabbed Jules by the helmet and started tossing him about. Jules could hear the water sloshing around as he was shoved and pulled.

"Merde," he thought and spit out his mouthpiece.

Bubbles exploded up and confused the Orcanum.

Jules had taken a deep breath. He swam back in the direction of the sub, ascending as he went.

There was a time when Jules Valiance could hold his breath for nearly seven minutes. Twenty minutes if deep free diving. This was not that time. His lungs burned.

He felt a powerful hand on his foot. He kicked away his flipper and was free. The Orcanum swam hard then and was on Jules before the old man had a chance to think.

The brute had him by the shoulders, but Jules could still move his hands. He pulled a circular tab on the bottom of his vest, and a white cloud burst out, enveloping them. The Orcanum squeezed. Jules thought that his shoulders were going to snap. Then, the strength was sapped out of the hands, and Jules was free. He popped up, spluttering for air just as his lungs were about to give out.

The sub was only a few meters away. He was away from the milky water. The Orcanum bobbed up behind him, face down and air-hole up, unconscious.

Elise helped Jules up the side ladder and onto the narrow deck of the Aquaboggin.

"An anesthetic cloud designed for a shark attack," Jules said, struggling for breath. "Good enough for our friend there."

"Will he be okay?"

"Of course. He'll be back up and terrorizing divers in just a few minutes. His breathing hole is at the surface, so he will be fine if nauseated for days. He was protecting this treasure, for some reason, a reason that we must deduce."

He presented the metal box to Elise. There was an ornate emblem on the top of the box.

"That logo is the insignia of Les Scaphandriers, designed originally by a hermit from Cassis and then re-imagined by Man Ray during an absinthe epiphany. The transponders of my team are in this box. Another puzzle to be solved."

And that's when the big fishing net fell over them.

Elise let out a little scream, and Jules pulled and tugged, but the net enveloped them. It grew tighter as those who had tossed it cinched in the ropes.

"We are waylaid!" Jules shouted. He had a knife in his hand and began to cut the net.

"Stop! You'll ruin our only net, you fool," a voice shouted. It was the skinny old Asian man in the faded Scaphandrier wetsuit.

There was a hand-rolled cigarette drooping from his lips. He ran up to Jules and poked a finger at him.

"Put the knife away."

Jules looked gobsmacked.

"North? North McAllister?"

The skinny old man glared at Jules and puffed his cigarette.

The other three stepped forward and onto the deck of the sub, dropping the net lines.

One, the Guyanese mystery known as Three John, was a towering black man dressed in old jeans and a tight sweater. There was a stovetop hat on his bald head and three pale scars across the left side of his face. The second was short and stumpy, a dumpling of a man with shocking red hair and a shotgun resting in the crook of his arm. The initiated called him Private Splatter, but only as a joke.

The third was Zuzu, a tall blonde woman dressed in a Scaphandrier issue jogging suit, the pant legs cut away as was the top at the shoulders, revealing strong muscles, a dive knife strapped to her thigh, and tan dark as burnished copper. She didn't look like someone you should trifle with, thought Elise.

None of them did, really.

"Mon Dieu," said Jules Valiance, "Les dead Scaphandriers."

"World killer," said Private Splatter as he shoved the business end of the shotgun into Jules's face.

Elise kicked the man in the shins. That was a bold move and ultimately a bad one as the stumpy man flinched, the shotgun blasted the air next to Jules's head, Private Splatter fell backwards into the ocean, and a hole was ripped in the net. The sound of shotgun pellets peppering a tin wall nearby could have been heard if the gun blast hadn't deafened them.

The party stopped, and hundreds of heads, human and not, turned in the direction of the shotgun blast.

Jules put his hands in the air. Elise moved in front of him, her ears buzzing. The dumpling man held his shin and cursed.

"She's brave but an idiot. Could have killed somebody," tall Three John said.

"You're an idiot, and who had the gun?" Elise answered in a low, angry voice.

The crowd turned away and resumed the party, the noise bubbling up again into a proper froth.

"Can we lower our hands and discuss the situation as rational human beings?"

Private Splatter slipped the shotgun into a back holster and made a face like he'd just eaten a rotten egg.

"Rational, he says."

Three John stared at Jules.

"Rational? From the man who convinced Farrah Fawcett to dive with snapping sea turtles for a Christmas postcard? From the fool who walked the Nile underwater? Backwards? From the maniac who couldn't keep his damned hands off of the cherub that destroyed the world?"

"Rational is another word for boring," North McAllister mumbled through a smoke cloud. Zuzu caught McAllister's eye and smiled.

They stared silently at each other for a long moment.

Jules clicked the latch on the treasure box, and it opened to reveal four silver watches. The timepieces of Les Scaphandriers.

"It was fortuitous that I found these buried under the sea in a little chest," Jules said, "and that their signal can last for so long, but to what point is this? Why did you bury your watches?"

"We buried them at sea along with the memory of Les Scaphandriers to wash the blood of the world from our hands," Three John said.

Elise watched Jules closely. Anger flashed in his eyes for a moment, and then she saw a sadness so profound that her heart skipped. The old man bit his lip and turned his face. His grip on the treasure chest weakened. Elise grabbed the box before it fell from his hands, and she held it close.

"We can still save the world," Jules said.

His voice was a whisper.

"Look around you, Jules Valiance," Three John said. "Do you have a bucket big enough to carry the ocean?"

Jules straightened.

"Nothing is impossible."

"I once believed that."

"Because it's true."

Elise saw something strange then. Jules Valiance was not a tall man in her estimation, but he stepped back from the group, turned to face them, and seemed to grow.

She had seen defeat in his eyes and fear. She had seen sadness. Now she saw something else. It wasn't anger exactly or pride. When she thought back on it, she believed that she saw the fires of imagination in his eyes, and when he spoke, he seemed to be a taller man than before with a voice that rang like the bells of Notre Dame.

"To rise from bed with a song and a hope, to boldly go under there and beyond, always with a smile, a laugh, and a dream. We sail so that all may profit from our explorations. We dream so that children may grow up to be us. We seek so that others are inspired to fly," he said. He paused for the briefest of moments, and North McAllister continued.

"We laugh loudly at quiet parties because someone must."

Zuzu stepped forward then.

"We go unafraid to the worlds below and between with song, fantasy, and wine by our side," she said in that thick German accent.

"We learn from our deaths and return with stories of love from the grave," said Private Splatter.

Three John held up his hand. They all turned to him, and it was quiet for a long moment. Then, Three John doffed his tall top hat and said,

"We are Les Scaphandriers, The Astonishing Aquanauts, and we dive into the deep, into the dark, into the mysteries and puzzles that God has left for us to solve."

"We are Les Scaphandriers," concluded Jules Valiance, "and we are impossible."

Jules went to Three John then and smiled.

"My friend, the code of Les Scaphandriers is a wee verbose and leaves out some important bits. Perhaps we should revise it. Who's to say? But I sailed here, to this world beyond ours, and found you somehow. If this is not impossible, then I do not know the meaning of the word."

"Les Scaphandriers were many things," Zuzu said, "but rational human beings? Not so much. This is Jules Valiance. He is our only hope, and he has returned. Now, this will be an adventure. Today is a time for celebration, for beer, vigorous love-making, and extreme violence. Rational? To Hell with rational."

Jules beamed and leaped over to Zuzu, embracing her in a bear hug. She resisted, then smiled, then hugged back. Old McAllister smiled so wide that his wrinkly face might split. Splatter continued to simmer but showed no immediate sign that he was ready to start shooting.

Three John stepped forward and offered his hand.

Jules took it.

"Zuzu is correct, my friends. Les Scaphandriers are many things," he said, "and dead is not among them."

Elise felt awkward and dropped back into the sub.

She went to the cold locker and stared at the colorless carcass of her friend.

Jules had his team again.

She was alone.

If this was as good as her life was going to get, she was not sure how she would survive.

*

CHAPTER THIRTY-EIGHT

At the Peak of Ebon

THERE WERE HEATED discussions over coffee and smokes.

There was also joyous dancing to the Wandering Haven bands, the sea monkeys with drums, and the grim humans with lively guitars.

It was quite a strange party, and it was non-stop.

Elise watched Les Scaphandriers argue and joke, and she even saw Jules slip away to kiss Zuzu that evening under the amber glow of the yellow moons. She was not surprised when she punched him. She was also not surprised but seriously grossed out when Zuzu picked him up and kissed him back.

Elise was "la petit Scaphandrier." They were kind to her and brought her food and drink. Three John pretended to be impressed by her adventures in Paris, her survival at the Eiffel Tower, and her courage at the Nursery. Private Splatter mumbled a compliment about her kicking prowess.

North McAllister offered to introduce her to some of the orphan children of the island, humans and Orcanum alike, who played and survived on the East side near the water pumps and greenhouses.

It was all well-meaning, and it was nothing to Elise.

That night, as the party continued to rage lit by torches and candles and the light of three moons, she sat on the deck of the Aquaboggin and stared off over the sea and to the black horizon.

She hated everyone and most of all herself.

Then, a moment later, she felt a sense of love and loss so strong that she cried.

Then, angry at her weakness, she bit her lip until she bled, and the crying stopped, and her vision grew sharp once more.

Then the cycle would repeat.

A cool breeze blew in from the sea. She wore her Scaphandrier gear. It was comfortable. Her old clothing from the Girl's Garden was stuffed into her backpack, unwashed, and it stank of filth and the fall of Paris.

Her blond hair tickled her face in the breeze, and she pushed it back into a ponytail.

Fish and other things jumped near her in the water and loudly in the distance beyond her sight. Here were two worlds forced to live as one. Earth drained of life, and that life forced upon Orcanum until she had overflowed. Billions were dead. Elise had not spoken a word since sunset, but she had listened. Glowing portholes had opened all over this beautiful place, and the oceans of Earth had surged in, a Biblical deluge that brought whales and sharks and all manner of creatures, even people who had been trapped in the vortex.

The Orcanum, though oceanic, breathed air and lived most of their lives on land. They had lost countless lives. The survivors here on Wandering Haven did not know if there were others.

It was a world without technology, no telephones or radios or electricity. As far as they knew, they were the last humans and Orcanum in the universe.

Les Scaphandriers argued theories and conspiracies and bizarre possibilities all day and into the evening, but Elise understood little of it and finally began to tune their chatter out, like radio noise in another language. She had finally escaped to the deck of the sub. It was nice and quiet there.

A little glowing squid popped up out of the water and accidentally landed on the deck next to her. It was the size of her hand, brilliant blue with shining eyes and flailing tentacles desperate to get back to the water.

Are you from this world or mine?

She gently lifted it up by the mantle and dropped the tiny squid back into the water, where it jetted off like a fiery rocket, leaving a cloud of sparkling, phosphorescent ink in its wake.

So beautiful.

Dad would love this place. He told me of worlds just like it, in his stories at bedtime, in those long car rides, or whenever we were just bored. Dad told me of these people, this place, this adventure.

How?

He gave her a blanket that kept her alive for ten years during the end of the world.

He told her of Jules Valiance.

How had he known?

Was she special somehow? There were books she had grown fond of where a single child or adult was designated as the chosen one, a special force, a savior. Was she the chosen one? She had slept for ten years and not aged. She was on a wild adventure into another world, and it seemed as if anything was possible.

But she had no powers. She couldn't fly or lift heavy things or read minds like in the comic books.

Her Dad had told her so much of this, and yet he had been so wrong.

It wasn't lovely or funny or innocent. It was death and sadness, and it smelled bad.

Her Dad was the best man she had ever known, and he had been so stupid.

She loved him, and she hated him, and then she felt something like a hand come up from her soul and grip her heart so tightly that she couldn't breathe.

Elise had built such thick walls to keep everything away, a dam against her feelings, that when they broke at that moment, she thought that her life was slipping, rushing, tearing away, like the ocean under the pull of the vortex, like her Dad's life at the beach.

There is that moment when you cry so hard that it feels as if your soul is being torn from you through your face. You can be so hurt, so overwhelmed, that a part of you, a special and irreplaceable part of you, feels like it's being murdered.

This was that moment for Elise.

She collapsed and fell asleep, alone on the deck and, in her mind, alone in the universe.

*

The ship's sails were embroidered fabrics as tall as the sky, suspended from masts of adamantine steel, and you could see her approach from a dozen leagues away.

The hull was glass forged in the heart of a distant star, tinted green from the life absorbed when in those far away fires the sands of Earth and the waters of Orcanum were wed and laced with the living technologies of worlds they had reaped.

And those sails, stitched from embroidered cloth that told the story of all creation when laid end to end, those billowing curtains draped and swaddled and protected the ship from time and space and injury of all kinds.

She was at anchor in a deep lagoon created when the Earth flood came to this ancient world, and the waters rose hundreds of meters. The cliffs and pillars of the volcano thrust up from the sea like the dark teeth of a god and framed the ship in ebony stone. This was the tallest volcanic mountain on Orcanum, the largest active volcano in the known universe, The Peak of Ebon in their language but a gibberish of clicks and sonar song in ours, a place of worship and sacrifice, a summit never breached because she was still alive with the roaring fires of creation and liquid rock still bubbled and burped along her rim.

An armada of air jellies floated in formation above and around the ship, each as big as a house and writhing with stinging tentacles that could grip and lift and destroy.

I'Masma stood at the bow of the ship and smelled the mist of the waves crashing on the rocks and on the hull, the sulphur of the mountain, the hint of death.

The deck at her feet was an amalgam of wood, star glass, and the gathered detritus of worlds far away, electronics made alive by the power of the Gods.

The sails made soft whipping sounds above and around her. She considered for a moment her fortune in having them, these tapestries woven from the strings of reality by The Ones Before. These were the most precious cloths in all the universe, and they were hers to use for a new and wonderful purpose, like every other bit of detritus that she gathered and absorbed and renewed.

The two suns shone soft light on her skin where it pulsed naked and exposed from her own shroud of the fabric. Her shroud had taken the work of a thousand weavers working a thousand days, and at the presentation ceremony, they had all been rewarded with sweet and liberating death. She had chosen a portion of the tapestry that told the tale of a star's love for a moon, a sweet and simple fable about rebirth through song. The One's Before had considered it their most elegant story, so it gave her such satisfaction to make it the last, horrifying thing that so many dying eyes would see.

Her skin was metal, wire, circuit board, and flesh because, like everything in her world, she was the sum of countless things, odds and ends gathered and absorbed and born anew as Her.

But what does it mean to be the most awful thing in all creation?

Born and killed. Born and killed again. Born and killed and ripped apart in agony again and again. In a thousand years, born stronger. Escaping death for a day, then captured crawling and mewling up a wall.

Ripped apart and killed again.

And so on, birth and murder and rebirth and adaptation and evolution through surviving then dying than being born again stronger, more full of hate each time. Imagine that over time, you have adapted to this pattern of infanticide, you have grown a day for every century, you have evolved, and the trigger for your evolution is pure hate.

She was the Herald for the Turning of the Sheets of Reality, and she had been created in a crucible of horror by beings known as The Torture Kings.

She sailed this ship under sails weaved from the stolen fabric of time, space, and reality.

She now went from world to world, razing and devouring technology that became new life and new power, tilling the soil, preparing everything as need be because the time was soon at hand. You see, everything built, no matter how mundane, was built of an imaginative spark, a desire to create, and all of those things would be harvested.

She was I'Masma, the Commander of The Ship of Dreams, and when she was done with Earth and done with Orcanum, she would sail on to the next, and then to the next, until all imagination's detritus was gathered and the last portal had been prepared for their return.

"Goddess, it is here with news of the little flying ship. It mewls and whines, but it knows."

The Crew Master was a fat blot of a human held up by two spindly legs. His one good eye stared at I'Masma, waiting for a response.

"Bring it, then, or wait for me to grow bored and put a pin through your brain. Either way, it's your choice," she said.

Her voice was so soft and elegant, so musical.

The Crew Master clapped his fingers and whistled. Two more

of the crew appeared, dragging a tortured Orcanum child between them. They tossed the creature to the deck at I'Masma's jeweled boots.

The Orcanum child's skin was battered and cut. A long slice had been drawn in the black and white blubber at its side. Water had washed the blood away, but the pink flesh was exposed beneath the skin. It was a deep and vicious wound. The Orcanum looked up at I'Masma with eyes hazy from pain.

"Well?"

The child clicked and sang, the voice cracking and bubbling.

"Where did we get this child?"

The Crew Master smiled.

"A cull of the tribes nearby. I promised to spare the beast's parents if it scouted for us."

"Oooh. Look at you, clever thing. Did you think of that scheme on your own?"

The Crew Master nodded.

"I should watch myself, with such a strategic mind onboard. Well played, Crew Master."

"Yes, your glorious elegance."

The Orcanum child continued to make soft singing sounds.

"Oh, you've told me what I need to know. Crew Master, there is an island near this planet's equatorial line, due south of us. Humans swept through the portals survive there, along with some of these beasts.

They have fashioned a crude little island of wood. Send a squadron and deal with them."

"Yes, I'Masma. Immediately."

I'Masma leaned down and took the Orcanum child's long chin in her hand. She looked into its tortured eyes.

"For your parents, child?"

It nodded.

"For them?" I'Masma pointed back to the deck, to a bloody pile of fin and bone, Orcanum so slaughtered, so chopped, that there was no longer a form or a shape.

They had been parents to the child, but they were now just a mess to be cleaned.

The child made a screaming whistling sound.

"I harpooned them myself, but I have had our chef clean them so that I might make musical instruments from their bones. You see, your parents' bones will join my symphony, and they will live on forever, bringing smiles to my crew through music. Isn't that nice?"

The young Orcanum looked up into the eyes of I'Masma.

"Yes," I'Masma said, "horror makes us and unmakes us, and we survive it, or we go mad. You trusted in the kindness of strangers, and that's the worst mistake that a young child can make. So, strength or madness. Which will it be, child? Make your choice."

The child's cry became an awful, high whistle through the blowhole, a scream so tortured that it ruptured the soft tissues, and a stream of scarlet began to mist out into the air.

"Will you survive this?"

The child tried to strike, but its swings were weak.

I'Masma easily pushed the clawing fists aside.

"Will you stitch together your sanity and become strong Will you grow up to be an assassin? Will you be the one that finally puts an end to me, years from now, in some epic battle yet to be told?"

The young Orcanum began vomiting.

"No. I don't think so. You were raised to play and to cuddle, and this is what you get. Take it away. And clean that pile of gore from my deck."

The Crew Master and the others pulled the screaming whale child to the rail and threw it over the side. They didn't bother to stop and see if it swam away or simply sank. If they had taken a moment, they would have seen it begin to drift, screaming and singing a song of madness, with the currents of its world.

I'Masma walked back to the wheel. The glowing tapestry cloak flowed behind her like a cloud; her legs were long and muscular, the calves wrapped in jeweled boots of leathery skin. Orcanum skin.

She watched as orders were shouted. A squadron of nearly fifty air jellies split off and up, catching the air currents that would float them south.

They were not fast, but they were strong and deadly, and there was no defense against them on this soft planet.

*

CHAPTER THIRTY-NINE

So You Want to Save The World?

"WAKE UP, LITTLE idiot. Do you want to save the world?"

Elise opened her eyes to the fuzzy face of Jules Valiance and the bright morning light of two suns. She stretched and rubbed the sleep from her eyes.

"After I poop."

"Well then, do as you must and make ready for the final absurd, and glorious mission of Les Scaphandriers. I am off for supplies. Food, Orcanum seaweed reefers, wine, and wine. Do you want anything?"

"A pizza."

He smiled and punched her lightly on the shoulder. She smiled back, suddenly feeling a lightness in her heart that hadn't been there when she drifted off into dreams. Jules was already off the deck and into the morning market crowd of Wandering Haven.

Elise went below and began her day.

*

The discussion to save our world took place the night before.

It was a good talk, and like all proper "let's save the world" discussions, it took place under atmospheric darkness lit by unusual means. The human survivors of The Turn had found that phosphorescent worms created wonderful little globes of illumination that looked like living lava lamps. So, as Elise slept, Les Scaphandriers met under the light of the moons, living lava lamps, and golden tallow candle glow.

Their discussion to save the world was long and heated, fueled by wine, passion, courage, and loss.

Notable moments are worth repeating and can be found here, transcribed for your benefit from the French, Guyanese Creole, Mandarin, and German.

"What do we know?"

"The Earth was drained of its ocean, but not all of its waters. How?"

"A particularly large suction hose?"

"An army with buckets?"

"A great sponge."

"The ocean is still there. This is all a dream."

"Nonsense. We saw what happened. We made it happen."

"A glowing hole opened in the floor of the Atlantic Ocean, and the waters were sucked in."

"It would take centuries or more for all of that water to drain through that one little hole."

"Pass the wine."

"Piss off. Get your own."

"How do they make wine here?"

"Sea grapes."

"You're joking."

"Sea grapes."

"Hmm."

"Madame De Laclos and others have told me that there were other portals. There might have been hundreds of holes then. Millions. All opening at the same time."

"Still, what force can create such a suction?"

"Black holes?"

"No, but something with tremendous gravity."

"Blue holes."

"There's no such thing."

"Could it be that the slight difference in gravity and atmospheric pressure between our worlds could be enough to act as a siphon?"

"Spanking good theory. However, it was accomplished, the result was catastrophic for Earth and Orcanum. These creatures had nothing to gain and everything to lose."

"Yes, the holes opened up into Orcanum, and our ocean was brought here in a flash flood the likes of which the universe has never seen."

"So, we are linked. Does Orcanum have the technology to steal our ocean? If so, we are at war!"

"Put a sock in it, Jules. No, these are a primitive people. They haven't even discovered how to harness electricity yet."

"And the temple on the ocean's floor, the cherub with the violin, that was the trigger."

"Somebody wanted us to press the button, and they knew that we would."

"Some entity creates this enigma, this anomaly at the bottom of the Atlantic Ocean, knowing that it would invite exploration. It was a trap."

"A villain!"

"Perhaps. Perhaps we are the villains for pushing the damned button despite the warnings."

"But it's what we do. Are we curious? Of course we are. When does humanity pay attention to warnings?"

"Did someone break wind?"

"Private Splatter, please put your shoes back on. I am offended."

"Go to Hell. I have an infection of the toes."

"An outside party created a massive web of heavy gravity portals designed to drain our oceans into Orcanum, and even now, I believe it is this same fiend that pilots massive bulldozers that are razing Paris. I saw one with my own eyes, and we barely made an escape in the Aquaboggin. It is a wall of black metal, plowing the city with enormous rotating blades, and on the deck, I saw slave humans and Orcanum alike."

"Conquer the Earth by draining her dry, then excavate what remains?"

"Strange times, I grant you."

"Aren't there easier ways to mine for resources?"

"Perhaps not. There wasn't even a war between worlds, so it seems to me that this is the equivalent of conquering a nuclear-armed planet with the push of a button. Or a flush."

"And what do these mysterious invaders excavate that's so precious?"

"I hope to ask them in person at some point. And then kill them with shocking sadism."

"Les Scaphandriers do not kill, and we particularly do not kill with shocking sadism, Zuzu. However, in this case, perhaps we make an exception."

"The portals are still active, then?"

"Yes, at least the one that we triggered. It is through that hole in space that the idiot child and I came to this place."

"Jules, stop calling her an idiot. She is twelve years old and will grow up with a complex."

"I have complexes, and I have achieved more than many noted celebrities and intellectuals."

"Could there be a central control point for these portals?"

"There must be. They are arcane, but they are a mechanism, and there must be a control point."

"So, we need only scour the entire known and maybe even the unknown universe for a reverse switch."

"Are you being sarcastic? I can never tell, Three John. You are indeed inscrutable."

"Yes, I am being sarcastic. How the Hell do we find the reverse switch?"

"Perhaps we need not scour the universe. The Orcanum swim the length, breadth, and depths of their world, and they come to us with shuddered tales of a death ship made of glass that's as tall as a mountain and sails on winds of fear at the top of their northern pole."

"The Orcanum speak in clicks, whale song, and sonar pings. How do you know what they say, shuddered or not?"

"North McAllister is a cunning linguist as you know and has fashioned crude methods of communication through trial and error."

"I've been bitten, piddled on, and thrown into the sea. But now I think I'm onto something."

"Thank you, Ensign McAllister. You are to be commended."

"Is the Aquaboggin fully functional, Jules?"

"Yes."

"And the Orcanum are our allies?"

"To a degree. Some still blame humans for this mess. But if we can show them that we have a common enemy..."

"And they swim this world's ocean by the millions?"

"Yes. With their lands flooded, they have returned to the sea."

"Then if this death ship exists, they should be able to track it, wherever in this ocean it sails."

There was silence for a long moment. The carnival had died down. It was nearly suns up, and the only sound other than the chatter of Les Scaphandriers was the soft lapping of water against the island's wooden floors.

Jules broke the silence.

"I propose an armada of Orcanum scouts search this planet's northern pole. When they find this ship, which I believe to have some link to the end of our world and the deaths of billions, we will launch the Aquaboggin on a kamikaze mission to destroy this goddamned devil and reverse the flow of the portals. We cannot bring the dead back to life, but we can avenge their loss and bring the ocean back to Earth."

Les Scaphandriers put their hands in the center of the wooden table, and their vow, though silent, could be felt like a brand in all of their hearts.

*

CHAPTER FORTY

Make Ready

OLD WICKET AND his partner were the first romantic coupling of Orcanum and human as far as they knew.

There might have been others, but here on the island, they were the first to find common ground in business sensibilities and, ultimately, lonely personal passions. Their romance had been awkward and stumbling, with more than a few moments of "don't touch that," "oops, I'll get a mop," and flustered sonar clicks.

Wicket was a thin fellow with as much meat on his bones as a chicken wing and a tendency to drink, while his Orcanum love, who Wicket had named Flipper as their names were incomprehensible and could not be pronounced by human tongues, was apparently something of a disgraced high priest in whatever odd religion the oceanic beasts observed.

So they had their differences, but they had in common a love of money. It was in the business of business they had found a niche.

The Octo-Thing had been a plaything of some Orcanum children, but a flash of Earth silver had pried him away, and now it was the featured attraction on the northwest side of the Carnival Midway, a musical peculiarity that brought in an astonishing load of trinkets and baubles every single night.

Old Wicket made sure that the Octo-Thing was properly fed

and was given a blanket for warmth in its rusted brass birdcage. The Orcanum found animal tendons that could be used to repair and renew the musical creature's violin and bow. Wicket never concerned himself with where the tendons came from, or whether they came from a willing and able volunteer, or they were pulled with great violence from some innocent. That didn't matter, really.

The Octo-Thing played its fiddle, people paid for the thrill and the laughs, and Old Wicket and his beloved Flipper made plans for a lovely retirement home on the sunny shores of a distant beach, perhaps next to a charming cafe with an ice cream shop.

Well, Wicket made plans; he wasn't entirely sure that Flipper understood him as they cuddled and dreamed. And all of that was on the assumption, of course, that there was a beach somewhere beyond the island. Or ice cream.

Details, after all.

Moonlight shone through the tent tarp onto Wicket and Flipper as they slept in each other's arms on the last night before the destruction of Wandering Haven.

Even if Old Wicket had been awake, he might not have noticed the black nylon rope that slowly descended from the center top of the tent, directly above the rusted cage of the Octo-Thing. Certainly, in the depths of slumber, Wicket didn't see the shadows moving along outside of their shelter slash theater. He didn't hear a softly cursed "merde" when the nylon rope slipped and dropped too quickly, smacking the top of the cage and rattling the bars. He didn't see the green eyes, white dreadlocks, and bulbous nose thrust in through the hole at the top of the tent, and even if he and Flipper had come awake, there wasn't much they could have done about the figure that shimmied down the line to the cage.

You see, Old Wicket and Flipper never noticed or bothered to care if the Octo-Thing was happy or sad, but Jules Valiance did, and Jules Valiance was a man of his word.

Jules carefully opened the cage and stared into the sorrowful eyes of the Octo-Thing, eyes that showed fear, then surprise, then something more.

A glint of hope, perhaps.

It clutched its violin and slithered out of the cage door.

The Octo-Thing wrapped its strange arms and feet and hands around Jules as he ascended the rope and stole him safely away into the night.

*

The rescue operation of the Octo-Thing was the final beat of their week-long preparation scheme.

Jules had made leaps and bounds in mastering the language of the Orcanum, spurred on by desperation and his unusually deviated septum, a physical deformity that allowed him to come close indeed to mimicking the clicks and bleats of the alien cetaceans. He had shared their plan with the old beast that was apparently in some sort of leadership role, and word was spread throughout the Orcanum that hope was never closer.

By the thousands, they had taken to the ocean, communicating over vast distances, searching for any sign of the mechanism that had caused such death and devastation.

It had only taken three days for a pod of Orcanum, swimming in the frigid waters of the planet's northern pole, to sight the massive sailing ship sheltered in the shadows of the volcano, the Peak of Ebon.

Word of the find made its way back to Jules and his team within a day, relayed from pod to pod.

The Aquaboggin had been made ready or as ready as could be, considering there was no additional ammunition or weaponry or fuel on the island. Les Scaphandriers stocked her with water and food.

Elise had been bored out of her mind at first but had taken one morning to playing with a few of the Orcanum children. She sensed that they were younger, or certainly less mature than she was, but soon found that their simple games of tag or stickball were more fun than she had allowed herself to have in a long time.

At first glance, they were all the same. Black and white, with those sharp eyes, sharper teeth, and smooth muscular flesh. Elise began to grow accustomed to them, though, and their differences became obvious.

This one thinner, this one thicker, the saddle patch patterns wildly different, the personalities as varied as a human's.

She was chasing two of the smallest Orcanum when she heard the sharp whir of helicopter rotors. Elise cut the chase and raced to the dock.

The Aquaboggin was in autogyro mode. She rested in the gentle sea just off of the dock, her propellers a blur against the morning suns. Three John was carrying a sack of something and making his way along the deck and into the hatch.

They're leaving without me? Her blood was up. She was angry and hurt. Elise ran to the sub as quickly as her legs could carry her.

The wind from the propellers whipped her face and hair as she stood at the end of the dock. The Aquaboggin was a dozen meters away and drifting. They were preparing to launch.

She screamed as loudly as she could, but her voice was lost in the rising noise of the blades.

Elise was so angry that she could spit.

After everything she had done and seen, they were leaving her without so much as a goodbye. Her bag was on that ship. She hadn't even buried her friend, the crab, and his frozen body rested in the cold storage.

This was wrong. This was insulting and wrong. She did the only thing that she could think to do at that moment. Elise dove into the water and swam toward the ship.

*

"Here she comes. Damned strong swimmer, that one," said Zuzu, looking through the starboard viewport next to her seat.

"You should let her come along, Jules. There's nothing for her on that island," said North McAllister.

"Strikes me as a fighter. Small, but a fighter," added Three John.

Jules sat in the pilot's chair and jockeyed the stick so that the Aquaboggin would be a bit further away from the island before launching into flight mode.

"Elise is a treasure, my friends. She is courageous and smart and good of heart. She has seen enough horror for a lifetime. If we succeed, we will return and ferry her like a champion back home. If we do not, she can live a life of simple things here on the island. I will not expose her to the awful things that we might need to do."

Jules began a visual inspection of the cockpit's control panel, making sure that all was in order. Private Splatter sat in the co-pilot's seat, and he eyed Jules with furrowed red brows.

"Soundtrack?" Splatter asked.

Jules considered activating the ship's entertainment system. While most of the Aquaboggin technology had kept pace with the times, Jules had steadfastly refused to replace his custom sound system. His collection of compact discs was vast, and he had no patience for digital this or cloud-based that. For launch into missions of extreme danger, he often chose a club mix of Bollywood show tunes that he had created for just such an occasion. This time, though, he looked back toward the rear of the Aquaboggin. There sat the Octo-Thing, buckled into one of the port seats. It held its little fiddle. Jules smiled at the creature and nodded, hoping that it would understand.

The strings of the bow touched the violin, and the Octo-Thing began to play a melody for their launch. The song was soft and slow, but the eyes of the Octo-Thing were happy.

Jules was lost in the song for a long moment.

What a wonderful musician for a cephalopod, he thought.

A tapping sound on the forward glass.

Jules looked up.

"Merde," he said.

"Zuzu was right; she's a good swimmer," said Splatter.

Elise floated in front of them. She rapped on the view glass again, harder this time. Her little fists made a soft thumping sound.

She made an angry gesture at Jules that was either a vulgar obscenity or a declaration that she was indeed "number one."

"Can't take off with her clinging to the ship, Jules," said Three John.

"Right. Zuzu, go peel the little idiot off of the viewing glass and toss her far enough away so that we can quickly launch," ordered Jules.

Zuzu started to say something. It was going to be a protest, an argument that the child should be allowed to come with them.

The explosive wave that flipped the ship interrupted her.

Shouts and noise from Les Scaphandriers. The music stopped as the Octo-Thing lost its grip on the instrument. Jules instinctively cut the engines. The autogyro blades weren't designed to work underwater. The girl. Damn.

His heart leaped. The blades were still spinning, they had been tossed upside down, and Elise was outside the ship.

Jules raced to the hatch, gripping seats as the ship righted itself. What the Hell?

He popped the hatch and clambered out onto the deck, followed by Three John.

Screams and sounds of destruction.

"Mon Dieu," said Jules.

Three John raised his pistol and fired at the colossal air jelly floating above them. The tentacles whipped the air around them then fixed on the hull of the sub. The bullets didn't do anything. The jelly began to rise into the sky, and the bow of the Aquaboggin lifted up and out of the water. Jules and Three John reached for the steel rails that ran the length of the deck and held on for life.

"Elise!" shouted Jules. Where was the girl?

More jellies, each as big as a bus, dozens of them, swarmed the skies over Wandering Haven. They were swooping and soaring, tentacles lifting screaming humans and Orcanum, ripping tarps and tearing wooden planks from the deck of the island.

"Elise!"

The air jelly above them descended, tentacles reaching for Three John. Zuzu popped her head out of the hatch, saw the chaos, and emerged with her knife.

She sliced at the tentacles that were lifting the ship's bow out of the water. The flesh was thick but easily cut, and the Aquaboggin fell free with a thunderous splash that knocked Three John into the water. Jules dangled from the side of the ship, one hand on a railing, eyes scanning the water for Elise.

He felt something grab his ankle. His blood went cold, and he reached for his dive knife.

Fingers? Feels like fingers.

Elise had him by the calf and was climbing up his leg.

He reached down with his free hand and snatched her up by the back of her Scaphandrier vest. With every bit of strength he had in his old body, he tossed Elise onto the deck and then followed, out of breath.

She punched him in the stomach, and he made a little "oof" noise.

"You left me!"

Jules couldn't speak. Zuzu took Elise by the hand and led her toward the hatch.

"Yes, and now we are under attack by an army of these giant floating monsters, so let's discuss this once we're inside of the sub," she said.

Elise turned and looked out to Wandering Haven.

The floating wooden city was being destroyed.

The people, the children, being dragged into the sky by creatures from a nightmare. The little shacks and huts and alleys exploding into sticks no bigger than kindling, fires erupting from candles and torches, everything dying.

Everything was dying.

*

CHAPTER FORTY-ONE

Choices

"WE DIVE. BUCKLE for safety," Jules said.

He dropped into the pilot's seat and grabbed the stick.

Three John towered over him in the small cabin. His eyes were anything but inscrutable. The Guyanese enigma was angry.

"No. This place has been our home for ten long years. These are our friends. We're not leaving them. We stay and fight."

Splatter flipped a switch and the rotor blades recessed.

Jules looked up at Three John.

"We defend them by going to the source of the flood, my friend," he said.

Zuzu shoved Elise into the seat behind Jules and clicked her safety belt into place.

"He's right, John."

"No, he's not," said Three John, and with that, the tall Scaphandrier climbed out of the sub and ran to the deck. He had a dive knife in one hand and his pistol in the other. He barely made a splash when he hit the water and began swimming back to the dock of Wandering Haven.

"Can't leave him behind, Jules," said North McAllister.

"Yes, we can. He's being a fool," answered Zuzu.

Elise watched the destruction of the island through the forward viewing glass until the sub descended and a wall of water replaced the horrible scene. The jellies, glistening blobs of purple and blue, hovered over the shantytown, ripping and tearing everything in their path with those long stinging tentacles.

She could see humans and Orcanum lifted screaming into the sky. Once inside the sub, she might have felt removed from the violence, as if the death was something she was watching on an old television show, but these were people and things she had known, if only for a short time, and the horror stayed real for her, sickening and real.

The sound of the sub's engines and the rush of the ocean drowned the cries of the dying as they descended.

"Three John is right. You can't just leave," Elise said.

"We help by doing what we must, and what we must do is travel north," Jules responded. His right hand shoved a throttle forward. They were pushed back into their seats as the vessel accelerated.

"They're dying. He's going to die too."

"Yes, and if we die trying to save them, we've wasted everything."

"You're afraid. You're a coward."

"Be still, Elise."

"No. You're a coward. You're all cowards. I hate you. I hate all of you."

"We must make choices, Elise," said Zuzu.

"So choose to help them. They're the last people, and they're dying. If you don't save them, then what good are you?"

Jules almost responded with an angry rant about the sacrifices they all must make, about the needs of the many outweighing the needs of the few.

He almost said all of that, but the logic of a young girl is as sharp as a surgeon's scalpel, and the weight of her look of disappointment could crush the strongest argument as a hammer smashes a nut.

"Valiance," said Private Splatter, "we are low on fuel. Once we're out of ammo, we're done. We can't waste any of it."

Jules pulled back on the stick, and the Aquaboggin began to rise. He flipped a switch, and the rotor blades popped out of their housings and began to spin.

Splatter shook his head and sank back into his seat.

"We won't waste anything, monsieur," Jules said.

The sub shot out of the water, lifted into the sky, and turned back toward Wandering Haven.

"Now you're talking," said McAllister.

Elise looked out of the side viewport.

"Oh," she said quietly.

The water was alive with Orcanum, hundreds of them swimming and porpoising toward the island. She could see that it was an army of the creatures, warriors, carrying swords and spears and other weapons. An Orcanum army had come up from the depths and from the sea all around and was rallying around the island.

"Hold on," Jules said, rather needlessly, as he put the sub into a tight spin, forward guns firing.

The bullets shot out of the guns in a thin stream, every tenth a tracer, so that the fire looked almost like laser beams from a science fiction film. Three air jellies caught in the strafe exploded into a mist of purple and blue that smeared the forward glass as they flew through.

Elise's stomach dropped and twisted as Jules piloted the Aquaboggin through the floating minefield of air jellies. Below them, she could see the Orcanum warriors were flooding onto the streets to defend the island.

She had argued to stay, and now she was terrified beyond anything she had ever known.

*

In the beginning, he had seen the humans that had been swept through the portals onto Orcanum as enemies to be destroyed. He killed a few of them before realizing they were victims, much like his people, and their world had fallen as well.

Then, he had encountered strange creatures that were alien to his world, and he had found an enemy for he and his legion to hunt.

He was Try-Ton, and he had been the mightiest warrior in the King's army until their world had flooded and civilization was lost. He had spent the past ten years searching for survivors, helping to build their floating islands from what driftwood and debris he could find, and hoping that someday he would have the chance to meet the thing that was responsible for the death of his world.

The quiver on his armored back carried a dozen spears, each made of the hardest driftwood and tipped with bone points so sharp that they could pierce the hide of a sealephant. He was down to his last spear, now, but the others had found homes in the flesh of these monstrous floating jellyfish.

It felt good in his hand as he raised and aimed at another one of the purple beasts. His legion was a thousand Orcanum warriors strong, and when this spear flew, he would scavenge for more in the carcasses of the dead jellies, and he would resume the fight until this island, his people and humans alike, were defended, or he was dead.

A tall, dark human stood at his side, wielding only a small blade and a little weapon that spat metal and made noise. The human was strong and determined. There were three long and faded scars on the human's face.

This must be a warrior of the race, thought Try-Ton.

They smiled at each other and fought on.

The Orcanum didn't write. Their legends, stories, and history were preserved in song, in their communal memories. There had been many wars in their past and many battles that had become epic tales that would take days to tell. After a hunt, over the communal fire pits, as the stars rose and the children lay down for sleep, the stories of their great history were shared by the Story Keepers and Mystics. No, the Orcanum didn't write, but they preserved their history with extraordinary care and grace, and as Try-Ton fought, he knew that whatever the outcome, this day would live on.

The strange human airship fired its tiny metal stings, the Orcanum brought down a score of jellies with their spears, and the tall, dark human Try-Ton would come to know as Three John killed a dozen or more in courageous battle before he fell.

Try-Ton saw the jelly take Three John up in its tentacles.

He saw the airship dive into the body of the jelly, trying desperately to stop it but failing in the attempt.

The dark human warrior was dead from the tentacle stings before he fell to the ground under the body of the creature that his companions had slain.

*

Three John, but of course that wasn't his real name, was born to a family who worked in the lumber fields of Guyana. He had two sisters and four brothers, and he had been nearly killed by a jaguar while saving his mother when he was only nine years old. Three John had been bullied because of his scarred face and his strange ways, so he had learned to fight. Then he had learned to learn. His mother loved books, and she shared these slender paperbacks with her son, these wild stories of adventure and mystery. When he read, his spirit soared, and that spirit carried him to University and beyond, to a research vessel where he first met Les Scaphandriers as they plucked pearls from the mysterious oyster squid of the hidden Arctic Sea. His mother's spirit had always lifted his, and Three John's spirit of adventure had carried him to other worlds. His knife was gone, and the chamber in his revolver was empty, but Three John smiled widely as he looked up at the air jelly that was killing him. He was soaring once more, flying above and beyond, to worlds below and between, as his mother had always dreamed. Yes, there was pain, but as his eyes closed for the last time, the spirit of Three John, the Guyanese enigma, soared on into his most wonderful adventure yet.

*

Try-Ton fought on for hours, as did his warrior armada and the strangely dressed humans from the peculiar flying vessel. They fought for their home, for their world, and for their friends who died.

And so, by the rise of the morning sun, the tide was turned.

The creatures from the sky were dead.

Try-Ton knew that the battle of Wandering Haven would be told again in song, down through the years.

He and his elite warriors watched respectfully as the humans bid farewell to their friend after the setting of the suns. The one known as Valiance led them as they set the warrior Three John adrift on a small pyre of wood, and that was then set ablaze in a glorious and fiery funeral. They said words that he did not understand and watched the fire drift into the darkness until it sank and disappeared.

This warrior funeral at sea by fire was new to Try-Ton, but he found it good and fitting.

There was a human child with them, a female with hair the color of sunlight and big, bright eyes. Try-Ton made a point to greet the child, as it had shown signs of courage during the aftermath of the battle when fires and screaming still reigned and the bodies of the dead were being sorted. She was an unusual child, this human, and Try-Ton stood before her with his arms crossed over his chest and head slightly bowed. He dropped to a knee and hoped that the child understood this gesture as respect.

She bowed her head as well, and with a smile, touched him on the shoulder with tiny pink fingers.

"I'm Elise St. Jacques. Thank you," she said.

He rose and smiled.

This was a strong human child, and he wished her a future full of whatever good things humans might desire.

Later that evening, over the warmth of a victory fire and drinks that inspired Orcanum and humans alike, the one known as Valiance told Try-Ton of an evil ship at the top of the world.

*

CHAPTER FORTY-TWO

To the North

ELISE SLEPT.

The soft ticking of the submarine's instruments were her lullaby, and the gentle rocking of the ship as she carved the water just below the waves comforted her as she dreamed. In slumber, she couldn't smell the sour stink of the unbathed Scaphandriers; she wasn't annoyed by Private Splatter's bad jokes or by the constant arguments between Jules and North McAllister about strategy. Eyes closed and mind detached, she didn't sense the sadness from the others at the loss of their friend, the Guyanese mystery they called Three John. When in dreams, Elise could just drift without care or fear, and sometimes, the dreams even welcomed visions of her Dad. He would be there, a voice mostly, a deep and warm voice, and she didn't even know what he was saying, but it was comforting and good.

Elise slept long and hard for great chunks of the first three days of their voyage, even though the seat didn't recline and the pillow was a rough bundle of her dirty clothes because sleep repairs damage and the things that she had seen were jagged cuts and deep wounds. She was a kid, and if she lived in a perfect house on a perfect street back home with her Dad, she would still sleep more than you or me because all children do. Every experience is new to a child, every emotion closer to the surface, every injury deeper and more raw. Kids sleep long hours because they must, and so Elise slept to close her wounds.

"Little idiot," came a voice, waking her, "you should not miss this."

She stretched, grumbled, and opened her eyes.

Jules was at the helm in the seat in front of her, and he was pointing to the forward viewing glass.

"Look."

The sea was dark. She didn't know if it was night or early morning. Through the deep blue of the ocean before them, she saw dozens of little lights glowing like fireflies. Elise unsnapped her safety belt and moved next to Jules so that she was closer to the glass.

"Oh wow," she said.

The little lights were in a swarm that parted and danced away as the sub moved through them. As they passed, the glowing creatures were so close to the glass that Elise could clearly see them.

"Sea monkey larvae," said Jules.

North McAllister was in the co-pilot chair, and he stared at the glowing swarm with wide eyes. Zuzu and the others were glued to their observation windows port and starboard.

"They're beautiful," said Elise.

The tiny sea monkeys were no bigger than your thumb, with frilly backs and curly tails and big round eyes. They were little living light bulbs that frolicked and played as they passed. One of them was clinging to the glass directly in front of Elise, its tiny arms and legs spread wide to hold on, and it stared in at her as if it was curious or amused.

Elise laughed. If this was still her dream, it was a good one.

The baby sea monkey released the glass and drifted off with its kin, spinning as it went.

Jules was lit by the golden light of the instrument panel.

Elise looked at him closely. His smile was wide, his mouth

half-open, and there was a single tear running down his cheek from eyes that brimmed with joy.

She saw him as if it was the first time, a child just like her.

"Such absurdity," he said under his breath, so quietly that only Elise could hear.

And then the swarm of glowing sea monkey larvae were gone, and the sea became blue-black once again.

"Are we there yet?" Elise asked with just a trace of comedic awareness.

Jules shook his head negative.

"Who's to say?"

Elise looked at the instrument panel. She knew it fairly well now, which button did what and which switch did which. The round sonar screen showed a blue dot at their location, center, and off to either side were bright yellow masses.

The armada of the Orcanum swam hundreds of meters away to their port and starboard, keeping pace with the slow voyage of the Aquaboggin.

The battle of Wandering Haven had saved hundreds of lives, Orcanum and human alike, but it had come at the cost of their ammunition and fuel. The flight to the Northern Pole was now a slow sail just below the surface of the sea.

They had some fuel for flight, but that was being saved should it be needed.

And so, Elise and Les Scaphandriers voyaged on for day after day, escorted by an ever-growing armada of Orcanum warriors that would soon be the largest that this world had ever seen.

*

CHAPTER FORTY-THREE

The Old One in a Jar

I'MASMA'S TALL BOOTS echoed and clicked as she walked the translucent glowing halls of the ship.

The walls were the green of distant seas and glass smooth, and she traced a slender hand along its surface as she moved. Buried within the glass were seemingly infinite bundles of wire and cable, tiny devices and metallic vials, and each of these pulsed and quivered as if they were alive, which in a way, they were because that was the point of it all.

Her skin was alive with wire and organic metal as well, the electronic detritus of lost worlds replaced flesh she had lost through the eons so that I'Masma was made beautiful and whole from the stolen waste of a dozen civilizations.

And make no mistake, she was beautiful beyond imagination.

You would think, wouldn't you, that a creature born from an eternity of torture and re-birth would be a twisted thing, a disgusting troll or foul lurching mound of ugliness. But that would equate beauty with goodness of character, and as I'm sure you know, that isn't always the case.

A trio of crew dressed in leather rags bowed and whispered as I'Masma passed, then scuttled off to continue whatever duties they were to attend. One of the three was human, thin and filthy, while the other two were yellowed humanoids from some other place and time, creatures that had been caught up in the mix, as it were.

The crew of the Ship of Dreams came from worlds below and between, worlds that had been razed and harvested by I'Masma and The Rolling Deep over many years. To the point, they were survivor slaves that had lost all hope and now lived only to serve.

Several species, now all surviving together, Humans and Orcanum and sea monkeys and more. They had survived the loss of their world's waters and had been wise or dim or cowardly or frightened enough to join rather than resist.

When portals opened up on a new, fresh world, when the Shock Tide drained the ocean, there were always survivors. They had never been a problem. Earth had been the most advanced civilization that I'Masma and the Ship of Dreams had harvested, and there had been almost no resistance worth mentioning. The humans had caved quickly.

Apparently, the sudden loss of your world's sea was always enough to demoralize you.

Once the portals opened and the ocean drained, the Razor Ships could enter and reap the electronic constructs and mechanical contraptions. The strongest of the survivor slaves captained the Razor Ships and were paid in power, food, pleasures, or in the survival of their loved ones. The detritus was then delivered to the ship through the portals to be used as food, to be transformed into new life, to power The Shock Tide.

Quite a simple thing, really, but the power that was required, oh that was a different matter entirely.

I'Masma's pace quickened as she went deeper and deeper into the belly of the ship. The glow of the green glass halls grew more vibrant as she descended. A deep, throbbing hum could be felt vibrating from the deck.

She came to an emerald portal. I'Masma spun the large metal lock. It opened, and she stepped inside the heart of her vessel.

A chamber, a cavern of emerald glass ten meters tall and a full twenty wide. A hum like a scream. Living, writhing cables of what had once been rubber and copper, hundreds of them, spilling up from the deck at the center of the chamber and running into a glass tank coruscating with electrical energy.

There was a creature inside of the tank, tentacled and horrible in its formless mass, five meters high with its single reptilian eye open in terror and a beaked mouth held wide in an eternal scream.

I'Masma stood before this strange and ancient creature, her lithe form in silhouette against the light from its holding tank.

The Ship of Dreams needed lots of power, so the cables at her heart ran deep into the molten depths of the Volcano of Ebon, sucked up the limitless energy of Orcanum and fed that power back into the ship.

The portals of space that drained oceans, the engines that could sail The Ship of Dreams across the galaxy through these holes in reality, the colossal storage batteries that drove the Razors to harvest entire planets, all of these things were fueled by the energy at the heart of conquered worlds like Orcanum.

And even more than that, I'Masma and The Shock Tide needed lots of power because this creature of eternal scream was an Old One from the universe past, the last of The Ones Before, and only energy beyond imagination could hold this ancient thing as a slave.

I'Masma smiled and tapped on the glass cage.

The Old One didn't respond. It wouldn't. It never did.

This thing that was there at the birth of this universe fourteen billion years ago was frozen in pain, and now it served one single purpose. The Ones Before had the power to open holes between worlds, and this was the last of its kind. These ancient gods could unmake the fabric of the universe, warp it, transform it at their pleasure.

That's why The Old One had been captured, and that's why

it was housed in its glass prison, connected to tubes that kept it harnessed, asleep and dreaming.

"The world called Earth is almost harvested, my old friend. Soon, we're on to the next," whispered I'Masma.

The room was lit by the green internal light of the star glass, but now darkness crept in from the edges, just out of sight, a skittering of shadow in the corners.

The shadows had many eyes and teeth like knitting needles.

The Men of Many Eyes crouched and skulked in the corners of the room.

I'Masma lightly kissed the glass as close to the open maw of the Old One as possible.

"New worlds are waiting."

*

CHAPTER FORTY-FOUR

Apparently, There's a Plan

THE AQUABOGGIN SURFACED from a calm blue sea under the fading light of twin suns.

A swarm of flying shrimp skittered across the surface, startled by the sub.

Elise looked out through the forward viewport as the waters receded.

The Volcano of Ebon towered before them. Elise had seen mountains, but none like this, not an ebony monolith that jutted out of the sea like a giant black hand that held the fires of creation in its palm.

"What we're seeing is just the top ten thousand meters. Sonar indicates that this volcano extends twenty thousand meters below the surface.

This thing is ten times more massive than Everest," said Private Splatter.

"That volcano's power is beyond imagination," said Jules.

Dark smoke billowed up from the caldera of the volcanic mountain and disappeared into the sky. Pulsing rivulets of liquid rock spat out and leaked down from above, streaking the obsidian sides of the black tower in fire. At the base of the mountain where stone met the sea, Ebon opened up into a vast lagoon sheltered on either side by walls of black.

The two suns of Orcanum were on the decline, their light a rich amber as they sank toward the horizon.

Elise pointed.

"Is that a pirate ship?"

Jules engaged the active view screen and zoomed in.

"Idiot child, this is not some cheap Hollywood popcorn thriller with zombie pirates and..." Jules stopped himself as the ship came into view on the screen.

"Ooh. I stand corrected."

They stared in awe at the enormous jade glass hull intricately laced with wire, copper, and steel, at the billowing gold tapestry sails that gleamed as if they were alive, and the hundred-meter masts of the Ship of Dreams. The vessel sat in the heart of the volcanic lagoon, protected on either side and above by the mountain and the roaring, molten volcano. Enormous pipes towered at the rear deck of the ship, and black cables as thick as rail tunnels snaked out from the pipes and descended into the water below. Steam leaked and billowed from the pipes and cables as if they were carrying a cargo of impossible heat from the heart of the volcano into the ship itself. Figures dressed in leather and rags patrolled the deck.

Great metal cannons protruded from the port and starboard hull. A host of the deadly air jellies hovered in the sky above the ship as if on guard.

"A warship of luminous emerald, larger than the mightiest destroyer in the French fleet, protected by man-eating flying jellyfish monsters. Strange times."

"It looks to be connected to the volcano as if they're using it as a power source."

"We're supposed to destroy that? With what? Insults?"

Elise manipulated the view screen and zoomed in here and there on the deck of the ship. There were humans, Orcanum, and other races that she'd never seen, dozens of them, and they all looked filthy, desperate, and dangerous.

She zoomed in on the tapestry sails. They were ornate, beautiful, intricate, with strange writing and figures in gold on a vast canvas of deep blue and purest white. There was something about the sails that seemed familiar to Elise. She couldn't place it, but there was something about the sails that seemed like something from another time, another life.

"I know that from somewhere, those sails, I know them," she whispered to herself.

She trained the camera higher. A single, angry sea monkey chattered and crouched on the top of the center mast. It was holding a spyglass and scanning the sea.

"A belligerent sea monkey on the lookout. That won't do," said Jules.

He activated the Aquaboggin exterior speakers and hoped that his message to hold position would reach the Orcanum armada that flanked them. He emitted a series of clicks, moans, and burps, a warning broadcast into the sea at high volume that they should submerge and stay out of sight. Or, if his crude Orcanum was off by a bit, he had just invited their mothers for tea and a massage.

"Submerge, Private Splatter. I have a scheme," said Jules Valiance. "Lovely."

The sub descended just below the waves.

Jules motioned for Les Scaphandriers to gather round.

Elise joined them, squeezed between Zuzu and Splatter.

"Let us count our blessings," Jules said, "there are four sets of mining charges onboard, each with shocking destructive power. We also have four of the personal, high-speed aqua sleds and corresponding dive gear. There is enough fuel in the Aquaboggin to sustain one high-speed flight, while there is ammunition enough for one, perhaps two, strafing runs. We have knives, two loaded pistols, a musical Octo-Thing, three rubber ducks filled with anesthetic powder, an armada of enraged and heavily armed Orcanum warriors, a delta wing kite with five hundred feet of nylon line and aluminum wench system, a carton of ten-year-old cigarettes, water-skis, and the least profound of our remaining wines. Have I forgotten anything?"

"Can I have a gun, too?" asked Elise.

Jules looked at her with a mixture of amusement and sadness.

"Oh, little one, I don't think that's a good idea."

"Give her a gun, you fool. We're all going to die anyway," Zuzu said. North McAllister laughed.

"Your logic is strong." Jules handed one of the pistols to Elise. He fixed her with a stern look that made her want to laugh, but she resisted the temptation and remained quite serious.

"The safety is there. Click it, and you can fire the gun. There are six bullets in the chamber, and the trigger is more sensitive than Private Splatter's toes, so take great care."

"Got it."

"I said take great care. Do you promise?"

"I promise, okay?"

"Secure the weapon in your vest holster. Safety on, please. When you fire, the gun will kick in your hand. Hold steady. Aim for the body, not the head."

"What if it's a zombie? What if it doesn't have a body? What if it's just a head?"

"These are good points. Use your best judgment."

There was a thunderous pounding on the starboard viewport.

Zuzu jumped, McAllister cursed, and Jules ran to the glass to see what was happening.

Try-Ton stared at him from outside of the sub, floating in the clear seawater. The Orcanum warrior pounded again on the sub. Jules motioned for the warrior to wait a moment and then began deeply gulping air, forcing it into his lungs. Zuzu moved to the rear of the sub and manipulated switches and twisted little metal wheels.

"Airlock, please," said Jules between deep breaths.

He stripped away his clothing.

"Oh gross," said Elise, shielding her eyes from the sight of hairy old man butt.

Within moments Jules was sporting the red, blue, and white wetsuit of Les Scaphandriers. No dive mask, no scuba gear, and no time. He slipped into the tiny airlock. Water poured into the chamber, the hatch opened, and Jules Valiance, lungs charged to capacity, swam out to meet Try-Ton.

The Orcanum warrior was massive and graceful in the ocean environment. Jules floating across from him and displayed a certain amount of grace as well. He motioned that they should swim to the surface and led the way.

Their heads popped up from the cold water, and Jules felt the warmth of the twin suns touch his brow. The salt air smelled sweet. Jules loved that smell.

Try-Ton stared at him, unsure of what to make of this strange human.

Jules clicked and burped and sang, his best effort at communicating a basic plan. Try-Ton reared back as if to strike Jules.

"Oh, what did I say?"

Try-Ton stopped and smiled, showing rows of conical teeth.

"Ah, amusing. So, I have a plan. Give us until the suns disappear below the horizon, then attack with all of your force. We will have a chance, my friend. We will have a good, courageous, and unlikely chance."

Of course, that's not what Try-Ton heard at all, but the intent was there.

To the Orcanum warrior, Jules had actually said, "Two babies farting. I will win. Go when dark and eggs drop flat magic. All of us frolic. All of us frolic unafraid and with vigor."

Not bad, considering, and Jules would still have been pleased at his quick but rudimentary understanding of the Orcanum tongue. Whatever the case, Try-Ton understood.

Try-Ton considered Jules Valiance for a moment, this frail, pink creature from a world called Earth. The old human was no warrior, but their flying vessel was a weapon mightier than any on Orcanum, a surprise tactic that might give them all an edge against the massive green warship. The Orcanum warrior had his own plans for success, but what a distraction a flying weapon would make.

So for that, Try-Ton would risk everything.

Try-Ton nodded at Jules and disappeared into the waves.

Jules took a deep breath and dived back to the Aquaboggin.

This was suicide, he thought. Ridiculous suicide.

But still, it will be memorable.

*

CHAPTER FORTY-FIVE

Raid on The Ship of Dreams

PRIVATE SPLATTER WAS born Philipe Devilliers to wealthy parents on sunny Cap Ferrat in the French Riviera.

He had learned to water-ski at an early age, as glamorous aqua sport was an iconic part of life on the Mediterranean. Sir Mick Jagger had even given young Philipe a few slalom pointers and a snifter of cognac one delightful afternoon during a break in the recording of "Exile on Main Street." Water-skiing wasn't enough for the thrill-seeking little red-head, though, and soon, inspired by photographs he had seen in magazines of daredevils performing stunts at Cypress Gardens in Florida, he experimented with flat kites towed by boats that would send him a hundred meters into the air attached to a line, where he could smell the salt breeze and observe beautiful girls sunning themselves on the shores of Villefranche-Sur-Mer.

The simple flat kites soon became complex Delta Wing Gliders that could catch air currents and propel little Philipe into the blue sky like a ginger Icarus. He was the spotty Superboy of the Azure Coast, Philipe the Impossible, a flying fireball of ego and daring that inspired postcards and the dreams of teenage girls.

And that's why Private Splatter was chosen to strap into Les Scaphandrier's bright white hang glider and soar on a terrifying mission that would undoubtedly end with him living up to his nickname.

The Aquaboggin surfaced. There was no other way to begin the flight of the hang glider. If they were seen, they were seen.

The kite was stored in a long tube that ran along the port deck. Jules retrieved it, beginning the process of assembling and unpacking. Zuzu fetched the heavy aluminum wench and a thick spool of nylon line. Hopping onto the deck, she began wrenching the contraption to pre-set connectors at the rear of the sub. The long kite was pulled out onto the deck then, and Private Splatter made quick work of extending the wide wings and checking the sailcloth and battens.

Elise sat in the co-pilot seat, staring at the active view screen, zoomed in on the sea monkey. If it made any sign that it had spotted them, she was to shout as loudly as she could.

The kite was assembled and tethered to the nylon line.

Splatter donned a lightweight dive helmet and a combination scuba tank/jet pack that could propel him through the sea at surprising speed, if necessary.

His trusty shotgun was strapped to a sleeve on his chest, and his bushy beard poked out from under the helmet like a rusty broom.

Jules patted his friend on the shoulder and smiled.

"Bon chance, mon ami."

Splatter glared at Jules.

"I'm dead."

"Probably, yes."

Splatter made a rude gesture at Jules Valiance.

"Then let's do this."

Elise called to them from below deck.

Jules and Zuzu scrambled back down into the sub, Valiance dropping into the pilot seat.

"The monkey," said Elise, pointing at the screen.

The sea monkey was jumping up and down on the top of the mast and pointing at them. They couldn't hear it, but all of them assumed a great deal of sea monkey chattering was going on.

"Off we go," said Jules. He activated the jet engines of the submarine. The hatch closed. Throttle down.

Private Splatter stood at the aft of the deck, the kite strapped to his back like four-meter-wide bat wings. His knees buckled slightly as the sub accelerated.

Jules punched a button on the control console. The Octo-Thing began to play a jaunty tune on its little violin.

A clip on the aluminum wench dropped. Splatter shifted the inclination of the kite, and the wind caught him. The sub continued to accelerate towards the Volcano of Ebon and the monstrous Ship of Dreams.

At speed and with the wind, Private Splatter lifted off of the deck and soared into the sky. The nylon line was attached to a harness near his waist, and it was playing out like a fishing line with a bluefin tuna on the hook.

North McAllister watched the old man ascend from the open bow hatch. A cigarette hung from his lips, and he kept his eyes locked on Private Splatter, periodically checking the wench and the line as well.

Warm wind lashed Splatter in the face. It felt good. He felt young again, a Superboy flying above the Riviera. Up and up, he rose as the line played out. The Aquaboggin diminished below him. From here, he could see so much. The clear waters of the Orcanum sea. The looming vastness of the Volcano of Ebon. The fast-approaching warship and its strangely tapestried sails; its tentacle tubes stretching out into the depths below, presumably into the heart of the volcano itself.

Where were the warriors? Splatter scanned right and left. His eyes weren't as good as they once were, but they weren't terrible either.

The Orcanum warriors should have been hiding, yes, but visible just the same from this great height. They should have been a commotion in the clear water, a shadow of movement beneath the waves, they should have been something, but they weren't.

The water was clear as far as Splatter could see.

Had they fled? Where the Hell were they?

No time for that. I've things to do, he thought. The line was played out, and Splatter was nearly two hundred meters above the surface. Time for the signal.

He crossed and uncrossed his bandy old legs.

North McAllister saw the strange kicking maneuver.

"The signal!" he shouted loudly so that those in the sub could hear.

"He has achieved release," Jules murmured.

Private Splatter triggered a catch on his vest, and the nylon line popped free.

McAllister watched as the long rope gently dropped and Private Splatter's kite flew free, untethered, catching the currents of the wind.

He scrambled over to the wench and cut the line. Won't need that again.

Far above the ocean, Splatter was now in control of his flight. He dismissed his search for the Orcanum warriors. There was only one job now, and that was to stay alive as long as possible so that the fool Valiance could attempt his ridiculous scheme.

"Into the ski sleds," Jules said. Zuzu and McAllister worked quickly, strapping themselves into the little portable jet packs no bigger than a scuba tank. They swapped their shoes for fins and secured dive knives to their thighs and explosive charges to their bellies.

The Aquaboggin was running just above the surface.

Valiance dropped the hatch, and the sub descended, increasing speed. He pushed the throttle as hard as he could. Ten knots. Twenty.

The engines hummed, and Elise could feel the vibration of their strain against the hull.

"Watches?"

"Synchronized."

"The charges will detonate in twenty minutes."

Zuzu and McAllister entered the airlock. They gave Jules a thumbs up. He twisted a wheel, and the air was sucked out of the lock.

Seawater rushed in.

The hatch opened, and the two Scaphandriers pushed out into the blue in an explosion of bubbles.

Once in the water, they activated their ski sleds.

Small jets kicked in. Zuzu and McAllister grabbed the control tethers and made themselves as hydrodynamic as possible. The ski sleds were self-contained underwater jet packs that had enough thrust for five kilometers at high speed. The two divers could feel the force of the water against their masks, digging into their skin, as they shot forward toward the looming mass of the alien warship. There was no way to communicate, no turning around, just a surge of impeller forced water at their backs and a rush of noise in their ears.

"If this bomb blows up right now, I'm a pink cloud of chum," thought Zuzu.

"That's a strange bird," thought the sea monkey atop the mast of the ship. It brought its little spyglass up to get a better look.

"That bird has captured a skinny old human."

A closer look.

"No, that human is wearing wings. Crap."

The sea monkey again began to chatter and chitter. It tugged on a rope near its tail, and an alarm bell rang.

"First, a weird sea creature with human heads poking out of it, now a flying human. Mother said that there would be days of high strangeness. This must be one of them."

"The monkey has seen him," said Elise, "it looks like he's screaming and ringing alarms."

"Cursed sea ape," said Jules, "but not unexpected. Our flying friend is not subtle."

The Aquaboggin powered on, throttle down, and engines at full, churning water through her twin jet motors.

The winds were wonderful. The temperature change on the water as the suns set along with the air currents whipping around the volcano made for fantastic flying conditions. If this were a joyride, Splatter would have caught a thermal and stayed aloft for hours to enjoy the beauty of the twin sunset and the turquoise waters below.

This was not a joyride. He swooped left and right, his eyes on the target as he flew closer to the enormous sailing ship, his hands tight on the aluminum bar in front of him that guided his movement.

The damned monkey had seen him, and now Splatter noticed that figures on the deck were beginning to point and shout.

Worse, one of the flying jellyfish moved in his direction.

"This will take some doing," he thought.

"Goddess, there is a flying human approaching from the west," said the swollen and pasty crewman as he ran into the control chamber of the ship.

I'Masma turned away from the glass tower that held the Old One.

"Seriously?"

The crewman noticed the moving darkness in the corners of the chamber, the many red eyes and shining teeth. He shivered.

"The human is hairy, old, and winged," he said.

"Deal with him, it, whatever. I'm a little busy down here."

She rolled her eyes and waved the crewman away.

I'Masma raised her hand and gestured at an arcing tube of energy on a small console of glass and copper.

One wall came alive with color and patterns and texture.

It was an entire shroud of the chromatophore flesh, a ten-meter video skin screen.

Praetor Agrunctus stared down at her, the image jittery and shifting between perfectly clear and garbled visual noise.

"Your brilliance," Agrunctus said, "Earth is razed. The Rolling Deep has harvested our fill. Mission complete."

"Lovely, Praetor, just superb. It's time to return to us so we may move on."

She gestured again, and the skin screen went dark.

I'Masma turned back to the bubbling, liquid-filled chamber of The Old One. She gestured delicately above a command screen at the base of the hideous aquarium, and three-dimensional shapes of light erupted around her. She manipulated them, controlled them, shifted them into patterns.

The liquid within the aquarium began to bubble and agitate around The Old One. The monstrous ancient thing did not move or show any sign of awareness or life, but all around it was glow and froth.

Then, the single nightmarish eye blinked. A low vibration welled up from the thing and rose louder, more violently, until the rumble became a shriek, an unending and uninterrupted scream.

The Old One screamed, and power surged out from it, fuel that was the only thing in creation that could rip the fabric of time, space, and gravity so violently that holes were formed.

At that moment, on what was once the floor of Earth's vast ocean, the mile-wide portals of blue energy, these two-way windows, these gateways between worlds, these tunnels appeared again.

There were twelve of the massive Razor Ships on Earth.

They all were positioned next to one of the holes in space, and they all entered the coruscating energy fields at the same moment.

Praetor Agrunctus held tight to the thick leather arms of his command throne. Riding the Shock Tide into the next world always made him sick.

His control chamber glowed for the briefest of moments, then everything shuddered and flickered. He felt a stab of pain, then blinding light, and then he vomited so violently that gobs of the stuff spattered the far wall.

Agrunctus opened his eyes, and everything was still once more. He thought he smelled the ocean in the air that drifted in from the ceiling vents.

It was pleasant.

Private Splatter was a hundred meters from the surface and from the sailing ship. The ship's forward railing was now a chaos of crewmen pointing and waving at him.

They didn't look particularly friendly.

"Well, to Hell with them," he thought, only moments before the waters of the lagoon around the ship began to glow and bubble.

"Oh," he said as the vast ocean expanse of the lagoon, a good five kilometers wide, erupted in steam and bright blue lightning.

He had seen that sort of energy once before when they had opened the portal at the bottom of the sea that had killed the Earth.

Enormous black walls rose up from the ocean all around, each as big as a skyscraper and smooth as ebony razor blades. There were twelve of these monoliths, and they ascended, six to a side, flanking the emerald glass sailing ship.

Private Splatter felt small.

"Something just appeared on sonar. Multiple targets. Huge," said Jules.

Elise saw white blobs on the sonar screen positioned all about the vast lagoon.

Jules sent the thin periscope up a meter or so. An image appeared on one of the console screens.

"Merde," he said.

Black ships had appeared like mountains out of the turbulence to either side of the glass sailing vessel.

"They're like the one that we saw in Paris. The one that was eating the city," Elise said.

Jules was quiet for a moment. The only sound was the intense whine of the turbines as they powered the sub through the water.

"Well, little idiot girl, how does it feel?"

Elise looked at Jules, not sure how to respond.

"How does it feel to ride with the legendary explorers, the daring scientists, the Astonishing Aquanauts known as Les Scaphandriers?"

Elise smiled in spite of her fear.

He was crazy, but she loved him.

"It's awesome," she said.

*

CHAPTER FORTY-SIX

Such Cost

ZUZU, BUT OF course, that wasn't her real name, grew up chasing king crab on the deck of her father's fishing boat in the raging seas of the North Atlantic.

There was more saltwater than blood in her veins, and by the age of twelve, she could pilot a ship, land a tuna, and cripple a grown man with two of her knuckles and a thumb. They called her Zuzu when she joined Les Scaphandriers because her father's favorite movie was a black and white old thing he forced the crew to watch every Christmas at sea, and that was many Christmas's indeed. She did not fear death because she had been raised around it, and the movie told her that it was how she led the life that she owned that really mattered.

North McAllister, and that was not his real name either, had been inspired as a child by a plastic frogman in a fish tank.

His family owned an aquarium shop in San Francisco, and he had always dreamed of being one with the fish, swimming in seas of blue surrounded by vibrant green plastic grass and frolicking in the bubbles from aerated treasure chests. When as a young man, he met Jules Valiance while on a reefer binge in Antigua, his destiny was sealed. North McAllister had been born to dreams of the sea and destined to be Les Scaphandriers.

Now, as the two of them piloted their explosives-laden Aqua Sleds through the darkening waters toward steaming black tubes that fed power to an emerald glass warship, they knew that this adventure would probably be their last.

They had only been happier once before, but that's another story.

I'Masma stood on the bow of the Ship of Dreams and took a moment to appreciate the view. The twelve Razor Ships were at their side now, ready to join the return home. The suns were setting, and the sky was every shade of purple and orange, the first stars just beginning to twinkle to life.

The hairy old man with wings swooped and soared in the beautiful sunset sky above the ship, pursued by the air jellies and just staying out of their tentacles reach.

It was lovely.

She was amused by the flying man and smiled at his sky dance.

The crew stood behind her on deck.

I'Masma had told them not to throw spears or fire arrows at the flying man. Surprises were rare on the Ship of Dreams, and she wanted to cherish this one as long as she could.

The Razor Ships were full of Earth's detritus. The Old One was secure in his chamber. The volcano fed the ship the energy required to keep its cage closed. Soon, I'Masma would use the harnessed power of The Old One to open the portals, and they would all ride The Shock Tide to their next harvest. This had been a strong and successful voyage, she thought, and watching this foolish old flying human die a humiliating death would be a delicious dessert.

"That good lookin' bitch must be in charge," thought Splatter.

Even from fifty meters away, he was impressed with her.

She was strangely beautiful and alien, cloaked in flowing fabrics that revealed her shimmering skin. She stood at a huge metal wheel at the bow of the ship and watched him with wonderful eyes, large and as emerald as the glowing glass and copper of the ship's hull.

Was she smiling?

"I think she likes me," he said. Splatter kept one hand on the base bar of the kite, and the other grabbed the shotgun from the harness sleeve on his chest.

The barrel went over the bar and slid into a half-circle notch. It was difficult to guide the kite with one hand, but not impossible.

He dipped, and the kite went with him, dropping from the sky toward I'Masma like a bird of prey. Private Splatter's stubby old finger rested on the trigger, and his eye spotted her through the scope.

"How 'bout a kiss," he said.

The surrounding sea was now dark with the setting of the suns, but the star glass hull of the ship glowed a radiant jade that lit their way.

Zuzu and McAllister split at the bow, one going to the port and the other jetting to the starboard of the ship.

Time was ticking away.

If Jules was correct, the ship was using power from the volcano to feed the ship, and if that was the case, those enormous cables would need to be severed.

Zuzu slowed her aqua-sled and came to a stop next to the starboard cable. The water around the massive pipe was warm, and at the hose itself, the sea was practically boiling. She attached the explosive to the slick surface with a suction cup and activated the timer. On the port side, McAllister did the same thing and then checked his watch. The two of them had one minute to get clear.

Zuzu and McAllister hit the throttle on their aqua-sleds and jetted away as quickly as possible.

They would be clear of the explosive charge's detonation radius. Zuzu counted sixty in her head.

The explosives blew. She felt the sound of the blast in her bones, a throbbing low-end pulse followed by a surge of water. Not bad, she thought.

Unfortunately, in their haste and anxiety, they hadn't considered the force that might be released when the hoses were ruptured.

Those tubes, those hoses, conducted the power and heat of the largest volcano in the universe into the energy chambers of the Ship of Dreams. The explosive charges were just enough to create tiny fissures in the port and starboard pipes as planned. The force within erupted from those tiny fissures with a blast of tremendous heat and energy, completely severing the pipes and turning the ocean into a bubbling maelstrom of steam.

That wave of heat and boiling water flooded out toward Zuzu and McAllister far faster than their little aqua-sleds could manage.

Zuzu and McAllister rounded the bow of the ship next to each other and looked back at the same moment. They saw the blinding light as the hoses fell apart and the shimmering white of the water as it turned into a bubbling wave of steam that roared toward them out of the deep.

They turned and gave each other a "thumbs up" gesture.

The wave of heat and churning water enveloped them.

Zuzu felt a burning sensation, then numbness, but she held tight to the throttle and surfed along with the blast wave as best she could.

North McAllister lost control, though, and his ski sled became undone in the turbulence.

He felt it rip away from his back, and then he was tumbling in the boiling maelstrom. There was pain, and then his vision began to fade.

The bubbles. Oh. He was a child again; he was a plastic frogman in a colorful aquarium surrounded by a wave of bubbles bursting from a treasure chest of gold.

What an adventure this had been.

I'Masma watched as the human went into a steep dive and swooped toward the deck. He was so charming and wonderful and unexpected. She loved the thought of him but knew that his approach wasn't without purpose. She sighed softly, and her smile faded away. I'Masma raised her hand and in it was a glowing globe that began to burn brightly with arcing energy.

Private Splatter descended, howling at the top of his lungs. He came right for I'Masma as fast and as straight as an eagle.

She aimed the globe at him, and a single bolt of energy lashed out. At that same moment, the old man's finger tightened on the trigger.

The energy bolt was not the last thing the great Philipe Devilliers saw.

The Superboy of the Azure Coast, the ginger dream of teenage girls along the French Riviera, the legendary flying impossibility, enjoyed the sight of the strange alien woman as she spun violently in a cloud of pink mist, her flesh flying into the evening air.

Private Splatter had become his code name because Philipe was an extremely good shot.

He saw twin explosions of steam and energy erupt from either side of the warship.

"Good old Zuzu and McAllister," was the last thing the old man ever said.

And then he saw a blinding light, and somewhere in the infinite, Private Splatter would fly on and on, forever, a hang-gliding angel with a shotgun.

Elise St. Jacques and Jules Valiance saw the sacrifice of Les Scaphandriers through the view screen of their submarine.

They watched Private Splatter's kamikaze charge at the deck and the twin explosions of steam to either side of the ship that billowed high into the night sky.

Elise couldn't blink. She couldn't move.

"Elise," said Jules, "please hold on tightly."

Jules adjusted the trim and throttled down. The Aquaboggin rocketed higher on the plane. The autogyro blades popped out of their housings, and the ship shot up into the sky with such force that Elise was forced down into her seat, her breath squeezed from her lungs, her pistol digging into her side like a nail.

The Aquaboggin flew towards the Ship of Dreams through a hot rain of water made boiling by the volcanic energy that surged from the severed power hoses.

Elise caught her breath. It was hard to see through the steam and mist on the forward viewing glass, but she could make out shapes and patterns of brightness. There was the great flowing emerald ship, and it was rocking back and forth, the strange tapestry sails rippling, the ocean below her hull a seething froth of boiling water.

The volcanic mountain that framed the scene was a black hand against a cobalt night sky, and crimson liquid rock was pouring down her slopes.

Her Dad never spoke to Elise about Heaven and Hell, but she had heard stories from her friends and others, she had seen paintings and stories and films.

This was a scene from Hell, she thought, and they were flying into it. She had never been so scared.

The speed of the ship's flight scattered the mist and water on the forward glass. Elise could see more clearly.

Something was moving in the sky around the ship, flying out from the slopes of the volcano.

Wires. Spears.

There were black and white figures on the slopes.

Orcanum warriors, a thousand of them, some riding great sea-lephants and even enormous land crabs far bigger than the creature she had befriended back in Paris.

The Aquaboggin soared over the great ship, higher than the

billowing sails and steel masts, and Elise could see the spears flying, thrown by warriors, lines attached. The spears bounced off of the hard shell of the star glass deck, but some struck and pierced the tapestry sails.

Elise remembered the time that she and her Dad had gone zip-lining at a little zoo near their home in Florida. Orcanum warriors began sliding from the slope of the Volcano of Ebon down the lines and toward the deck. They had created zip lines.

A loud bang. The Aquaboggin shuddered then rocked violently. A slick purple tentacle slapped the forward glass. The ship spun. Jules fought the controls. Through the side glass, Elise could see the dark mass of an air jelly. The thing had them, like a squid enveloping a fish.

"Of course, why not," said Jules.

Elise felt her stomach drop as Jules sent the ship into a tight spiraling dive. The turbine engines were screaming.

He steadied her, evened her flight, but their speed was accelerating. Elise thought that her face was going to smear onto the back of her seat.

"You are a good and brave little idiot," said Jules over the noise in the cabin.

She didn't know what to say, because she was only a kid and she knew that she was about to die.

She could see the ship looming faster and faster through the squirming tentacles in the forward glass as they spun forward, then Jules wrenched the control wheel, and the ship angled sharply to the port side.

He shot the Aquaboggin on a line toward the starboard hull of the Ship of Dreams and turned at the last possible second. They were jetting like a rocket alongside the hull, and they peeled the air jelly away as they went. The creature was smeared against the glowing green hull of the warship like, well, like jelly on toast.

Jules pulled the stick and throttle hard. The Aquaboggin screamed as it rocketed into the sky.

Elise smiled through her fear.

Jules Valiance really was epic.

The Ship of Dreams was no longer connected to her power supply, the unlimited energies of the volcano.

Jules had thought that perhaps by severing those power hoses, he would disable the ship.

That wasn't entirely accurate.

The ship was powered by the energies in her engines and the natural electrical fields of the star glass that composed her hull. She could sail forever along the seas of Orcanum.

But that wasn't her purpose.

The power of the volcano wasn't for the ship.

It was used to keep The Old One's prison cell strong and to keep the ancient thing enslaved.

The Old One was the force that could open up the portals between worlds.

It was the last of its kind in our universe, a God from another time, and The Old One's enslaved energy was the only living thing in all of creation that had the power to warp reality.

The Old One's prison chamber could stay strong for a short time without the volcanic energy, but certain measures needed to be in place.

Back-up power would need to be engaged.

Those things did not happen.

When Zuzu and McAllister severed the power hoses, the energy that contained The Old One stopped instantly and forever.

And within that chamber of glass, a single ancient eye moved, blinked, and saw.

Within that slave cell, an ancient mind became aware.

Try-Ton stood on the back of his sealephant. He raised his spear and threw it with every muscle in his being. He had seen the first spears strike the deck and fall. He had noticed that the spears could hold in the tapestry if they struck it at a good angle and with force. Warriors had died and were dying, and this battle would determine so much for the fate of his people.

His spear hit the tapestry at the top of the mast, and it held tight. Try-Ton quickly tied the line off on the back of his saddle and threw a leather strap over the wire.

The angle of descent would be steep, but it would do.

He sang a shrill song, a prayer, and began his slide to the ship.

The night air whipped him as he went. The water below was not bubbling as violently, the tubes having dropped into the depths and the energy drain from the ship becoming less with every moment, but there was still steam, and the air was hot.

The mainsail mast was coming fast. His spear was embedded in the strange fabric near the very top. He would either find the strength to grab and hold there, or he would shoot past into the sea.

This was his only chance.

He prayed for strength.

The howling scream of the Aquaboggin engine died without warning.

She had been a good ship, but she had never been built for this.

Her engine froze up under the strain just as Jules brought her around for a final strafing run at the deck of the ship.

His hope had been to fire all of his guns as he landed.

Instead, Jules fought the controls as the ship began to drop out of the sky. She was not aerodynamic by any means. There were no wings, no mechanism to prevent her from just plummeting.

One chance.

The sail.

*

CHAPTER FORTY-SEVEN

Destroyed

THE AQUABOGGIN HIT the Sails of Eternity like a missile and tore through them at an angle, ripping the fabric and then catching in a twist of the material that was held tight to the steel mast.

Elise didn't have time to think. She was upside down, sideways, and then back again, spinning as the Aquaboggin careened to the glass deck of the ship. Emerald shards flew as the great old vessel skidded along, sparks and flames and pieces of the Aquaboggin exploding as she crashed.

Orcanum warriors leaped out of the way, and the sub tore along the deck with a deafening shriek.

Jules jammed a button and pulled a lever next to his seat, fighting the g-forces that were pushing him back. A loud bang and the capsule holding the pilot and co-pilot seats was ejected. Jules and Elise caught a flash of the rest of the Aquaboggin slamming along through a whirlwind of debris then they were shooting backwards along the deck. A parachute engaged but didn't catch, the lines twisting, and the escape pod slammed into and through the thick jade glass of the main cabin.

Silence but for the ticking of equipment and the soft sound of shattered star glass falling. Elise opened her eyes. She was dizzy but alive. She looked at Jules and saw that he was already unbuckling.

He kicked the forward viewing glass away.

"No time for daydreams," he said.

Elise smelled smoke. She unbuckled. Jules grabbed her, and they jumped from the cabin pod just as flames erupted and enveloped it.

Elise fell into a swath of the sail tapestry.

The embroidery was glowing. The fabric was so soft.

Wait. I know this cloth.

She held a piece of the sail to her face.

This was the same fabric as my blanket.

My blanket.

The blanket my Dad gave me, the blanket that kept me alive for ten years while Paris died all around me.

How?

She remembered something else then, something important.

Her legs were wobbly, but she staggered forward, looking for Charlie.

The Aquaboggin had crashed along the deck for twenty meters or so, leaving bits and pieces of itself as it went. The torn, smoking, and burning hulk of their trusty submarine was at rest against the forward glass of the Ship of Dreams.

And there, on the deck half-buried in a sheet of metal and torn cloth, was the dead crab from the storage freezer.

Elise knelt beside Charlie's cold gray shell.

This really was goodbye, she thought.

Something slithered up next to her. The Octo-Thing, still carrying its little violin.

The strange cephalopod squirmed quickly beneath a metal sheet panel from the Aquaboggin and hid.

The deck of the ship was a war zone.

The Orcanum warriors were flashing blades and swinging bludgeons.

Elise had loved pirate movies. Her Dad would sit with her in the theater, popcorn in hand, and they would cheer and applaud as old wooden galleons came alive with glorious battle. Now she stood on the deck of the ship as the warriors fought around her, and she would have been thrilled never to see another pirate movie for the rest of her life.

There was blood and pain, screams and voices begging for mercy that wouldn't come. There was no stirring music as soundtrack, no reassuring moments of comedy. The warriors of Orcanum were taking back their world. There would be no prisoners, no kindness, and no surrender.

It was horrible.

"Take out your knife and your pistol, little one," said Jules. Elise did as she was told and pulled her dive knife from its sheath at her thigh, the gun from her vest holster.

Her hands were shaking uncontrollably.

The old Scaphandrier had no weapon. His pistol and knife were lost in the wreckage of the Aquaboggin. Jules moved to a dead crewman of the Ship of Dreams that lay in a pool of blood with an Orcanum sword sticking out of his side.

Jules gripped the sword handle tightly and pulled.

The blade slid out of the corpse with a wet sound.

Jules walked toward the bow. Elise followed at his heel.

There were a dozen Orcanum warriors at the bow of the ship.

Dead crew littered the deck. The warriors were about to leap into the water when a small portal opened by the ship's wheel.

I'Masma rose from the portal. Her shotgun wounded arm was repairing itself, the cables and wires twisting along the deep cut and stitching it together, becoming vein and glistening flesh. The final shot of the great and legendary Private Splatter had done its damage for a moment, but now there wasn't even a scar.

She held a glass globe in each hand, globes that blazed with white-hot energy.

I'Masma smiled and lifted the energy globes high above her head.

One of the Orcanum noticed her. He made a frenzied clicking sound, and the others turned to I'Masma.

"Sizzle, roast, and die," she smiled.

Jules and Elise were knocked backwards by a concussion of light and sound. Roaring lightning bolts of energy erupted from the globes and struck the Orcanum warriors, who were vaporized where they stood.

Elise had spots in her eyes from the brightness, and her ears rang and bled from the loud thunder crack. She looked around, feeling sick from pain and shock, and saw that Jules was already up and approaching the woman with his sword held in both hands.

She wanted to scream for him to stop, but Elise couldn't find her voice.

"Consider this your warning, madam. I am Jules Valiance, Commander of Les Scaphandriers, leader of the League of Astonishing Aquanauts, and preferred dance partner of Madonna," he said as he approached.

I'Masma looked at him with a half-smile on her beautiful face, one eyebrow cocked up from curiosity.

"Oh," she laughed, "you're the one who couldn't resist pushing the little button. Thank you so much. You gave me your world. What a lovely gift."

I'Masma didn't speak English or French. Elise saw that her lips were moving, she heard a pleasant sound, and the voice was suddenly in her head.

Jules continued his approach. Elise felt cold dread in her belly. This wasn't going to end well.

"Why do you do this? Such terrible things. To what purpose? Is it sport?"

"It can be fun, yes," smiled I'Masma, "but that's not entirely why we're here. We harvest the technological detritus of worlds. We are built of such things. We make them come alive, and they join with us."

"Wait. You're etoiles de la éboueurs? Intergalactic rubbish collectors?"

The smile on I'Masma's face disappeared.

"Who am I to judge? So, now to your trap. The cherub at the bottom of the sea. In a similar manner, the anglerfish of Earth's ocean dangles a little glowing niblet to attract its prey. Curious things go to marvel at the glowing niblet, and they are devoured," Jules said.

"Why, yes, that's wonderful," came the voice of I'Masma, "the predator uses curiosity as a weapon. A trap. Curiosity kills the weak. There's a pretty thing, says the curious. Let me touch it. Oh no, it's killed me. So brilliant."

Jules stopped and threw his head back as if looking straight into the twin suns.

Was he looking up at the top of the mainmast? Elise couldn't see anything there, but the fabric was billowing and could conceal much.

The old Aquanaut spun around and began twirling the blade like some sort of aging, bandy-legged Shogun warrior listening to a silent war chant.

What's he doing? This was no time to be so strange.

He stopped and looked straight into the eyes of I'Masma.

"You run a beautiful game, my dear," he said, "you plant your trap in a place so deep in the ocean that a society needs to be advanced enough to find it. Your trap can only be found by someone with the electronic and metal creations you need.

We descend in our Aquaboggin to explore a curiosity. I ring the dinner bell in a cathedral at the bottom of the Atlantic, and you come to eat."

I'Masma smiled, and her eyes softened. She looked almost pleased.

"Yes. Don't you think that's clever?"

"Clever, but you took cruel advantage of my curiosity. Shameful. Presumptuous."

There was a shuffling sound near Elise.

What?

She looked at the smoking piles of debris.

Was something sneaking up on her?

The sound became brittle, like something breaking, and it was coming from Charlie.

His shell was cracking.

He's falling apart, she thought.

A piece of the gray shell fell away, and Elise saw vibrant purple beneath. Another piece was shed, and there was blue, then orange, pink, yellow.

Charlie the crab was molting, and beneath the gray shell, he was the color of a rainbow.

The legs kicked. The pincers opened and closed. Elise felt her heart thundering in her chest, and she cried with joy.

The little eyes on stalks spun around and looked right at her.

The crab clambered up, shaking away the rest of its dead gray shell.

He was every color at once, a rainbow crab, and he was beautiful.

Elise hugged him, unsure if it was okay to hug a crab but doing it just the same.

She looked up to Jules and saw something so unusual she sputtered something that would have gotten her mouth washed out with soap if her Dad had been around.

Jules continued moving forward toward I'Masma, but this time he lifted his legs unusually high and kicked them out at odd angles.

He was walking in a silly way, a halting, staccato, exaggerated way, a ridiculous stride that made no sense whatsoever, a walk that would have been funny if Elise wasn't so scared.

The expression on I'Masma's face went from pleasant to confused in an instant.

"Oh, he's gone crazy," thought Elise.

"Humans are born to create. We build things because we must," Jules said, "and we are inspired by our imaginations to dream, to explore, to scratch the itch of curiosity. That is what makes us noble and good. Curiosity kills? Yes. But it also saves."

I'Masma lifted her arms and held the twin globes of energy high above her head. They turned white and made a sound like skin burning.

"You are amusing, but it's time to end this," she said.

"But aren't you curious?" asked Jules Valiance.

Her eyes went wide. What did that mean? She hesitated because, of course, she was curious.

And that's when Try-Ton leapt from the topmast directly above with a blade in either hand and lopped off I'Masma's arms at the shoulders.

*

CHAPTER FORTY-EIGHT

Bloody Death and Rainbows

FOR THE BRIEFEST of moments, I'Masma saw her home and the cradle nest where she was born, the many kin of her brood basking in the warmth of their mother sun.

It was a flash of a vision, and she did not know why it came to her at that moment, but it did. That was a pleasant time but short-lived time before The Torture Kings had taken her and remade her, and she had become one with the technology of The Shock Tide.

The thought was nice, and it lasted for a split second but felt like a wonderful eternity in her mind.

Then there was pain beyond imagination, and the air around her was an explosion of her dark purple blood erupting out of the stumps where her arms had just been.

She fell to her knees. Bright, blinding pain. There's my arm, she thought, still holding the weapon. There's the other one.

Oh yes, they've really done it now.

Try-Ton rolled onto his back, showered by the blood of the female creature. He was in agony. His legs were broken and useless. He shoved himself back and along the slippery glass deck with his elbows, the twin blades still held tightly in his hands. The ornate and brilliant tapestry of the ship sail billowed above and around them. He could hear the voices of his warriors, and they were singing the songs of triumph.

He might die this day, but this strange ship of glass would be theirs.

The night was clouded with steam from the roiling sea, so Try-Ton could not read their victory in the light of the stars, but he knew how this night would end.

The monstrous female creature, her slaves, and her Ship of Dreams were no match for the warriors of Orcanum.

Elise ran to Jules and wrapped her arms around him, not minding the stink and the blood and the sweat. She sobbed hard and held him tightly.

The old Scaphandrier smiled and hugged her back.

"Oh, look at you," he said when he saw the rainbow crab scuttle close, "you were molting. Tricky old crab."

"Can we go now?" asked Elise.

Copper wires and metal tubing snaked from the star glass hull of the ship and reached out, searching. I'Masma's arms continued to twist, and her hands held the energy weapons tightly. The detritus of worlds was food for The Shock Tide. That was the reason they went from world to world, gathering up old technology and waste; that was the stuff that made them strong.

Like rubber and metal worms, the wires and loose bits of metal leeched onto I'Masma, onto her arms, reforming them, reforming her, and she smiled because she could feel the pain drift away and the hatred return.

Her arms were dragged quickly, almost instantly to her shoulders. The wires writhed as if they were thread being stitched by a hundred invisible hands.

The stitching felt so good.

Her un-makers, the Torture Kings who had spent countless years raising then destroying I'Masma, had mocked her as weak because she had moments of humor and passion. I'Masma laughed then because this would be a brilliant joke.

The humans were busy celebrating with each other.

The Orcanum warrior that had wounded her was injured and lying nearly unconscious on the deck.

And she absorbed the detritus from all around, as was her nature, and in the blink of an eye, she was reborn.

Elise saw the evil woman stand whole, not dead at all, not sliced into pieces.

Jules was facing away, holding her tightly, but Elise was facing the bloody deck where the monster had been killed, or so it had seemed because now her arms were a part of her once more, and she was looking right at them.

Elise screamed then, louder than she had ever screamed before.

Jules felt his heart kick in his chest. He didn't look back. Holding Elise tightly, he dove forward and away into a chaos of shattered deck glass and torn sails.

The air burned as energy bolts struck only inches from his head. The sound deafened him. He couldn't hear a thing, and he was dizzy.

He looked back. The female creature was slowly walking towards them, and there was nowhere to go. Jules tried to stand but couldn't find his feet and fell backwards.

Another blast of energy, and this one hit Jules Valiance on his leg.

He groaned.

Elise saw it happen, the light, the burning, the smell of the wetsuit and his skin.

She did what any child would do when the monster came.

Elise grabbed the sheets of the sail and pulled those soft covers over her and over her friend Jules, hiding beneath and hoping that the thin fabric could stop the world.

A blast of energy. Heat, but not a burn. Jules was shaking with pain.

Elise pulled the Fabric of Eternity around them and held it as tightly as she could.

I'Masma fired again, but, of course, she cursed. The sails showed no sign of heat.

The fabrics of the sails had been created by The Ones Before and stolen by I'Masma from a world long ago and far away after many horrific battles. Many slaves had died to secure them, a treasure worth more than the gold of a thousand planets. They were resistant to the energy of The Old One, they showed little wear and tear, and they were glorious to see when billowing from the masts of their ship.

Some even said that the material could resist time itself. The fabric could be torn and cut, it could be punctured, but the strange seamstresses of The One's Before had woven them so that no energy could make the fabric burn.

No worry, thought I'Masma. There were other ways to kill.

She looked left and right. The Men of Many Eyes were on deck now. Six of the Lurkers had escaped from the Orcanum warriors, and now they were on her flank.

She pointed at the mass of tapestry cloth.

"Pull those humans out of the sails and bring me their eyes."

Jules had never felt more pain.

He bit his lip until it bled, then leaned in close to Elise.

"You are a good girl, Elise."

He smiled at her and pushed aside the sailcloth. His leg

throbbed, but he jumped to his feet and opened his arms wide to I'Masma.

"Bonjour, mon ami, a good trick, no?"

Elise scrambled up out of the cloth and reached for him just as an energy bolt hit him in the chest.

Jules fell next to her with an awful sound, and she covered him with her body.

The Men of Many Eyes moved towards Elise and Jules, but they stopped and turned when they heard an odd popping noise from where I'Masma had been standing.

One instant, she was looking at the humans; the next, she was upside down and spinning round and round.

"Did the ship capsize?" she thought.

Then, she was looking at the deck from a strange perspective.

Her vision faded.

"What?"

Just before a wave of black washed over I'Masma and took her away forever, she saw colors, so many colors, all the colors of a rainbow.

She smiled because rainbows were beautiful.

I'Masma never knew it, but this rainbow had been a large, extremely protective crab that had skittered up her back and lopped off her head with its massive, powerful pincers.

Try-Ton couldn't stand, but he could sit up. He threw one blade, then another, and two of the slender dark creatures dropped dead.

The others moved toward him, and there was nothing that he could do to stop them.

Jules was still breathing. Elise could feel his heartbeat and could see the fog from his breath in the cold night air. She turned and saw the Lurkers moving toward the warrior who had tried to save them.

Elise pulled the pistol from her vest and fired. The pistol kicked hard in her hand, and the bullet flew far from its target.

The noise hurt her ears, and the flashes of light blinded her, but there was something else. She was dizzy. No, it was the deck, there was a rumble below them, and it was getting louder.

The star glass deck of the ship exploded upwards and out.

The Old One roared up from the depths of the ship, and now it was free, growing larger by the moment, thick tentacles flailing, body like a misshapen oak, single enormous eye red with rage.

Elise fell backwards and rolled to Jules. She held him tightly and closed her eyes because if this thing was going to kill them, there was absolutely nothing that could stop it.

*

CHAPTER FORTY-NINE

Ancient

THE MEN OF Many Eyes turned and attacked The Old One.

Their claws flashed, their teeth gnashed. They were ferocious, and their bladed fingers sliced the thick mottled skin of the old god.

Elise opened her eyes and watched, holding tightly to Jules.

If the dark demons were trying to kill this strange new giant, then it must be good. It looked like a monster, but what if it needed her help? She rolled away from her friend. Elise had run in terror from the dark lurkers before, but now she ran toward the Men of Many Eyes, and she was not afraid.

She fired her gun again, and this time her aim was true.

She wounded one of the slender demons.

It turned to attack, to kill.

The Old One came fully awake then, and He saw.

He had been there, at the beginning of this universe.

There was no understanding something so ancient, so powerful, so alien, but Elise watched, and she thought she could sense what The Old One was feeling, what He was thinking.

That single eye, an eye that had seen the birth and death of galaxies, now stared down at the shattered and sinking remains of a ship that had been its prison, its torture chamber. It gazed at the living things scattered about the deck; it looked out at the other monstrous black ships in the sea beyond and up at the fiery glow of the volcano above.

In that moment, The Old One remembered everything.

It knew all, every horror, every humiliation that these creatures had visited upon Him. They had used Him to kill billions of living things. They had perverted His power. They had butchered and mocked Him.

He was a god from the universe before, and He had been made to dance for monkeys.

Now, this tiny pink creature was trying to protect Him.

A child. She was good. These others, they all had the same smell, and they were not good at all. They were destroyers.

They would be unmade, and He would go home.

With but a thought, The Men of Many Eyes ceased to exist.

They became clouds of vapor, instantly drifting up into the night sky.

The corpse of I'Masma, too, became a mist that was there and gone like fog.

The deck of the ship, the bow, the hull all around, everything except the sails dissolved into cold clouds of formless matter.

Praetor Agrunctus, on the deck of his beloved Razor Ship, didn't have time to think, or scratch, scream, or fart. He was gone, and then so was his ship, and then the others.

The Old One continued to grow as the ships and murderers of The Shock Tide faded away into the air as if they had never been.

The Old One was as tall as a ship's mast, and He became taller by the second.

Elise held tightly to Jules Valiance as the mighty Ship of Dreams disappeared around them, and they fell into the sea.

The impact of the water was hard, and it stole her breath for a moment.

Elise saw a flash of white. A part of the sail. The tapestry was floating, and she gripped it like a life raft.

A rainbow appeared next to her.

Charlie. Its strange eye stalks looked at her, slightly bent, curious.

She smiled at him.

The eyes moved in close, and they stared at each other for a moment.

"Thank you," said Elise.

Then the crab raised one of its pincers as if in salute and dropped below the waves.

The sea at night was dark, but if Elise could have seen through the murky water, she would have watched with a joyous heart as the rainbow crab descended gently toward the bottom, back to its home beneath the waves.

She shivered. The water was cold. Jules was barely breathing. His face was pale.

"I don't know what to do," she thought.

"Use the retrieve button," Jules said quietly.

"What?"

His finger pressed a button on her Les Scaphandriers watch.

"Perhaps we can dream of one more impossible trick."

*

CHAPTER FIFTY

She's Changed

THE LIVING DETRITUS of a dozen technological worlds had brought about the evolution of The Shock Tide.

They had used the power of the enslaved Old One to merge with the old technologies, to become something new.

The detritus that had been scavenged from different worlds and brought to crude life by the power of the Old One wasn't picky, however.

The bits of shattered televisions and toasters, the cars, the blenders and computers and talking action figures, they didn't care what or who they merged with, they just writhed about until they found something organic or just interesting in some way, and joined, merged, became new.

The warriors and slaves on the deck paid no attention to the scattered and burning wreckage of The Aquaboggin as they fought. If they had been watching those smoldering sheets of metal, they would have seen something strange and wonderful happen just moments before The Ship of Dreams and her crew were dissolved into nothingness.

The Octo-Thing saw, though, and the little creature was quick to go along for the unexpected ride.

Jules Valiance had always considered his ship a friend, a companion, an honorary member of Les Scaphandriers.

To him, The Aquaboggin was alive.

The weird organic technology of I'Masma's ship, or perhaps The Old One in a final act of kindness, must have thought so too.

A shark. Oh my God.

A shark.

Elise thought her heart would jump out of her chest.

Something big had bumped her from below the surface.

Jules was bleeding, and so was she. They'd attracted sharks.

They were going to die. They'd gone through all that, and now they were going to be eaten by sharks.

Elise became angry then, furious, and she kicked out, thrashing the water with her feet.

"Stop it," came a voice.

Zuzu was next to her in the water, her head barely above the swells.

Elise reached out.

"Careful, little one," Zuzu said. Elise could see that the left side of her face was shiny and swollen. Her hair was gone in places, and the revealed skin was wounded.

"You're burned."

Zuzu smiled, but there was tremendous suffering in her eyes.

"Yes, and what amazing scars I'll have to show for this adventure."

There was a sound of water sloshing, and an enormous shadow rose out of the deep beside them. Elise could see by the light of the volcano, the fires, the stars.

"Oh," she said.

The Aquaboggin surfaced next to them.

The submarine of Les Scaphandriers was born anew, her shattered hull reformed and held together by the countless strands of copper and wire that had fused with her. There was more than that, though, something new. There were pulsing ribbons of phosphorescent coral, of thick and living tissue, stitching that had put the ship back together, into one piece, almost as she had been. She sparkled here and there where her metal had been replaced with emerald star glass.

Elise heard the soft voice of Jules Valiance.

"Ah, my beauty. She's alive, Elise, and she found us."

Something terribly bright erupted then.

They looked off to where the Ship of Dreams had been.

The Old One had grown to tower over the Volcano of Ebon, and the ancient god was emitting a radiant golden light, its tentacles stretching up to the stars.

The single eye, ancient beyond our time, stared down at them.

It winked. And then, The Old One returned to the universe in a single burst of sparkling shimmer that reminded Elise of a Christmas tree. More light transformed the sea all around them, the portals opening once more in thousands of places along the seafloor of Orcanum and on Earth as well.

The sea began to churn.

"We must hurry," said Zuzu.

"Yes, but the cloth, I want the cloth," Elise said.

The sails of the ship, the Fabric of Eternity, floated nearby and glowed an amber light. It had protected them, and it had saved her.

Zuzu dove, knife in hand, but returned in a heartbeat.

There were tears in her eyes.

"I can't, Elise, it hurts. We must go."

"Give me the knife. I'll be fast."

Elise dove into the blackness and pulled on the billowing sheet of white. The dive knife cut easily through the Fabric of Eternity, and she quickly sliced away a long swatch of the cloth. She surfaced next to Zuzu, out of breath and with eyes that stung from the saltwater.

"We really need to go," Zuzu said through clenched teeth. The churning of the ocean was expanding around them, and they could feel the tug of the tide.

The hatch of the Aquaboggin opened. Zuzu gasped in pain as she summoned the strength to lift Jules into the ship. Elise helped as best she could, and in seconds they were inside.

Elise heard the sound of a tiny violin playing. The Octo-Thing sat in one of the seats with the safety harness strapped tightly around its mantle.

Zuzu collapsed on the floor of the sub next to Jules.

"The medical kit," she said, her voice a hoarse whisper.

Elise quickly retrieved the kit and gave it to Zuzu.

"You'll need to pilot her," said Zuzu.

Jules was dying. Elise knew this. The wound in his chest was awful, and his breathing was thin. Zuzu covered him with the sail-cloth for warmth then wrapped a blanket around herself.

Jules looked up and smiled at Elise.

"It is time to return to the Hall of Les Scaphandriers. Autopilot and homing beacon," he whispered with a smile, "little blue button next to the altimeter. It's labeled in French, so there can be no mistake. If it still works, it will be a miracle, but today seems to be a day for miracles. And if not, what new adventures might await, eh?"

Then, the old Aquanaut closed his eyes.

Through the viewing glass, Elise could see the night come alive with light as the portals to Earth opened, and the ocean began to drain.

The water pulled them under, and the Aquaboggin rode the maelstrom down, deeper and deeper.

"I've got this," thought Elise, and she truly believed it.

*

CHAPTER FIFTY-ONE

Be Impossible

DAD ONCE TAUGHT Elise to surf.

She surfed again now, from the pilot's seat of the Aquaboggin, pulled into the trough of a mile wide maelstrom of starlight, and pushed out at the crest of the wave.

They were enveloped as they rode the surging power of the portal's relentless pull. The interior of the sub was the same but different, lit now by phosphorescent creatures.

She had no power, her fuel was exhausted, but the gravity of the portal between worlds pulled her along faster than she had ever gone.

Elise didn't know how long they rode the tempest, but when they finally emerged from the pounding white wall of surf, there was only a single, brilliant sun, and there were birds and a red sandstorm sky.

Uh oh. We're really, really high, she thought.

The ship shot out of the portal at the crest of the wave like the front car on a roller coaster. Elise held tight as they dropped in and rode the force of the massive wall of water, everything whitewash and thunder.

When the waters finally cleared the view screen, Elise saw gray stone seawalls to either side of the ship.

Where are we?

The portals were returning our ocean to us, to Earth.

It would take days, but it would happen.

Some of our whales and fish and sharks would be swept back as well as strange and odd things of Orcanum.

There were miracles, too, on that other, distant world.

Try-Ton survived. He couldn't swim with broken legs, but his arms were strong, and he clung to the rocks at the shore of the volcano and would soon join his warriors once more.

His legend would grow until it went beyond Orcanum and into the stars.

Both worlds were being given a chance to heal.

The Aquaboggin rocked as she surfed along at the head of the storm surge, and Elise looked out to the seawalls and the sand swept skyline beyond.

"Ah, she still sails. Good ship," said Jules in a harsh gasp of a voice.

Paris.

They were surfing a wave down the Seine as the river returned to the city of light.

"Elise," said Zuzu. Her voice cracked.

Elise St. Jacques went to Jules Valiance and knelt by his side.

"You are a good pilot, little idiot."

"Thank you."

"Now, you must promise me some things. There can be no argument."

Elise began to cry.

"Play. Explore. Chase the stars. Be absurd. Be impossible. Do this, and you will never grow old. You are Scaphandrier now. Protect your wonder with all of your might, Elise, because imagination..." He coughed hard, and Elise was afraid that his breath would not come back.

There was a sparkle in his eye when he found the strength to continue.

"Imagination," said Jules Valiance, "makes us beautiful."

"You'll be alright. Please. You'll be alright."

"Oh, I've been more than alright," he said, "there are no perfect endings, my friend, but there can be good ones."

*

CHAPTER FIFTY-TWO

Good Night and Sweet Dreams

THERE WAS RAIN on the day Elise and Zuzu buried Jules Valiance.

This was the first touch of rain Paris had felt in ten years.

They stood in that wonderfully cool mist over the fresh mound of earth at the cemetery of Pére-Lachaise.

The coffin was the wood of old ships, and Jules was dressed in a shroud of the Fabric of Eternity. The beautiful sail cloth did not glow that day, but Elise could dream of miracles.

Elise said some things, and her words were well thought out and composed. She also danced a silly dance as the Octo-Thing played a jig, and she made an odd face as well because Elise was certain that Jules would prefer it that way.

Elise St. Jacques created the tombstone of her friend from a slab of fossil rock she found in the Hall of Les Scaphandriers.

She used an iron stake to engrave a few simple words.

"Jules Valiance Forever. He Brought Back the Ocean."

Plastic flowers, a good bottle of wine, and a rubber duck were placed at the foot of the tombstone.

Strangely, several cats arrived and sat by the grave.

Perhaps they were drawn by the music or by the voices of kind humans.

Were they the cats of Jules Valiance?

Of course they were.

Elise cried that day in the rain.

Then, Zuzu escorted her back to her new home.

But there was one more adventure to be had that year.

There were books and magazines in the Hall of Les Scaphandriers. There were games and puzzles too. Elise had much to occupy her time there, but she was a child of the television age, so she was drawn to their video monitor and their vast collection of old discs and tapes.

One night, Elise found a collection of old video discs that bore the label "Unreleased Documentary Films."

She slipped the first disc into the player and sank into the plush recliner, nestled with pillows and blankets.

The grainy video began with a percussive soundtrack and fast-moving images of the deep ocean, of exotic foreign markets, of mountain climbing and water-skiing, and well-dressed people in posh casinos.

"For one full year," said a deep, rich voice, "the secret society of Aquanauts known as Les Scaphandriers hired our film crew to document their adventures. We traveled with them around the world and experienced things beyond our imagination, things I would have sworn were impossible."

Elise soared then, her smile so wide that it reached to the moon and back.

"The team has determined that these films will never be seen by the public. They will be the stuff of legend, just like this extraordinary, silly, and courageous group of men and women. Our crew was honored to work with them, if only for a short time. And if for some reason you are watching this film and you are not Les

Scaphandriers, please believe me. Every bit of it, every moment, no matter how absurd or unlikely, is completely true."

The film continued.

There was Jules, and Private Splatter, and Zuzu and North McAllister and the Guyanese mystery known only as Three John. They were young and fantastic.

Sister Viverette was there too, younger, not stern at all, laughing and adventuring with the rest. Oh, thought, Elise, oh my. The dive helmet medallion she wore, her insistence that Elise be tucked away in the blanket every night. Sister Viverette was Les Scaphandriers, and she had wrapped Elise every nightfall in the Fabric of Eternity. She saved her in a blanket of time when the ocean was ripped away.

But more and beyond all of that, there was the voice on the video.

The narrator of the documentary had a warm and familiar voice, one she had listened to every night before bed, one that weaved silly and scary and impossible stories.

So this was how he had known of Jules Valiance and Les Scaphandriers.

This was why he had placed her in the care of The Girl's Garden and Sister Viverette.

Oh, that voice.

Elise laughed with joy until tears ran down her face.

www.ingramcontent.com/pod-product-compliance
Lightning Source LLC
Chambersburg PA
CBHW020231180626
46810CB00006B/2142